Barbara Gamble, runner-up for the Constable Trophy in 1984, was born in Belfast and took her BA at Queen's University there. Since then she has worked as a journalist in London, and taught English to students in Spain for a year. Married to a journalist, she now lives near Middlesbrough and teaches creative writing to young offenders in prison.

BARBARA GAMBLE

Out of Season

GRAFTON BOOKS

A Division of the Collins Publishing Group

LONDON GLASGOW
TORONTO SYDNEY AUCKLAND

Grafton Books
A Division of the Collins Publishing Group
8 Grafton Street, London W1X 3LA

Published by Grafton Books 1986

First published in Great Britain by
Constable and Company Limited 1985

ISBN 0-586-06843-0

Printed and bound in Great Britain by
Collins, Glasgow

Set in Times

To Tony, Alex and Alison
and
in memory of my Grandmother

1

George died. He choked to death on a peanut, on the eve of his sixty-seventh birthday. Such a ludicrous way to die, I have often since reflected, as unexpected as dying from earache. We were at a dinner party at the time, waiting to sit down to eat, and the peanuts, lying innocuous in little silver dishes, were but a prelude to the meal.

People, I find, are curious not about death, but about the manner of dying. 'Was it a particularly *large* peanut?' I was often asked.

'Not large,' I would reply, 'but stubborn.' The peanut lodged in George's windpipe and he could not breathe. Our hostess telephoned for an ambulance while I patted George ineffectually on the back. Someone suggested George drink a glass of water but by then his lips were already marked with purple.

He was dying by the time the ambulance arrived. And though I could not be sure of the exact moment when he died, I know it was very far from the hospital. I asked the driver to stop the ambulance and after he did so, I realized we were close to the sea, for I could hear the waves licking at the promenade walls.

At the cremation I watched George's coffin slide slowly behind a red velvet curtain. The service took twelve minutes, which is the time it used to take George to eat breakfast. But he was a practical man, not given to wasting time, and would, I imagine, have approved of the efficient manner in which his body was reduced to fat and to bones and to ashes.

George's ashes were scattered over a bed of overblown

roses in the cemetery garden. The wind blew in from the sea that morning and his ashes did not stay coffined in the full petals for long, but flew haphazardly through the air.

People, as they say, were terribly kind. I received several cards of condolence and some letters. Most of the letters – from George's lifelong friends, from distant relatives – were short and brisk but one or two were mawkish. 'We are all diminished by George's sudden and tragic death,' one letter from an old schoolfriend incomprehensibly suggested. I am not a sentimental woman so I did not keep the letters long; I detest clutter.

A lady from Oxfam came two days after the funeral at my request to take away George's clothes. She was earnest and middle-aged; she wore her hair in a bun and was dressed unbecomingly in a green trouser-suit. She offered me her condolences and I offered her a cup of coffee. Together we emptied George's tall-boy, his wardrobe, his chest of drawers. 'We have a famine,' she told me, 'a drought, two civil wars and an earthquake to contend with.' I tried not to smile but nevertheless the thought of an African peasant wearing George's fully-lined waistcoat was ludicrous, appalling but ludicrous. 'No,' she gently explained, 'we will sell the suits in our shops and buy maize with the money.'

After she had left, I collected together all George's papers from his study; his files, his notes, his annual reports, his minutes. And I made a bonfire, at the bottom of the garden. The paper burned readily and I added the ashes to the gardener's compost heap behind the small orchard.

Some of my friends were horrified by the apparent ease with which I resumed life, begrudging me this return to normality. 'You ought to cry,' one suggested. 'Even at the funeral you did not cry.' I explained that tears did not come easily and that those who wept readily were undoubtedly immoderate in their emotions as well as in their habits. But eventually people left me alone and I became simply one widow amongst hundreds in this large seaside town.

I have been a widow now for seventeen years and widowhood is a state to which I have become thoroughly accustomed; it is not a tragic state, nor is it particularly disagreeable; it is rather like living with chronic sciatica – one becomes used to it, one accepts it, one accommodates it. My life is, of necessity, solitary. I am eighty-four years old and one of the more discouraging aspects of my longevity is the fact that most of my friends are dead. Of those who remain alive, one is severely crippled by arthritis and lives in a bungalow several miles away, imprisoned by her pain. The other was removed, some eighteen months ago, to a private geriatric home when senile dementia was diagnosed. I visit her occasionally, but the visits are distressing for us both. She mistakes me for her elder sister, and asks me in plaintive and then in bullying tones for the china doll she mislaid as a child.

So my closest companion in the ebb of my years is the sea, and it has been my custom since George's death to walk to the sea each day. The walk is not arduous – a mere quarter of a mile – but it is sufficient to exercise my lungs and my legs. I wear a warm mink coat – one of four George bought me – and a pair of comfortable stilettos. Sometimes people stare at me in the street and I daresay find me odd, thinking a woman of my years ought to have no business striding along the promenade.

They would prefer to think of me remaining at home, sitting before a fire, wearing sensible slippers, enjoying the simpering company of innumerable cats. My daughter Jean has on several occasions offered to buy me a cat, but I have always refused. She and I rarely see eye to eye

9

and besides, I have never been partial to domestic pets. On the whole they are indolent creatures, unruly during the mating season, sybaritic, self-absorbed.

This morning I walked to the sea as usual, but the water was not companionable. By this I mean that the waves whispered no warning, gave me no indication that the tenor of my life, unchanged for seventeen years, was to undergo such an extraordinary upheaval.

Last night I slept so deeply that my sleep was almost a drowning. When I awoke the day had dawned without me, a fact which I viewed with some irritation. I regard missing the dawn as others do missing a bus, knowing they will have to stand and wait for the next. By their very nature, of course, dawns are considerably more reliable than municipal transport, but at my time of life to miss even one sunrise is inexcusable. I cannot think why it was I slept so deeply or so late; perhaps it was the warm cocoa that coaxed me into eight and a half hours of unconsciousness – but when I woke I felt bereft, cheated by nature, deprived as I was of watching the dawn enter the bedroom through the partially closed curtains.

It was five-and-twenty past eight when I opened my eyes, a fact in itself worth mentioning as I am usually up at six, and breakfasting in my bed-jacket by half-past. Insomnia is a privilege for those as old as I, I could not think why it had bypassed me. Jean, who is middle-aged and impatient with life, often complains to me of not having slept a wink. (It is one of her more dreary complaints about her life.) 'I could do absolutely nothing,' she will grumble, 'but lie awake and think of all the things I could be doing if it weren't the middle of the night.' When I explain to her that I feel something akin to gratitude for my own insomnia for providing me with extra hours, she looks at me with an expression of pitiful condescension.

So. Five-and-twenty past eight. My morning routine is reliable, reassuring, constant. I rose, slippered my feet, pulled back the curtains, opened the window, smelled the day. During the night it had rained and the smell was of damp grass, the sea, autumn. The view from my bedroom window is always pleasant and occasionally even now it makes me gasp. You can see the water, the harbour, the strand and, closer, the horse-chestnuts that line the street. The water looked calm, the harbour was deserted, on the strand a man threw pieces of driftwood to an obedient dog. I left the bedroom window open to air the room and walked across the landing to the bathroom to wash.

While washing, I listened to the small radio – I must remember to call it a radio and not a wireless – that Jean bought me for my eightieth birthday. The news headlines were being read out, and I found them remorselessly dispiriting. I recall George saying some time after we met that after the Great War there would be no other wars like it, that war would never be fought again on such a large scale. But each news item was of conflict, of disaster, of violence, of several small wars being fought all over the world. I turned the radio to a different station and listened to a man with an effete voice and little grasp of English grammar introduce a record by a singer with an unpronounceable name. I cannot think why Jean bought me the radio. I turned it off and then switched it on again, hoping to exhaust its batteries.

I breakfasted in what used to be the morning-room and what is now my sitting-room, the place where I carry on my secluded intercourse with the world, where I read my morning paper, listen to the lunchtime weather forecast, hear the shipping news, watch the television. The room is small, comfortable, undemanding. I ate crispbread,

11

honey, a piece of fruit and I looked out towards the garden while drinking my lemon tea. The fruit trees of the small orchard are blighted now, and I cannot think why. Whatever the reason, they suffer from a chronic affliction which means they no longer bear fruit, have not borne fruit for many years. Perhaps they are simply a testimony to my widowhood.

Outside, the air was cold for September, scissor-sharp on my cheeks. I passed houses, walked under trees, turned the corner beside a pillar box, crossed the road near a parked car. I saw a woman cleaning the downstairs windows of her home, a young child playing with a plastic toy, a man waiting by a bus-stop, a leaf falling from a sycamore. I heard a lorry rumble past on the main road, a bicycle bell ring, someone running in heavy shoes, the distant thrum of a vacuum cleaner. I smelled the sea.

I was fortunate to find my favourite promenade bench unoccupied. I am proprietorial about this bench, one of a dozen that punctuate the length of the promenade. Territorial, my daughter claims. She says I am foolish to think of a piece of wood as mine, that everyone who lives in this town has a right to sit on it. I think what she means is that because I am an old woman, a widow, I have less right to it than I believe. This is one of the innumerable and trivial matters about which we argue. My daughter calls herself a liberal and talks about equality a great deal, and her earnestness baffles me. When I find teenagers sprawling upon my bench – as I do often in the summer – I chase them away and tell Jean later of my triumph.

I had only been seated for a few minutes when I noticed an old man in a grey hat walking slowly towards my bench. Behind him, the sea too was grey, the colour of slate, and the seagulls' calls so shrill that my ears rang. On the beach, a small child was digging a sandcastle with a blue spade; a few yards away its mother watched, her legs wrapped in a red blanket. The man walked slowly in my direction; his steps were cautious, aided by a stick. He was followed, less cautiously, by a small black terrier dog wearing a tartan coat.

When the man sat down beside me, I continued to look out at the sea. 'Good morning,' he said, raising his hat. I did not smile, merely acknowledged his greeting with a nod of the head. I am not partial to strangers, on the whole I find them guilty both of impertinent behaviour and dreary conversation. 'A dull day,' he said in the loud voice peculiar to the rather deaf. 'Those clouds over there,' he added, prodding at the air with his stick, 'they may well bring rain.' I nodded, but said nothing. Jean talks of the weather often – a subject she feels ought to interest me simply because I am old – and I had no wish to discuss the possibility of rain with an old man partially deaf and carrying a stick.

And then he leaned towards me, looked intently into my face and spoke once more. 'My name is Jones,' he said. 'Henry Jones.' I drew my library book from my bag, opened it, read a paragraph, and when I looked up again, the man had gone. I felt oddly as though the future had whispered something to me, some words I could not yet understand. But I dismissed the thought as fanciful, and immersed myself in my novel.

On the sea-front, on the opposite side of the road from the promenade, are several shops. One sells rock with the words '*A present from the seaside*' embedded in red letters, and infants' dummies made of red toffee, and sweets that mimic the creatures of the sea – crabs, shrimps, mussels – and edible pebbles and home-made fudge. Another sells gimcrack rubbish made in Oriental countries – donkeys and plastic key-rings and pencils and ashtrays. A third sells hot dogs and coloured ice-creams and a violently hued drink of melting ice. After watching the sea from my bench, I walked past these shops and it was as I passed the toy shop that I slipped on the pavement and fell.

I cannot think why I fell; the pavement was only a little damp from the earlier drizzle, my shoes were my most comfortable pair, I did not lose my balance. But fall I did, outside the toy shop, near the amusement arcade, hearing the call of the seagulls, the noise of the fruit machines, the concerned cry of the complete stranger who helped me up and who, before I could stop him, ran to the nearest public telephone box and called an ambulance.

When the ambulance-arrived, I had perfectly recovered. 'The gentleman who rang you was too hasty,' I explained. 'I am not in the least hurt. I simply slipped on the pavement.' The ambulancemen – there were two – glanced at each other and despite my vociferous protestations led me ignominiously towards the open doors of the ambulance. I rewarded the man responsible for this unwarranted ignominy of mine with a glare of true malice. Some compensation, but not enough to assuage my anger.

The ambulance driver constantly exceeded the speed limit as he drove to the hospital. He swerved with unnecessary carelessness at every corner and even had the temerity to add the sound of the siren to the noise of the screeching tyres. 'I shall report you,' I said, on our arrival at the hospital, 'for dangerous driving.' The man paid me scant attention, gripped my arm and led me towards a door marked Casualty Department. 'You'll be all right, luv,' he said, with a familiarity I found objectionable. In the casualty department, I spoke to a girl I presumed was a nurse. 'I wish to be allowed to leave immediately,' I said, and then I very foolishly fainted.

2

Several people saw the ambulance race along the sea-front, scattering seagulls and late holiday-makers alike, and several more heard its siren. Two typists working in the social security offices at the corner of Promenade Way heard the siren and used the sound as an excuse to leave their typewriters and their swivel chairs and to peer eagerly out of their second-floor window. Too late to see the ambulance, they stared instead out towards the sea, counting the number of tankers waiting to be admitted into the already overcrowded harbour, and thinking longingly of five o'clock.

In the sportswear shop on the other side of the amusement arcade, the noise distracted the assistant long enough to enable the young female customer he had been serving to slip quietly out of the shop wearing a neatly-pleated tennis skirt under her cotton dress. The assistant did not miss the skirt until his weekly stocktaking at closing time, six hours later, by which time the girl was already one set up at the municipal tennis courts behind the putting-green.

The seagulls, hovering greedily above the pier end for elevenses, shrieked on hearing the siren, their shrieks proving that nothing in the seaside town could make as much noise as they could, not even an ambulance.

In the amusement arcade, a few yards from the spot where Grace Hopkins so inelegantly fell and so churlishly received the aid of the passer-by and the ambulancemen, the sound of the siren was not heard at all. This was undoubtedly because of the racket emanating from the ten Space Invaders and the seven fruit machines that were in use at the time. It was claimed by the leader of the local ratepayers' association that the noise from the amusement arcade equalled in decibels the sound of Concorde landing at the bottom of one's garden, and very few people disputed this claim. In the time it took the ambulance to get from the sea-front to the hospital, eighteen adolescents lost between them £20. And although a notice prominently displayed at the entrance to the arcade plainly stated that nobody under the age of sixteen was permitted to enter the place unless accompanied by an adult, it was obvious that the instruction was seldom, if ever, adhered to. Most, if not all, of those pressing buttons and moving dials and holding levers and staring at the various electronic galactic missiles of the Space Invaders were boys between the ages of twelve and fifteen. Most of them were losing money at an alarming rate and at least half a dozen ought at that very moment to have been learning how to make a bookshelf in the woodwork class at the local comprehensive.

The arcade manager knew his clientele were underage; he suspected the money they used to feed the machines had been deviously acquired; he didn't trust any of them an inch. The Space Invaders which lined the sides of the dimly lit arcade were chained to the walls with heavy industrial padlocks, their screens protected by thick glass, the money in their innards inaccessible. They were, in fact, impregnable. The same could not, however, be said of the change machine which squatted in the centre of the arcade beside a pin-ball machine that nobobdy but the infrequent over-thirty-year-olds used. Mr Potter was certain this change machine was tampered with daily, and that meant he was being robbed. But he also knew that the money these juvenile thieves coaxed from the change machine was, in turn, wasted in the

16

arcade itself and this knowledge was some compensation. 'Fair exchange,' Mr Potter was in the habit of muttering to himself, 'no robbery.'

When the ambulance pulled up only a few feet from the plastic booth in which Mr Potter sat, he looked up briefly, sighed, and returned to his tabloid crossword. He was a man of little curiosity, a small man with the evidence of over-eating and disappointment on his face and a persistent ear-infection which had bothered him for more than four years and which made him reflect on how much he would welcome a ride in an ambulance and a short spell in hospital, if only to escape from the caverned existence of managing an amusement arcade.

Mr Potter was still sighing when, a few minutes later, a fight broke out five feet from his plastic purgatory. He watched the two teenage boys punch each other in the face, chest, arms, groin and stomach, in much the same way as he watched Grandstand on his Saturday off – with little interest in the action and even less in the result. The fight, accompanied by the sort of language and threats Mr Potter had grown to associate with his clientele, continued for between three and four minutes, time enough for Potter to finish the 'Across' clues and proceed to the 'Down' section. While searching for a five-letter word meaning 'luke-warm', he saw the two boys grab each other in an absurd and pugilistic embrace, fall backwards against the pin-ball machine and from there to the floor.

Addressing two pairs of boots, Potter raised a fat and ineffectual fist and promised – in a voice wholly devoid of threat – to call the police. The two boys got up, sneered at each other, gestured crudely towards Potter, and walked out of the arcade.

One of the boys was called Roff.

Roff was not his real name – he had been baptized as

Michael – but it was the only name he would answer to. He had chosen it for himself two years before, in an attempt to stop his mother calling him Mikey. He had chosen it because the name was tough and uncompromising. And he had chosen it, above all, because he craved to be different.

His mother continued, however, with the persistence of mothers everywhere, to call him by a pet name. His teachers still addressed him by his surname, and his friends would always think of him as Mick. Roff alone used his new name, and did not appear to notice that it sounded like the bark of a particularly bad-tempered dog.

This is what Roff looked like, running along the promenade, running away from the arcade in case the police came, running from Potter's resigned threats. He looked like a teenage boy with too many spots around his mouth and on his chin, a boy who had not thought it worthwhile to wash that morning and who would not bother to wash that night. He looked like a sixteen-year-old who wished he were twenty and who acted often as though he were thirteen. Discontent growled at his eyes and ganged up with the spots to make his face appear ugly and unendearing.

But when people saw him, they noticed only his hair. And it was indeed remarkable, worthy of a second or even a third glance, fully deserving of the attention it received from strangers. It rose from his scalp, from the centre of his head, in spikes six inches high. There were five of these spikes, each so stiff, so disciplined, that even in the severe gales of the previous winter they had remained perfectly upright. The gales had blown down fences, loosened slates from roofs, blown at least three frail pensioners off their feet. But Roff's spikes had remained unscathed, oblivious of the Force Eight winds that swept along the promenade, as though held in their rigid positions by faith. Of course faith could not be held responsible for keeping that aggressive, taunting hairstyle in position, for Roff was without faith. No, the secret lay elsewhere, in a drawer in his sister's bedroom, underneath her tights and her underclothes and a photo of the first man she had ever slept with, two years before. The secret was Sheila's contraceptive jelly, which Roff took from the drawer every morning, used to stiffen his spikes, and replaced again. Sheila had slept with other men since the one in the photo, and, well, if she was to get herself knocked up at seventeen, it wasn't his fault, was it? He didn't need much jelly, anyway, to keep the spikes stiff, just a blob or two for each one.

The colour of these spikes also drew the attention, for they were not black or brown or blond, as might be expected, but a bold and somehow dangerous shade of yellow. The day he blew two week's dole money on getting his hair dyed and spiked at a posh hairdresser, his Mam went wild. She covered her face with her hands and cried. She screamed and stamped at the kitchen floor with her foot. She yelled at him and threw a mug. Roff was forced, eventually, to make her a cup of tea to calm her down. Drinking the tea, she looked sorrowfully at him, shaking her head. He waited for her to tell him she'd get used to it, that the colour was nice, but when she opened her mouth again it was only to say something stupid. 'How'll you sleep?' she wanted to know, 'with all them spikes sticking into you?' The question was funny and Roff laughed. Everyone knew that if you was tired enough, you just went to sleep, no matter what. Mostly he slept on his stomach, and the spikes never bothered him. Besides, he'd seen his Mam go to bed with rollers in her hair, pins and clips; he didn't see there was much difference. Once a fortnight he washed his hair and on those occasions he put the jelly on while it was wet and dried the spikes with a hairdryer so they'd stay upright. Once, after this, Sheila had collared him on the landing and asked if he'd seen her tube of jelly, but he'd only shrugged. 'You want to lay off screwing around so much,' he told her. 'That way you wouldn't need the stuff.'

The tide was on the wane, and the high-water mark disfigured by cracked paper cups, sweet wrappings, gulls' feathers clotted with brownish sewage. Roff stopped to lean against the promenade railings. The air smelled faintly of salt and – because the sea-front pubs had opened their doors – more distinctly of beer, sharp and close. On the beach, on sand littered with cigarette butts and mislaid buckets, three children bounced on trampolines, watched by a bored attendant and three anxious mothers. Roff watched the children. He was hungry but it was too early to go home. He was tired, but had only got out of bed two hours earlier. He was bored, but he didn't think it was a good idea to return too soon to the amusement arcade.

He watched. Up the children bounced, down again, up and down, with the regularity of metronomes. The girls wore shorts and T-shirts and one of them had her hair done in a pony-tail, tied with a red ribbon that matched the colour of her shorts. The girl smiled at her mother with the innocent arrogance only the under-eights are capable of, and bounced. Roff could not even remember having been that age and he thought it a stupid thing to do, to spend your time bouncing up and down on a trampoline like that, looking so bloody pleased with yourself.

He would be glad when the season was over, the holiday-makers gone home. When he could reclaim the sea for himself. He did not like these people, these tourists. They cluttered up the beach, their children cried and they looked at Roff – the mothers especially – as though they and not him had a right to be there.

The girl with the pony-tail bounced higher, her feet curled beneath her.

Roff waited for the right moment, waited until she was a foot, eighteen inches, from the canvas, and then he called out to her. 'Hey,' he shouted, 'hey you!' The girl turned her head in his direction, lost her metronomic rhythm, fell backwards against the metal bar of the trampoline.

He didn't bother to wait for the girl's scream, the mother's outrage, but walked quickly along the sea-front towards the town, smiling to himself.

The town's new shopping arcade was busy that afternoon, its human traffic moved quickly, purposefully. Fat, well-dressed women entered the only café in the arcade serving freshly baked Danish pastries and emerged again half an hour later with their lips tasting of icing-sugar. Young mothers, inevitably harassed, pushed toddlers in push-chairs with one hand while in the other they carried the family's weekly groceries in plastic bags. Supermarket check-out girls stared blankly at their cash-registers and dreamed of fame. Businessmen strode briskly across the arcade, using it as a short-cut between their offices and the bank. Roff sat down on an unoccupied concrete bench in the centre of the arcade, removed from the concrete waste-bin beside him the early edition of the evening paper and read the television page, the sports page and a particularly full account of the inquest of an old man who had knifed his wife in eighteen different places. He heard, but did not listen to, the whining of infants, the bickering of the unhappily married, the chatter of women, the gossip of men, angry quarrelling, gentle coaxing, veiled threats, sighs of delight, the ring of the supermarket cash-registers, the clacking of an electric typewriter behind a distant closed door, the chirrup of a radio disc jockey from a nearby transistor, the rumble of a double-decker on the High Street.

At two o'clock, Roff fell asleep on the bench and dreamed of the sea.

At three, he woke up, yawned, lit a cigarette and stretched his legs in order to trip up a shopper.

At five he got up, stopped a passer-by, asked him for a light, and returned to his bench with a ten-pound note from the man's jacket pocket.

At half-past five, when the arcade was just beginning to empty, Roff took out the Thompson sub-machine gun he had kept concealed under his jacket all day, pointed it towards the nearest crowd of people, and fired. He killed fourteen – eight women, two children and four men. He watched these people dying in slow motion, with several action replays, and heard a television news reporter tell the nation of a daring act of urban terrorism while the camera's lens lingered caressingly on the dead bodies.

At six, bored with his fantasy, Roff made his way back to the amusement arcade. He spent five of the ten pounds on the Space Invaders and the other five on amphetamines.

At midnight, Roff went home.

The house where Roff lived was terraced, brown-bricked, mean in appearance, carelessly painted, grimy-windowed, numberless. It was damp and inadequately heated and even, where the floorboards upstairs were loose, dangerous. At the front of the house was a small square garden, a nasty scab of earth where in the spring a few courageous crocuses sprouted on clay soil beside a brown drainpipe.

Once, all the houses in the street had looked like this one. Once, they had all squatted together, sharing the same brown paintwork, the same drab exterior, the same

22

unprepossessing appearance. Once, when none of the houses boasted numbers on the front door, it was easy to mistake Mrs Brown's house for Mrs Jenkins', and the Baileys' from the Colts'. But this was no longer the case. The other women in the street, once young and careless of the value of their homes, were now widows, and widowed, had begun to look to the town's tourism to augment their widows' pensions. Painters had been hired, gardening manuals consulted, net curtains bought from mail-order firms, three-piece suites paid for on hire-purchase, wash-basins installed in every bedroom. And, finally, advertisements placed in front windows.

The homes had become guest-houses.

One or two of the more enterprising widows had even approached their bank mangers for loans, pestered the planning department of the local council with applications for extensions, badgered builders to make two rooms one, or one three, or three five. Gradually, these houses acquired names, lost their drabness, proclaimed their individuality. Holiday-makers came at first to this street in trickles, and then gratifyingly in streams. They stayed in the Seaview, at the Anglers' Rest, in Primrose House, behind the gleamingly white curtains of Well Come.

The Jenkins' house, however, remained unkempt and – it was generally agreed by the caucus of widows – lowered the tone of the street. Even the fact that the sea was a twenty-minute walk away was seen as less disadvantageous for business than the proximity of this house. It was a blight and an eyesore and a disincentive to the more discerning kind of boarding-house guest. Roff despised these women, greedy for guests and extra cash, with their net curtains and their six pints daily. They were old and lived in bodies misshapen by over-eating. When he passed them in the street, they talked loudly about bringing back conscription.

He hated them. Their lives were neatly parcelled and he wished them dead. He didn't believe people over fifty had much right to live, anyway.

Inside the house, silence lay like dust. Roff scattered it, banging closed the front door, stumbling over a chair in the hall, weaving against the wall, switching on the television at full volume. The images on the screen were gaudy. A man with a red face kissed a woman wearing a dress the colour of artificial grass. They lay on a bed, the woman opened her mouth, showed teeth that were pink, embedded in maroon gums. Slumped in an armchair, Roff wasn't sure whether the gaudy colours were due to a fault or because of the speed in his brain, not caring much either way. The scene bored him, the sort of stuff his mother enjoyed. He changed channels, watching the late news for thirty seconds, a documentary about the Third World for two minutes, an advertisment for a bathroom cleaner.

He turned the television off.

The room stifled him. His mother said it was cosy, and it stifled him. In a brown plastic pot on top of the television a plant had died. Beside it, the clock gave the time as twenty past five. It had been twenty past five for months now, nobody bothered to wind it up. The three-piece suite was covered in a floral material; red roses, their petals blighted by cigarette burns. The curtains were brown, the ceiling the shade of nicotine, the carpet green. The colours and the patterns threatened to choke Roff.

Sometimes he would lie awake in bed, thinking how quickly the three-piece would burn if a lighted cigarette were left on it, how soon the curtains would go up in flames.

On the mantelpiece stood a photograph of Roff and Sheila. The picture had been taken long ago by his mother. Roff and Sheila standing, stranded, on a large log in some park. One of his teeth was missing and Sheila wore a headband in her hair. Looking at the photograph was like looking at a picture of strangers. 'You were a lovely lad then,' his mother would say, lifting up the picture, taking it to the window to examine it more closely. 'A great kid.' Roff would shrug when she said this, knowing she was talking about some other kid. 'When you was five,' she would say, 'you run off. Nobody knew where you'd gone. The police found you by the canal, playing with some rusty old cans, throwing them into the water. You got such a belting when they brought you back.' His mother was keen on the past, flinging it in his face like sand, making him feel uneasy. When he asked about his father, she said nothing. It was the only segment of the past she never discussed, the only part that Roff wanted to hear about. He sighed and went to bed.

His bedroom smelled. Of rich, adolescent sweat, of stale cigarette smoke, of the slowly rotting apple-cores that stood like trophies on the windowsill. Of grubby T-shirts and of the rubber-soled boots Roff wore everywhere but in bed. A small, dirty, stinking room, like a fox's lair, a badger's set. A radio-cassette beside the bed, a pair of earphones on it, a guitar underneath, a mildly porno-graphic magazine. He had tried to teach himself to play the guitar, but found it too difficult. He had, another night, cut off the breasts of all the nude girls in the magazines, using the same scissors he had used to sever his acquaintance with the guitar. He had enjoyed cutting the guitar strings, hearing the twangs, knowing that if he couldn't learn to play it, nobody would be able to.

Roff undressed slowly. The speed had almost worked through his system, now he was tired. He got into bed, pulling the sheets over him, inhaling deeply as if inhaling the smell of a dawn sea. He fell asleep quickly, as does a child or an animal, without reflecting on the past, the present or the future.

At four-thirty in the morning a distant fog-horn nudged him from deep unconsciousness into a dream. He dreamed he possessed a singular power, a power so unique, so extraordinary, so devastating that it made grown men and women scream and children weep and tremble. In his dream, Roff walked by the sea-wall at the southern tip of the town. It was summer, for the sun was strong, thumping down on his back, his arms, his head. The tide was high, the waves tumbled at the sea-wall, noisy and insistent. Roff placed both hands on the sea-wall and pushed, hard, against it several times. The force of his body made the wall give way, the stones crumble, disintegrate. Water, tons of it, the whole ocean it seemed, poured over the disintegrated wall, pushed its way towards the people in the town. Two old men sitting in deckchairs were carried off by the water, rafted on their deckchairs, their arms trying to say what their mouths could not. The water climbed and clambered and soared and pushed along the sea-front. It overturned cars, it drowned women, the promenade was flooded. Roff heard the screams of children, the terror of adults, as the water slashed into them, seizing – it seemed to him – its rightful place, reclaiming what was rightfully its own.

When he woke, Roff thought he could still hear the noise of so much ocean causing so much damage, damage he himself had unleashed. But it was only the sound of the blood rushing to his head. He was soon asleep again, but the dream, the feeling of power, stayed with him in his sleep, clinging to his unconsciousness like a limpet to a rock-pool.

Roff's mother Annie heard Roff climb the stairs, walk past her bedroom door, use the bathroom and then step into his room, closing the door behind him. The boots he wore were heavy and she could hear the floorboards of his room grumble at their weight. Sometimes she wondered if he slept in his boots and she had thought of asking if he'd had them specially welded on. She never did, though; they never talked much, her and Mikey. She'd called him Mikey ever since he'd been a baby, but these days when she used his name he would scowl and grunt and tell her he'd changed it. 'It's Roff, see,' he'd say, glaring at her, not seeming to think it was funny, changing his name like that. 'Okay,' she'd said once, 'you're Roff and I'm Gladys.' But he hadn't got the joke, hadn't even smiled. But then, he rarely smiled, like smiling cost him, like it hurt him to smile. 'There's nothing to smile about,' he'd said the other day, and she'd thought it was sad, a boy Mikey's age, his whole life in front of him, thinking there was nothing to smile about. When she was sixteen she'd smiled all the time. Her teeth had been better then – that was before the two pregnancies, the one miscarriage – and she'd smiled to show off her teeth. 'Nice tits, nice teeth,' she'd overheard a boy say one day in the street, and he'd been right. But since she'd had kids her tits had got smaller and her teeth looser in her gums, and these days nobody looked at her long enough to make any remarks about her.

She heard the boots drop to the floor and then she heard him switching off the bedside light in his room. Once, when he was little, she'd gone into his room every night, leaned over his cot, close enough to smell his breath – sweet and milky – long enough to know he was deeply asleep. That was after Bob had walked out, when the kids were all there was to stop life turning sour. She and Bob had been together two years – not long, but long enough for her to have got pregnant twice, long enough for her to think they'd stay together. The day he went the sun had been shining, hot and strong, making

27

the brick walls of the back yard warm when you touched them, making the bin smell, making Sheila grizzle and the milk on the step go off a bit. A Saturday it had been, a Saturday in the summer, and when Bob said he was off to the pub for a pint she didn't think nothing of it. 'A pint,' she said, knowing that meant two or three or even four, but she didn't mind. Bob brought her his wages every Friday, and all he ever kept was his beer money. 'See you later,' he'd said, and off he'd gone.

The sun had still been shining at eight o'clock that night and Bob still hadn't come back. She put Sheila to bed, made a bit of supper, turned on the telly. 'He'll be back soon,' she said to herself, and though she said it again on the Sunday and on the Monday, Bob never showed. He didn't show on the Tuesday neither, or the Wednesday, and by the time Saturday come round again she knew he wouldn't be coming back. 'He's buggered off,' her neighbour said, and Annie just nodded. The neighbour talked about getting the police in, and about maintenance and about how you couldn't trust men, and Annie kept on nodding. She cried herself to sleep for a fortnight, until at the clinic they said all that crying was bad for the baby and it was time she stopped thinking of herself and living for her kids. So that's what she did. She got a job charring and then another in a pub, and when she wasn't working she made sure the kids was clean and neat and contented.

But Mikey wasn't a contented baby, no matter how hard she tried. He cried a lot, and was sick, and when he couldn't get what he wanted, he had tantrums. 'You're like your Dad,' she'd say, but the truth was she couldn't remember after a while what Bob had been like. One thing was certain; he wasn't like the man in her book. This man was almost six feet, with deep blue eyes and a wonderful smile. Bob's teeth had been bad, his eyes a sort of muddy colour and he'd not smiled that often for her to remember whether his smile was wonderful or not. The man in the book – the title was *A Ticket to Paradise* – was a widower, having lost his three children and his beautiful wife in a tragic accident. What the accident had been, Annie wasn't sure, but D'Arcy was still stricken by grief over the deaths in the first chapter. As a successful financier, he travelled over the world, and had recently bought himself a ticket to the Seychelles, where he intended to spend a long holiday trying to recover from the awful tragedy that had struck him down. The girl he met on the plane going out was the heroine of the book and she was blonde and slim and men always fell for her. She was a journalist, on her way to the islands to write a travel feature, and Annie guessed that she had just got over an affair, or that her past held a secret she had revealed to nobody. She was rude to D'Arcy on the plane, but there was no doubt that he found her attractive. Annie couldn't tell what might happen when they arrived in the Seychelles, or whether the girl would fall in love with D'Arcy, or even if he would be able to stop thinking all the time about his beautiful dead wife. She'd read the next chapter in the morning before she went to work. Books, well, they kept her going. You needed something to make life exciting.

3

Something woke me. My watch said five-and-twenty to five. A few feet away, somebody was snoring. George used to snore in the twin bed next to mine. Snore, whistle, grunt. Men are such selfish sleepers, and George was no exception. 'Do be quiet, George,' I said, but remembering then that George was dead.

I lay awake for an hour, possibly more, listening to the vowels of illness.

The hospital smelled of milk puddings and of dedication, both contributing equally to my feeling of biliousness. The ward was draughty and the nurses wore heavy shoes and unbecoming hairstyles. I had entered the ward in a wheelchair, an indignity I did not take kindly to. The bed was too high, not sufficiently wide and blankets scarcely adequate. A gaggle of nurses gossiped in a corner beside a table of vased dahlias. When I awoke again at six the flowers had gone but the nurses were still there. One of them disengaged herself from the group and advanced upon me with a thermometer; this instrument was placed in my mouth and left there so long I feared the mercury might melt. When I removed it and placed it on the table beside my bed, the nurse chastised me.

'We must take your temperature, Mrs Hopkins. You know we must. We want to see how you are.'

'I am perfectly well, thank you,' I replied. 'I slipped yesterday on a wet pavement and I have quite recovered. I had quite recovered last night, but I was forced to occupy this bed – '

'Observation,' said the nurse.

' – and I should like to go home as soon as possible.'

'Home? You want to go home?'

'I have no intention,' I explained, 'of staying here. I have never had a day's illness in my life and I am not now going to change the habit of a lifetime. Perhaps you would return my clothes to me, and when you have done that, a porter can call me a taxi.'

'This isn't the Grand Hotel, Mrs Hopkins, you know. It's a hospital.' She looked at me in some amusement, as though my request to leave had not been made in earnest, was but some frivolous eccentricity. 'You can't leave yet.'

'Why ever not?' I asked.

'It's not allowed. No patient can be discharged until after breakfast.'

'Very well then,' I conceded. 'In that case, I shall leave after breakfast.'

' – And until after the consultant has made his rounds.'

'The consultant.'

'Yes. Mr Johnson.'

'And when does Mr Johnson makes his rounds?'

'Eleven,' said the nurse. And then, after a pause, 'Or twelve.'

'I see. I am to be incarcerated here until noon, am I?'

'Well,' the nurse smiled, moved away, 'it might be longer. Your results aren't through yet. You never know,' she added, with some malice, 'you might be here for some time.'

I ate my breakfast in bed. I ate an egg that had been hastily and inefficiently scrambled and a slice of soft toast. The other women in the ward ate, too. I watched them eat, dressed in their cotton nightdresses and their cardigans, illness marking their faces, pain accosting their bodies. And I recalled something George had said, not once but many times. That dying in a hospital was to allow oneself to be defeated, not only by death, but by life as well.

I have never been able to decide whether George was as wise as he pretended or whether he had merely perfected the execution of a succinct turn of phrase.

At eight, the nurse returns. She is smiling, and really rather a pretty child. I expect she finds me a difficult patient, possibly even obstructive, certainly irritating. George used to say that when I grew old I would become argumentative, even waspish. He knew, of course, that he would not outlive me. But George was waspish even when he was young, and when he predicted I would be argumentative he knew I would have to argue without him.

'If you can just give me your next of kin', says the nurse. 'For the records.'

'I have no next of kin,' I explain. 'My husband is dead.'

I notice the nurse is wearing an engagement ring, a diamond solitaire. 'I lost my engagement ring,' I tell her. 'Mislaid it in a public lavatory. I removed it to wash my hands, forgetting to put it on again. George was rather cross. He bought me another and when I lost that – I quite forget where or how – he said ours must have been the most expensive engagement in history. Will you lose yours?'

'Oh, no. I never take if off.'

'Are you engaged to a doctor?'

'A teacher. We're getting married next year. In April.'

'I married in November. During the ceremony the rain made the most frightful din on the roof. George was suffering from a heavy head-cold at the time. During our honeymoon he was quite impossibly cantankerous.'

'When did your husband die? Was it long ago?'

'Oh yes. A very long time ago. So, you see, I have no next of kin.'

'But you must have children. A son?'

'A daughter.'

'So your next of kin is your daughter?'

'Yes,' I concede, 'I suppose she is.'

'Can you give me her address? We need it for the files.'

'I can,' I say. 'But I would rather not.'

Jean and I do not get on. We bicker. I am sufficiently acquainted with my own shortcomings, I hope, to realize some have been inherited by Jean; a tendency towards brusqueness, an intolerance of the idle and the stupid. I am brusque and intolerant with the staff of department stores and with representatives of minor officialdom – with railway porters and electricity men and the like – but that is only because such people often serve to hinder rather than to help. Jean, while kind to shop staff, attentive to the needs of electricity-meter readers, pleasant to recalcitrant railway staff, is brusque with me. She treats me as one would a wayward infant – with a mixture of impatience and forbearance, and with the accompaniment of too much sighing.

But Jean is worthy; she believes in duty. And here we are most unalike. She believes in duty as others believe in God or in democracy, and worse, she proselytizes about her belief. 'You are old,' she tells me with unremitting regularity, 'and it is my duty to see you look after yourself.' She invites me to Sunday dinner when I wish only to remain alone; she calls at the most unsuitable hours to inquire after my health; she brings me pots of homemade gooseberry jam during the summer and bunches of artifically grown flowers in the winter. She suggest I have central heating installed. She advises me to refurbish my wardrobe. She recommends a hairdresser who will remove the unsightly yellow stains of age from my white hair.

She interferes, and her interference borders occasionally on harassment.

So I explain to this nurse that I will not give her Jean's address; I tell her I would prefer Jean to remain ignorant of the fact that I am in hospital. 'She will only interfere,' I explain. 'She will want to come and visit me.'

I can see her with perfect and frightening clarity, striding up the ward in her smart two-piece, bringing with her several books, a box of fruit and an armful of exhortations to behave, to do exactly as I am told, to allow that the doctors know best. The nurse, infinitely patient, is still standing by my bed and I am reduced to bargaining with her.

'If I give you Jean's address, I shall expect to see a doctor within an hour.'

The doctor arrives. He has sallow skin and is supported by an entourage of students. He examines me, talks of more tests, peers benevolently towards his students.

'How are we?' he asks.

'We are in perfect health,' I retort. 'We are in such perfect health that we wish to remove our person from this hospital bed as soon as possible.'

'Do we, now. We tripped, I believe?'

'We did.'

'And we fainted.'

'We did not faint. We lost our balance.'

'When you fell on the pavement, did you faint then?'

'I did not. The pavement was wet. Had it not been for the enthusiasm of a middle-aged Samaritan, I would now be at home, and this hospital bed would be vacant for those who are really ill.'

'You can't faint without good reason. We'll take some blood tests. You may be anaemic.'

'I am not,' I assert, 'anaemic.'

'We'll find out whether you are or not. Keep you in another night, just to be on the safe side.'

Presently the nurse returns, consoling me with the menu for lunch. 'Cottage pie and chocolate pudding.' It is as she is telling me how favoured chocolate pudding is among the patients, that I decide to discharge myself. I have never eaten chocolate pudding in my life and I have no wish to eat it now. I have only the hospital garb I am wearing, but my handbag is on the small table beside me with sufficient funds in my purse to get a taxi home.

I pull back the meagre bedclothes, walk slowly down the ward towards the bathroom, take the lift to the ground floor, pass two porters discussing football, go through the main door. I am lucky – a taxi is letting out a passenger and I lean over and tell the driver I am in rather a hurry.

Outside my home I give the taxi-driver a more than generous tip. He looks both gratified and bemused, but he says nothing, excusing my bizarre appearance on the grounds that I am old and wealthy and possibly not perfectly in command of my faculties.

Jean called this morning. She disturbed both my breakfast and my peace of mind. And in her behaviour and her manner, she reminded me quite chillingly of my mother.

Naturally I recall my mother. A sepia face, black garments, a grey sternness. She wore shoes that would last a lifetime and her voice carried through the large rooms of my childhood.

In the year in which I was born, fashion dictated female children be called by the names of flowers – Primrose was a popular choice, Violet and Marigold, Lily, and Rose. Perversity led my mother to eschew fashion, to call me not after a flower, but after an attribute. She called me Grace. Need I add that I was not a graceful child? That I felt misplaced in my name, mocked by it, that I was large and clumsy? That vases fell at my touch, glass shattered in my hands, that in my presence spillages at the dining-table were common? That my mother held herself aloof from my clumsiness and habitually called me 'child' and rarely, if ever, used my given name?

Perhaps that is why I so enjoy my solitary old age. Because my clumsiness is not witnessed, because I accept it, because it is not an affront to others.

But, my mother. For most of her life she was nagged by illness. Yet she always held her head high, her back straight, and though she spoke seldom of her pain she carried it everywhere with her, a reproach to my father, to me, to anyone foolish enough to take their health for granted. Our large house was dark, airless, chilled by an eastern wind. The curtains were brocade, the furnishings dour. Only the maid's room – which smelled comfortably of cheap facial powder – was bright and airy. The maid's name was Isobel and she came from County Down; her vowels were long and open – howls between sharp consonants. I spent most of my childhood asking her questions, the remainder of it attempting to decipher her answers. She was kind and thin, and when she kissed me on the cheek a smell of warmth would remain. But she did not kiss me often, for my mother frowned on such intimacies.

On my eighth birthday I was permitted to eat with my mother and father, instead of in the breakfast-room with Isobel as was customary. Of all the rooms in the house the dining-room was the darkest. I remember the rectangular dining-table, a slab of mahogany in the centre of the room, the leaded windows, the clip-clop of the grandfather clock, permitting time to pass like a weary dray-horse.

Before dinner, Isobel gently sang a 'Happy Birthday',

but during our meal there was silence. I found the cutlery heavy, irksome to use; I was frightened of knocking over the mustard-pot, a plate, the water-jug; and conversation was not encouraged during meals. I spoke if I was spoken to, and as my mother and father both retained their silence, so, too, did I. Nervousness made me eat more than I intended and unease caused me to eat too rapidly. I remember I was wearing a dress which itched around the neck and which was fractionally too tight around the bodice. And I remember, also, my father permitting me to drink one glass of ginger wine after the meal.

I do not know whether it was the tight bodice of my dress or the ginger wine or the unaccustomed meal which caused me to be sick over the white lace tablecloth. I had seldom been ill before. I cried. My mother beckoned me towards her with a grim index finger and, while Isobel was clearing up the mess, she slapped me, hard and accurately, across my left cheek with the palm of her hand.

It was Isobel who comforted me, secretly, when I had been sent to my room, and Isobel who explained to me that life was not as easy as we expected it to be, and who confided that mothers and daughters sometimes did terrible things to each other without knowing why.

Before I was twelve, my mother died of one – or several – of the illnesses that had plagued her since my birth, and Isobel returned to County Down. My father went to fight in the Great War and an aunt moved in to supervise my upbringing. I have not thought of my mother for many years and it frightens me to realize that my daughter has more in common with her dead grandmother than I would ever have thought possible.

When Jean called this morning, I was placing a blackened saucepan in the back garden to smoke. I had left the saucepan to boil with my breakfast egg in it while I

37

went to the door to pay the milkman. It had taken me some considerable time to locate my purse and when I bade the milkman good morning, having paid him, I returned to the kitchen to find my breakfast egg cracked, my saucepan burnt and the smell of scorched eggshell quite overpowering.

I do not normally eat eggs for breakfast, but my ordeal of the previous day had left me with a larger appetite not only for life, but for breakfast as well. I was looking forward to my boiled egg, its accompaniment of dry toast (I had forgotten to purchase butter), to a pot of tea or coffee. I was going to eat my breakfast slowly while looking out on to my overgrown back garden. Then I was going to telephone the hospital and arrange for my clothes to be returned to me, before visiting the public library to change my books. My morning was arranged, ordered, it lay reassuringly ahead of me. Jean's arrival naturally upset my plans.

She was wearing a suit I had not seen her wear before and she carried a bundle, wrapped loosely in brown paper, in her hand. It was not yet nine o'clock, but she looked at my stockinged feet and my dressing-gown and she shook her head. And then she sniffed.

'What on earth is that dreadful stench, Mother?'

I confess her greeting put me out of countenance. 'You might say good morning, Jean,' I remarked with some asperity, 'before you start commenting upon the smell of my home.'

She sighed. 'Good morning, Mother,' she said crisply, inviting herself in, placing the bundle on the hall table, leading the way to my sitting-room.

'Do come in,' I said, following her.

I realize I ought to have expected this visit. That the hospital would have informed her of my disappearance. That she would have asked innumerable questions, been supplied with innumerable answers, that she would have felt it her duty to apologize for my behaviour. And that she had come to my house to demand an explanation for that behaviour.

She sat down at the breakfast-table. 'Mice droppings?' she said. 'Is that what the smell is?'

'Mice droppings are odourless. The smell is burnt eggshell. The saucepan is smoking in the garden and I am about to eat breakfast. Have you eaten?'

It was a foolish question to ask and it earned me a look of frostiness. Jean eats at seven o'clock, preparing one of those frugal breakfasts which are supposed to be excellent for the bowels but which are most unappetizing.

'I ate', she informed me (as I knew she would), 'at seven. With Alan. I ate and then I cleared away the breakfast dishes and then I made the bed and then I came over here as soon as I could. Why are you still wearing your dressing-gown?'

I explained that I had not yet had the opportunity to dress. 'I woke at six and read in bed. My book was an interesting one, a story about a man who murders his wife and who places her dismembered body in the chest-freezer in their garage. It was rather gripping, so I got up only when I had finished the last page. I was about to dress when the milkman called. He is a disagreeable man and I'm quite sure he overcharged me. It was he who made me burn the egg.'

'Really, Mother,' said Jean, laughing as if at the vagaries of a child, 'what stories you concoct.' She laughed again. She seemed to think it not at all improbable that a man would murder his wife and dismember her body and place the pieces in a freezer, yet she did not believe that the milkman had been responsible for my burnt breakfast.

'You think me incompetent?' I said. 'Unable to cook my own breakfast? You may share it if you wish,' I offered, waiting for the toast to scorch. 'You can have some toast. Or an egg. I can easily burn another egg for you.'

'No, thank you. I'll watch you eat. And after your breakfast, we can have a little chat. I have something to say to you.'

I smiled. 'How nice,' I murmured, spreading marmalade on my toast. My breakfast afforded me scant enjoyment. I do so hate to be *watched* while I am eating, and that is exactly what Jean did during the course of my meal – she watched me. My boiled egg was hard and tepid. Not how an egg ought to be at all; and for this I blamed Jean. I said she had spoiled my breakfast.

'Why have you come?' I asked.

She smiled, such a weary patient smile. I watched a blackbird in my back garden and heard the sound of leaves dying.

'I've come to see you. I come every week, twice a week if I can. Half the time I call you're out.'

'I am usually in. Particularly at this time of the morning, breakfast-time. And sometimes I simply pretend to be out. Sometimes I simply have no wish to answer the doorbell. It rings far too often,' I said. 'Religious fanatics call, wanting to convert me. And men in ill-fitting Romanian suits, wanting to sell me something called double-glazing.'

'I called this morning,' my daughter said, 'for a reason.'

'Yes. I expect you did. Have some tea.'

'It's not tea, Mother. It's coffee.'

'Have some coffee. The taste is so similar between supermarket tea and instant coffee, it hardly matters.'

But Jean refused the coffee. Coffee, she said, was bad for you; a stimulant. 'It makes me edgy,' she explained. I made no commment. Jean has always been edgy; restless, over-active.

'You can tell me why you called once I am dressed.'

I took a considerable time over dressing, and I put on a frock I knew Jean would dislike – a red frock with long sleeves, a garishly gold belt, one of my favourites. And I added several strands of red plastic beads that had caught my eye in one of the trinket shops near the sea-front. Jean finds plastic jewellery offensive, an affront to the eye. She herself wears discreet, organic jewellery – silver bracelets, small wooden brooches on the lapels of her suits, tiny ceramic beads around her neck. She will want to tell me my red beads look cheap, hang vulgarly around my neck, do nothing for me, but she will not.

When I come downstairs again, the room has been spring-cleaned, the dishes washed, a week's supply of newspapers removed, the carpet hoovered, the windows washed.

'And that saucepan. The one you left in the garden. I've cleaned that, too. It's spotless now, but there's a small hole in the bottom.'

'You ought not to have scoured it so hard,' I say. 'That was my penultimate saucepan.'

Jean tells me she will buy me another. 'Something in non–stick,' she says, challenging. 'A saucepan that will be immune to your carelessness. If I were you, I'd throw that saucepan away. It won't be any use to you now.'

'I hate waste,' I assert. 'I shall fill it with earth from the garden and when spring comes I shall plant marigold seed in it. Marigolds, or those new petunias. The striped ones, red and white, like the colours of a rugby club.'

'Football, Mother.'

'Or lobelia,' I say. 'The dark-blue lobelia, the colour of midnight.'

Presently Jean speaks, says what I imagine she has been waiting to say all morning. She stands in the doorway between the sitting-room and the kitchen in her brown suit and her cream roll-neck jumper and her brown leather boots. She looks like a complete stranger, an alien. I wonder for a brief moment how I can have permitted a stranger to come into my house.

'Eccentricity, Mother, is not a virtue,' my daughter tells me. 'And unless checked, it can spread.' I notice the saucepan in her hand. Is this kitchen utensil to be used in my daughter's argument; is it in her hand to testify mutely to my eccentricity? Apparently so.

'Burning eggs,' says Jean, flourishing the saucepan, 'mistaking tea for coffee, growing flowers in pans with holes in them, reading grisly murder stories.' Here, she pauses, but only to place the saucepan on the table. I peer towards the saucepan. Through its bottom I can see a circle of tablecloth the size of a florin. 'Discharging yourself from hospitals,' I hear Jean say.

'From one hospital, not several.'

'They rang me. A consultant spoke to me on the telephone.'

'I was rather afraid they might get in touch with you,' I say. 'The nurse was most insistent about my next of kin. The hospital was over-heated and draughty. A comfortless place, quite comfortless. The nurse wanted to keep me in that narrow bed to eat cottage pie for lunch. Cottage pie and chocolate pudding. Naturally, I refused.'

'The consultant told me you were wearing four-inch stiletto heels when you collapsed on the pavement. He told me that for a woman of your age to walk about in heels that size was the absolute height of folly, the absolute height.'

'A man', I say, 'with a sense of humour.'

'What? He also told me that you left the hospital without your clothes. That you simply walked out of there with nothing on but a hospital nightdress. I had to apologize on the telephone, it was most embarrassing. I had to say it was not the kind of thing you normally did – '

'I am not normally deprived of all my clothes – '

'He spoke to me quite harshly. As though I was partly responsible. As though I somehow condoned behaviour like that from my own mother. How could you do it, Mother? How could you walk the streets half-naked, like some sort of destitute? How could you?'

Reaching over, I move the saucepan slightly, sliding it along the tablecloth until another florin-sized area – a flower this time – is visible through the hole. Outside, more leaves die from the fruit trees. It is September, I think to myself, the tenth of September, shortly after ten in the morning, and my daughter is about to lose her temper, to say something I will later regret.

'I shall return the nightdress,' I said to Jean, wishing to distract her. 'I have no earthly intention of keeping the wretched thing. It doesn't even fit me properly – it gapes at the back and the sleeves are much too wide. And I did not walk the streets, Jean. I hailed a taxi.'

Jean snorts, and I suspect she does not wish to hear how I hailed a taxi, how the taxi-driver talked to me about his daughter, how he dropped me at my front gate. She much prefers her own version of my behaviour.

'I had to go to the hospital before I came here,' she tells me, 'to collect your clothes. I left them in a bundle on the hall table, wrapped in brown paper.'

'How kind,' I exclaim. 'Thank you so much.' Sometimes it is wise, on such occasions, to preserve the proprieties. I like to pretend, no matter how angry I am, that I still retain the capacity for politeness. I like to pretend my daughter and I can bicker in a civilized fashion. I like to pretend we are discussing nothing more important than a bundle of clothes wrapped in brown paper.

Jean has not, however, forgotten that to discharge oneself from hospital one has to have been a patient, however temporarily. She wishes to know when it was I collapsed, and where, and, of course, why. Her face is concern and anxiety and puzzlement, for she prefers her life to be uncomplicated, she does not take kindly to hospital consultants speaking harshly to her over the telephone; she does not realize that a lifelong aversion to chocolate pudding is sufficient to make me discharge myself; she cannot understand why I do not behave as do the mothers of her friends – contented in a garden, complacent, discussing geriatric ailments.

And she is worried about my health.

'Did you break anything, Mother, when you collapsed?'

'Do try to be more precise, Jean,' I snap. 'I did not collapse. I slipped on a wet pavement – '

'You collapsed in the hospital – '

'Again I slipped. The linoleum had been newly waxed; it was slippery. Afterwards I complained to the Sister. I told her the linoleum was dangerous. She quite agreed.'

'Bones? Did you break any bones?'

'No.'

'You could have. You might have fractured your hip, or broken your arm, or sprained your foot. At your age – '

'Whenever you begin to talk of my age,' I retort, 'you make me want to reach for the sherry bottle.'

We face each other. Outside it has begun to rain. Jean shakes her head and the room still smells very faintly of scorched eggshell.

My daughter tells me I behave as though I were eight, or eighteen. Walking out of a hospital semi-naked is the kind of thing she would expect from an eighteen-year-old. 'An act of rebellion,' she says.

But she is mistaken. And I have never rebelled. How

splendid to have been a suffragette, to have manacled myself in chains to some municipal railings, to have shaken my fists at bemused police constables.

Instead of having married George.

'You simply won't accept the fact that you're over eighty.' Jean looks exasperated. Has she no job to go to, no good works, nothing else to occupy her time?

'I know what age I am,' I reply. 'I don't even mind being reminded of it. What I do object to is the way in which you manage to equate my age with eccentricity, as you call it, or with the absence of good sense. Or with infirmity. If you wish so keenly to discuss age, may I remind you of the time when you were six and emptied the contents, the entire contents, of not one, but two bottles of your father's ink all over the sitting-room carpet. Or the time when you went to that fancy-dress party wearing my – '

'Don't be childish, Mother – '

'Ah!' I pounce. 'Because I am eighty-four, I am childish. Because you are fifty-nine, you are sensible.'

'My childhood was a long time ago; it's not relevant. We're talking about the present now. About the fact that you collapsed twice yesterday. About the fact that you hid your stay in hospital from me as though it were some shameful secret. About the fact that you are no longer as healthy as you once were.'

'As young. You mean I am not as young as I once was. As for my health,' I assert, 'it has never let me down; I do not expect it to start now.'

Jean's eyes scan the room, they search for inanimate witnesses to an old woman's stubbornness. The carriage-clock ticks, the gas sighs. The thick autumn rain still falling outside reminds me of the galoshes that I will have to don for my walk to the sea and the likelihood that the roof is leaking. I think how tiresome it will be to have the

45

roof repaired; workmen on the roof making a clatter, demanding cups of over-sweet tea, listening to music from a transistor perched in the guttering.

'We want you to move in with us.'

'Move in? Leave this house?'

'Alan and I discussed it last night. We think you'd be better off with us.'

'Better off?'

'Looked after. Cared for.'

'Ah.'

'We'll build you a granny extension.'

My internal organs lurch, become displaced in the orbit of my body. I do not know quite what to say, how best to express my repudiation of Jean's offer. I tell her about the flock of geese I saw the day before yesterday. How I was walking towards the sea-front, how I chanced to look up towards the sky, how I suddenly noticed the geese. 'Migrating south,' I explain, adding my hope that the geese were not too late. 'The winters here are too harsh for them,' I say. 'Too brutal for such birds.'

Jean has no wish to hear about flocks of geese; she thinks I am rambling. Geese are not important to her, and the only bird she can instantly recognize and name is a robin.

'We'll build a granny extension,' she tells me, 'above the garage.'

I am perfectly candid. I sit down at the table, my elbow near the saucepan, and I explain that I have no desire to live above her garage. I am not the sort of woman who takes kindly to an offer of residence above someone else's garage. Jean ought to know this. Besides, I have my own home; large, rather empty, a little damp, but my home. I am not to be uprooted. And I have a particular objection to living in a place known as a granny extension. 'Such a *silly* phrase,' I say. 'Did you make it up?'

'No, Mother. People live in granny extensions all the time.'

'People?'

'Grannies. Elderly relatives.'

'A sort of out-house, is it, a granny extension?'

'Now you're being absurd. A flat. Self-contained. Your own living-room, bedroom, bathroom. Even a kitchen. You would have a wonderful view of our back garden. You'd become quite fond of the cherry-blossom tree, I know you would. Pulling back the curtains every morning, it would be the first thing you would see.'

'I dislike cherry blossom. Such a frivolous tree. Pretty for two weeks of the year before the May wind blows its petals away. And I have my own view. Here, I can see the sea.'

'You would be near me and Alan,' she pursues. She has inherited my persistence. Was she as persistent as a child? I cannot remember. 'We could watch television together, the three of us. You could join us for our evening meal. And if you wanted to be alone, you would be. Neither I nor Alan would dream of interfering. You would live your own life, just as you are now. The only difference is that you would eat properly, have more comfortable surroundings. And if you ever had another fall, some kind of accident, and illness, we would be nearby to look after you.'

'Yes. I see. I am to be mollycoddled into my grave.'

'Nonsense, Mother.'

'I am perfectly capable of looking after myself.'

'No. You live on tinned food and bananas. You use those dentures of yours as an excuse for bizarre eating habits. Before Father died you used to eat properly. Roast pork and apple charlotte. Engraved napkin rings and bone china. French wine and good brandy. Now you eat sardines out of their tins. And you have mice in your kitchen. When Father was still alive you ate properly, the house was warm, the mice stayed in the basement where they belonged. Everything has changed now.'

'Naturally. Your father has been dead for a long time. Things *ought* to change.'

'Not like this. An old woman shuffling about in an even older house.'

'Don't be unkind, Jean. You will only cement my resolve to remain here.'

'But it's my duty. To look after you.'

'Your offer is most generous, but I cannot accept it. I intend to remain in this house until I die. Nothing will make me leave it. And please don't talk to me about duty. I was dutiful to your father for far too long; it brought me nothing but pain.'

'So you won't move out?'

'That is correct.'

'You'll change your mind.'

'That I doubt. Now, do you intend to stay for lunch, because if so it will put me to considerable inconvenience.'

I show Jean to the door, watch her walk quickly to her car in the rain. How richly the air smells of decaying matter – dying leaves, a neighbour's compost, roots rotting quietly beneath the surface of the soil. I wave cheerfully to Jean as she gets into her car, wishing to pretend I am neither frightened nor alarmed by her offer.

At lunch, I find I am not hungry. Jean, while intending to deprive me of my privacy, my freedom and my independence, has also deprived me of my appetite for food. I scatter breadcrumbs beside the refrigerator for the mice and place the saucepan in the back garden to rust.

Later, my telephone rings and an acquaintance reminds me that the bridge club is to meet, as usual, next Wednesday.

4

On the harbour wall Roff sits, angry, wanting to maim the water, throwing objects towards it – empty cans, hunks of seaweed, stones. But the sea, too, is angry. Slate-grey, ramrodding the harbour walls, soaking the shoes Roff wears, telling him to piss off.

Never having met his father, Roff tries to imagine him. A tall man, bearded, Roff's grey eyes. Average height, glasses, a short nose, a full laugh. Fat, two-chinned, cheerful, the sort of man who tells jokes. Annie never tells jokes and is thin in her black waitress outfit. When he asks about his father, she shrugs. 'Went off,' she says, as though discussing sour dairy produce. 'Just went off.'

Roff used to wonder why; still does. At school he invented several different fathers for himself. He had been a gambler. Not an everyday sort of gambler, losing on the horses, throwing money away at the dog-track, but a man who lost thousands in casinos up and down the country. 'He gambled away our house,' Roff once told his friends, with inspired embellishment. 'We had to live in the back yard for a fortnight till he won it back.'

His father had had two other women in the town, both younger, both richer, both prettier than his mother. When his mother had discovered this dual deception, she cried solid for two whole days. Three boxes of tissues she went through.

He had emigrated, when Roff was only four, to Australia, where he now lived in a house with a swimming-pool and a barbecue and where several hundred men worked for him.

He had committed a dreadful crime just before Roff was born, had been forced to flee the country and had not been heard from since joining the Foreign Legion.

He had gone to work as a diver on an oil-rig and had died in the most tragic accident. When his body had been recovered from the depths of the North Sea, his face had been so swollen as to be quite unrecognizable.

Some of Roff's stories about his father were believed, but most were swept aside with adolescent scepticism. The only story that Roff gave out consistently was the one in which his father had been in a pub fight many years before, had threatened another man with a broken pint glass, had accidentally turned the threat into fact and been convicted of grievous bodily harm. He was now in a high-security prison.

The sea slams against the harbour wall. Roff thinks of his father sitting on the bunk of his cell in Durham jail reading pornographic magazines (perhaps the same magazines he himself reads). He sees him, a small man with muscled arms and a face without a smile, eating in the prison canteen, dreaming of the reunion he will soon have with the son he has never seen.

Roff does not know, and will never find out, that his father walked out on Annie because of boredom. And that the nearest he has ever been to a high-security jail was the day after he walked out, passing Wakefield prison on a bus on the way to Leeds. That he now works with a small building firm in Leeds, lives with a woman called Vera, and drives a small saloon car. Roff's father never thinks of Annie, or of Roff, or, indeed, of the eighteen months he spent living with Annie in a seaside town on the east coast. When he and Vera take their holidays they go to Blackpool or Morecambe, avoiding the eastern coastal resorts, his secret and almost forgotten past, and the possibility of ever having to remember it.

50

This is how Roff likes the sea to be – angry, belting its waves against the rocks, the screeching furious froth, the rain pockmarking its surface. When his father gets out of prison, this is the first place he will show him – this harbour wall, this angry water. In the winter nobody comes here, not even the fishermen. People have been known to drown here, swept from their feet, too busy admiring the view. Annie tells Roff often not to go there; it is dangerous and, besides, a boy his age should be out with his friends, not spending his time staring at the sea.

When the tide is high, Roff runs the length of the harbour wall, jumps on to the sand, watches the water tease the shore, feign retreat, rise again, lick the pebbles shiny. Under the shelter of his jacket, he takes out a tin of Cow Gum and a plastic bag and inhales. It is not long, not yet quite dusk, when he sees with his dilated and mildly demented eyes various monsters, brown and green and uniformly huge, emerge from the sea.

5

At my bridge club we play for fifty pence a rubber. The stakes are small, the bidding cautious, the sherry dry, the conversation drier. I smoke a cigarette, and this intemperate behaviour earns me the widows' raised eyebrows. Rain pelts against the long windows and the room smells sadly of damp macintoshes.

I have always been fond of bridge. George was a very fine player, particularly at duplicate. In Rome one summer we won an absurdly large amount of money from a minor member of Romanian royalty. I remember how gleefully I greeted this triumph of ours. (I was quite young at the time.) Of course George returned the money the following morning, leaving it with the hotel desk-clerk, adding a courteous note. 'You ought not to take it so seriously,' he chided. 'It is, after all, only a game, and one governed more by luck than skill.' Nevertheless, George was generally a very bad loser. In the evenings when we used to play canasta, I invariably had to let him win. I often think that is why he became so very wealthy – because luck, not skill, was on his side. When his luck changed, when the war came, he changed too, and our games of bridge, like our travelling, and our friends, were consigned to the past.

But I do not wish to dwell on that; on the changes wrought in George. Some memories are best lying dormant, like slugs under a garden stone, where they can do no harm.

We are about to begin to play the first rubber. Mrs

Willow has the score card; she is a weak player, indecisive, and I rather suspect that when scoring she cheats. She is partnering Mrs Simpson, while my partner is Mrs Davies.

All three women wear hats of felt in dull, muted colours – beiges, browns, greens. Though I have been a member of this club for over ten years, I cannot count these women among my friends. And their bridge game is poor, lacking in both discipline and concentration. Often when one of them makes an incorrect bid, while I frown, the others giggle. All this – the felt hats, the giggling, the incorrect bids – serves to irritate me, to put me off my game.

Mrs Simpson shuffles the cards, Mrs Davies cuts them. We are ready to play. I think, while adding up my points, of how my aunt would warn me of the dangers of living too long. She would warn me of impaired hearing, weakening eyes, an incautious bladder, an unpredictable heartbeat. Of the death of friends, of boredom, of the fear of dying in the street, of dying in one's bed, of endless illness, of chronic discomfort. Of watching the world move too quickly – she herself detested trams, was afraid of ever stepping on one – of becoming an observer of life, a mere spectator.

She never warned me about the tyrannies of one's children.

Mrs Willow starts the bidding. 'One heart.' She speaks in a fragile voice, as though she is frightened, not by having to open the bidding, but by life itself.

'Two diamonds,' I say, and glance at my partner.

Mrs Simpson says no bid. Over luncheon she talked about her dead husband and her distant grandchildren in a low and melancholy voice. 'A heart attack,' she said, 'at sixty-seven.' We had, all of us, heard this detail

53

before, but our sympathies were again sought. 'How frightful,' Mrs Davies said. 'How ghastly for you.'

'I do so hate to be alone,' Mrs Simpson says now.

'Yes, dear,' Mrs Davies nods. 'Two spades.'

'And the crime rate.' Mrs Simpson shakes her head. She has read she tells us, of the most horrendous attacks upon old women, upon men in their seventies, upon ageing couples living in insecurely locked flats. 'The old are under siege,' she says, giving details of these attacks, of pensions stolen, lips split, broken bones, faces requiring stitches. Her hands are shaking so badly she accidentally permits Mrs Davies to see her cards, though she is too distressed to notice this. The world, she asserts, has become a terrifying place in which to live, so terrifying that she has placed her name on a long waiting-list for sheltered housing. 'One would be safe there,' she claims. 'Money would not be stolen, bones would not be broken, a woman would not be – ' and here she pauses, delicately ' – interfered with.'

'Raped,' I insert.

'Well.' Mrs Simpson turns to give me a look of distaste. She is coy about matters touching upon sex; she dislikes me because I am outspoken, because I refuse to wear a hat, because I do not feel, as she does, that widowhood is a form of amputation.

Mrs Willow cannot decide how to bid. She looks nervously at her partner, seeking surreptitious guidance. Blinking, she says she thinks she might as well pass, her hand is very poor, and was not the lamb cutlet at luncheon ever so slightly underdone?

'Raw,' I say.

'It does not help my complaint,' admits Mrs Willow. She suffers from a bowel problem, one that necessitates the constant wearing of a bag into which her body's waste must pass.

'It's rather uncomfortable,' she says, and I sigh elaborately, not wishing to hear details of her intestinal disorders, wondering why I should be subjected to it. 'I change the bag regularly,' she says.

In my irritation with Mrs Willow, I bid foolishly. 'Three hearts,' I say, and earn Mrs Davies' disapproval.

'Really, my dear,' she chastises, knowing Mrs Willow and Mrs Simpson will go on to win both the game and the rubber.

After the rubber we take a break for afternoon tea. We eat in the adjoining room, a room as indifferent to human aspirations as an airport lounge. On first joining the club the room struck me as dreary, cold, comfortless, and it has not changed. Endless summers of afternoon sun have drained the colour from the brown velvet curtains, and the table upon which we place our teacups is stained, marked, unpolished. The chairs are uncomfortable to sit on, and discourage drowsiness; yet only last month one of our members died in one. This is a room ready for death, a room in which the past is too easily accessible, a room furnished for widowhood.

The tea is only warm and our sandwiches filled with limp and bitter greenery. Mrs Davies, irritated by the loss of the rubber, complains about the lack of a pot of hot water to the waitress, who is surly and indifferent.

'In our day,' Mrs Davies recalls, 'we had respect for our elders and betters.' There is general agreement that this respect has vanished, that the old are treated as burdens, that the quality of life has been diminished by too much traffic, by pre-packaged food, by the reliance of the young on a spendthrift Welfare State. I do not join in the discussion but pick instead at the crust of my sandwich, shedding crumbs on the sombrely patterned carpet. The arguments of these women are badly thought out, their opinions as stale as the bread, their statements unreasoned. The Empire is frequently referred to, and the War.

'The young have no sense of direction,' says Mrs Davies.

Mrs Willow simpers. 'The price of eggs nowadays!'

'On the television,' says Mrs Simpson, 'men and women kiss and undress and there is never, any more talk of love.'

I pour out the tea again. In the fireplace someone has laid sticks, a white firelighter, crumpled newspaper. When the waitress remembers to light the fire, one of us (Mrs Simpson? Mrs Davies?) will sigh and look towards the flames and speak of the exorbitant price of fuel.

'A cake?'

'Thank you, no. The currants interfere with my dentures.'

'A slice of gingerbread?'

'The doilies are soiled. I would not be surprised to learn that they have been used on a previous occasion.'

'The tea is cold.'

'Where *is* that girl?'

'And how', Mrs Davies inquires, 'is your daughter?'

The question, so cunningly inserted between the eating of sandwiches, the exchanges of trivia, catches me unawares. Mrs Davies is a devious woman and because she has not yet forgiven me for bidding three hearts, her revenge is, under the guise of a pleasantry, to ask after Jean. She knows we rarely agree, Jean and I, that there is pain in the relationship, anger and distrust. She knows, because I do not believe in keeping secret my dislike of my only daughter.

'She is perfectly well,' I say.

Childless Mrs Davies smiles. She says, 'She is devoted to you, is she not? Often, when I pass your house, her car is outside. How lucky you are to have such a daughter.'

'Yes.'

'I was never blessed with children,' she tells me. 'When I die, my carriage-clock and my silver will pass to a great-nephew whom I have never met.'

'I'm sorry,' I say. My words are inadequate; Mrs Davies sniffs and I notice crumbs of gingerbread cling to her mouth, coat her lower lip. The women at the table think me selfish, deficient in ordinary, decent human kindness; I have no compassion, for all compassion in me has been spent.

The waitress brings the pot of hot water, but by now we have finished our tea and she is told to take it away again. She moves out of the room and we know that she will not now light the fire. Having seen our fur stoles, our pearls, she does not think we require a fire, or even that we merit one. It is perfectly possible that these assumptions are correct.

Adjourning to the bridge room, we change partners. Partnering Mrs Willow I know we cannot win the next rubber, given her memory and her lack of skill, and I bid cautiously now. In my hand, the cards are slightly sticky; they have been used too often, by too many women, but they will not be changed until the end of the month. Between the faded velvet of the curtains the rain smears the window and I watch it, thinking how dreary the afternoon is, how dull the game, how insignificant the companionship I had hoped for. I imagined these women returning later to their homes, to their past, to their memories, holding these memories to them as a child does to a teddy-bear that has long since lost all its fur.

Mrs Davies is in better spirits now that winning has been guaranteed to her. Of the four of us, she gives the impression of being the most robust; she nods her head vigorously while listening to Mrs Simpson talk of her dead husband and her distant grandchildren.

'The young deserve success,' says Mrs Willow, nervously, hearing of a grandchild's hard endeavour, a university degree completed, a well-paid job in the catering industry.

The clock on the wall tells me it is thirty minutes past five. Through the doorway I see the waitress take off her white apron, push it into her coat pocket, put on the coat. In a few minutes, she will go down the stairs and join the bus-queue, stand in a street wet with rain waiting for a bus that will have been delayed. We will finish playing the rubber and, at dusk, smile our farewells to each other, each of us making our solitary way home.

But now Mrs Simpson continues to talk of her grandchildren. Mrs Willow smiles too much and fiddles with the jewellery at her neck, and Mrs Davies coughs to warn me not to light another cigarette. I stare at my hand, clubs, diamonds, hearts, spades, and I realize that I am afraid of becoming like these women, widows who want nothing more from life than the happiness of other people.

After the final rubber Mrs Davies unexpectedly suggests we walk part of the way home together. Her offer discomfits me; I am used to walking home alone and have no desire to talk widows' talk with her on a wet evening in late September. Generally, after bridge, I walk home via the sea-front, watching the few lights from the harbour boats, inhaling the brine. This walk is a reassertion of my solitude, a pleasant, undemanding ritual to which I invariably adhere. Besides, the fresh air and the brine give me an appetite for my late tea and the walk restores the circulation to my legs.

But Mrs Davies links my arm. 'A walk by the sea-front,' she claims, 'would be delightful.'

Though several years younger than I, Mrs Davies' step is slow. She suffers, she tells me, from an arthritic knee, and though I feel some sympathy for anyone in pain, her slowness irritates me. The tide is low and even in the dusk it is possible to see the insufficiently treated sewage which trickles from a brown pipe inset in the promenade wall. I fancy I can even smell this human waste lying on the beach, waiting for the next high tide, and the smell is offensive, reminding me of hamburgers and fried food and insufficiently digested hotel breakfasts. It is the smell of inadequate lives, trivial miseries, loveless marriages.

'They say the sea is polluted,' Mrs Davies remarks.

'So I believe.'

'Even dangerous to swim in.'

'Yes.'

I notice a figure on the beach near the rocks that guard the harbour; his walk is unsteady, and he throws stones towards the water, several at a time.

'A drunk.' Mrs Davies snorts her disapproval. 'The resort is not what it once was. Forty years ago the water was so clear the stones were perfectly visible underneath. And the debris on the beach – cans of lemonade and packets of cigarettes and the wrappers from sweets; there did not use to be debris. Or drunks. I wonder,' she says, inevitably, 'what this place is coming to? My departed husband used to swim regularly before breakfast. Were he alive today, he would be scandalized by this.' She indicates, with a sweep of her arm, the beach – the raw sewage, the empty tins, the drunken youth, the barely visible mounds of dog excrement. 'Were I a younger woman, I would write to the appropriate authorities about this disgrace. I would protest. But we are too old, you and I, to protest about anything.'

59

Listening to Mrs Davies, I understand that she is waiting only to die, and that if we continue to walk together for another few yards she will begin coyly to discuss the arrangements she has made for her own funeral. 'I must go,' I say quickly, walking off, fearing the contagion of her company, her mute acceptance of an unwarranted death.

The telephone rang later, while I was immersed in a television programme about natural history. I let it ring, fearing it would be Jean, and I continued to watch the television. But Mrs Davies' words returned, swooning in my ear, and I wondered if she was right and if I, like her, was too old to protest about anything.

I was a girl of eleven years old when Father went off to fight in the First War, almost fifteen when he returned. Two months before the outbreak of war, Mother died and I went to live with my aunt. It was she who assumed that Father, too, would die, she who informed me he had little to live for. 'He has me,' I claimed, with the egocentricity of girlhood, 'and he has his country.'

'Pshaw,' said my aunt, as though neither merited further discussion.

During those years of the war, I learned to play the piano and to play bridge. My aunt, already accomplished in both, learned only patience. Letters from the Front were infrequent, their arrival unpredictable, their contents distressing. Often one letter written in May would precede another written in April; the war made the post cruelly capricious. When a letter did arrive, it was presented to my aunt over the breakfast-table by the maid with a mixture of temerity and reverence. 'A letter,' my aunt would redundantly remark, 'from your father.' I was not informed of the contents of these letters – it was held that I was too young to learn of the doings of war –

but my imagination compensated me. I would lie on my stomach in the garden with an unread book by my side, a paper-knife dangling idly in my hands, and I would think of my father. I would smell the honeysuckle and I would wonder what my father was doing. Would he be sleeping now? Fighting? Would he be wounded? I tried so very, very hard, to imagine the trenches, the dug-outs. Wars were not then fought on the television as they are now, to an international audience; one still required imagination to conceive of its horrors. Was his trench long? Deep? How deep? How muddy? Were there many trees by the battlefields of France, farmhouses? Did rabbits scamper through no man's land? Did birds sing?

My aunt's maid – less loquacious than Isobel had been, of an altogether more sullen disposition – refused to answer my questions, shaking her head at my curiosity as if at some unpardonable offence. My aunt shrugged. 'They say the greatest enemy is boredom,' she told me, a fact I could not make myself believe. 'Your father sends his good wishes,' she would add.

'Will Father die?' I asked, but this question, too, remained unanswered.

'Your time might more profitably be spent at the piano,' suggested my aunt.

The honeysuckle flowered and faded and flowered again. In those years of the war I became a woman, though I now have little recollection of the process which today appears to cause the young so much anguish. I continued to play the piano – a modest skill I have long consigned to the past – and I was playing it the day Father returned from France. The morning – it was October – had been damp, and the sound of the rain upon the windows in the drawing-room tampered with the rhythm of the Chopin sonata I was attempting. In my efforts to blot out the rain I played the piece loudly, far too loudly, not as it ought to have been played at all. And so it was that I did not notice Father until he was standing at the door of the drawing-room.

'You play that piano,' he said, 'as though it were your adversary and you wanted to thump the very life out of it.' I rose, went to kiss him. I remember how well he looked, how bright his eyes, and I remember that his cheek smelled faintly of earth.

It was some time later, as we sat down to luncheon, that I noticed my father's right arm was missing.

Nobody spoke of his maiming during the meal. My aunt drew attention to garden flowers and silently handed my father a spoon with which to eat his vegetables. 'We had an excellent crop of gooseberries last season,' my aunt said, and my father nodded but otherwise took no part in the conversation. I did not know whether it was the presence of his family which caused his muteness, or the absence of his right arm. Later that month I heard my aunt speaking of my father to a friend. 'It is not his missing arm that concerns me, though that is tragedy enough,' she confided. 'No, it is the amputation of his reason.'

So Father returned from the war in a state of physical and spiritual mutilation. Of course I did not realize this, and my aunt, who did, was unable to help. Father took to sitting outside in the walled garden, shrapnel in his knees, a book of poetry in his left hand. His view embraced the bare cherry-blossom tree, the wooden gate at the end of the path, a street lamp-post. He was angry with his disability and he was angry with the world. I began to collect stones from the sea-shore – even then I liked my solitary walks – stones that bore the hallmarks of the sea, stones pockmarked by time, stones worn round, smooth by the ineluctable movement of the waves upon them. When I returned, I would give these stones to my father. I would sit beside him in the garden and pass them to him, one by one. I would watch him smell, feel, scrutinize, even lick them. 'Your little gifts from the sea', he said to me one afternoon, 'diminish my anger for a few moments.'

They took my father away some months later. Even now I do not know where exactly he was taken. He had become a danger, my aunt claimed, to himself. He died in the winter of 1918, of the influenza, and my aunt said his death was a blessing. But I had already mourned his death.

I often wonder what Father would have made of life today, of a world excited by ephemera, of a world morally anaesthetized, of a world where certainties no longer exist. It is when I think these thoughts that I am reminded of my age, reminded of the fact that it is not only Jean who sees me as a stubborn and peculiar old woman.

6

When Roff came home from his evening on the beach he noticed two things. He noticed, first, the stranger who sat in the best chair. He was a man in his early forties, heavy but not fat, with short, dark hair and a brown suit. He presumed this stranger to be selling something – brushes, insurance, replacement windows – and was puzzled by the absence of the man's briefcase, samples, insurance form. People were always coming to the house wanting to sell things, and though Annie was rarely persuaded to buy, she almost always invited these people in for a cup of tea. But this man was not drinking tea, and he appeared too comfortable, too obviously at ease, to be selling anything.

The second thing he noticed was that Annie had been drinking. Now Roff knew that his mother never drank, for she talked often about her dislike of the taste. 'Bitter,' she said, 'horrible,' condemning spirits, beers, wines alike. Yet his mother was standing by the mantelpiece, swaying slightly as if in tune to music only she could hear, and when she spoke her words were not distinct. Seeing the stranger in the best chair, realizing his mother was drunk, Roff felt that some law of his universe had been broken. He felt much as a very young child feels when, expecting a gesture of affection from a fond parent, he is rewarded instead with a slap. He felt confused, disorientated and angry.

Long after dusk, long after the two old women had passed him by, mistaking him for a drunk, Roff had remained on the beach. Squatting on the pebbles, throwing stones into the empty pot of glue, hearing the sea slush a few feet away. In the dark he had heard a dog sniffing, its paws on the pebbles, forefeet scraping sand. He had not wanted the dog around, but the stone he had aimed at the animal's head had missed, slapping instead into the shallows of the water. The dog had barked and shortly afterwards one of the town clocks had struck several times, though he had lost count after six. Roff shrugged, thinking how little it mattered what the time was, which day tomorrow would be, the week, which month, the year.

By the time the dog had padded off, the effects of inhaling the glue had begun to fade, though a dizziness persisted. This was the dark time, these the moments when the only coherence Roff could make out of life was through his anger.

Enraged, he threw handfuls of pebbles into the water, remembering a story he had been told once in school, a story about a man who could part water with a stick, divide a sea with a word, a story about some magician. He thought the story stupid, for everyone knew nothing was more powerful than the sea. He hated, during the summer, to watch the water being kind to stupid kids, allowing them to paddle at its edge, even to swim out of their depth without coming to harm. He didn't believe the sea ought to allow itself to be treated like that, just another holiday amusement, cheaper than the big wheel, less exciting. Tonight he had wanted the sea to be angry with him, but the water was calm and almost silent, and little waves licked patronizingly at his sneakers.

Annie spoke first. 'This is Dave,' she told Roff. 'We got acquainted in the Rose and Crown.'

'Oh yeah?' Roff did not smile. He thought he would stop sniffing, for each time he came down he felt sick and

– much worse – alien, as though he had borrowed the body of a stranger and the limbs did not quite fit, the eyes were too heavy, the mouth too small. He had thought, walking slowly home, that his mother would not notice anything strange about him, would simply smile, make tea, say, 'Nice night out, son?' He hated her for bringing this man back, for talking the way people talked on television, for trying to make out she was better than she was. '*We got acquainted in a pub.*'

He watched his mother looking over at Dave, smiling too much at this man with his dark hair and his brown suit. He could see he was probably the sort of man women like his mother would go for, lonely women – the suit, the short hair, the plain brown eyes. He imagined his mother coming home from the hotel, smelling slightly of the food she had just served to the hotel guests, stopping off at the pub to buy some cigs, being bought a drink. He saw how, in a couple of hours and after a few rum and blackcurrants, such a man had commandeered her interest.

'Dave's in town for a while,' Annie said. 'He's in cement. Travelling. All over the place – Birmingham, Carlisle, Manchester, Swansea. Cement's big business these days.'

Annie smiled. She hoped Roff was not going to be difficult. She'd only nipped into the pub for some lemonade to take home, she hadn't meant to get chatting to this bloke at the bar, God knows her opinion of men wasn't high, not after Bob had walked out all those years ago. But she had taken a liking to this Dave, he'd insisted on bringing her home, it was only polite to ask him in. He'd kissed her just before Roff had got home, and the kiss had excited her. She sighed, thinking of all the time spent working as a waitress, all the years bringing up

Sheila and Roff, all the penny-pinching – after all this, surely she deserved some joy out of life?

'Cement,' said Roff, thinking how sudden and perfect was his hatred for this man.

'That's right,' said Dave, talking about a contract his firm had with a local builders, how many bags of cement were required for even the most modest of housing, how much each bag cost. 'Cement's under-estimated,' he said. 'People don't realize, see, how important it is. There'd be no houses without cement, no offices, no pubs, nothing. England would be a wasteland.'

'Yes,' said Annie, liking the sound of the word. 'A wasteland. I see what you mean.'

Roff wanted to turn on the television. When it wasn't on, he had nothing to look at, boredom assailed him, restlessness. He focused his eyes on Dave's shoes – black, highly polished, laced shoes that looked as though they'd never been near a bag of cement. If this man were not here, he could watch television, Annie would make tea, they would laugh at the advertiments, he would not feel angry. At the small hardware shop where, earlier, he had bought the tin of glue, the Asian had overcharged him. He had wanted to smash up the shop, scatter the bags of nails, put one of the hammers through the glass, rip apart the wooden counter. But a middle-aged man had come into the shop at that moment, and Roff had had the opportunity only to knock off a pair of garden pliers. He couldn't remember where he'd left them – the beach, the harbour, the arcade – and this saddened him, when he thought of the damage he could have inflicted on this Dave with one pair of pliers.

Dave said, 'What about some tea?' and Roff thought that the way he said these four words, the rapidity which his mother walked into the kitchen, indicated that this man intended to stay the night with his mother.

In the kitchen Annie filled the kettle, poured milk, added sugar, found the tin of biscuits, and thought how pleasurable these unthinking tasks became when done for a nice-looking man. She rinsed the best cups under the tap and removed the dust from the saucers and plates, while waiting to hear the sound of conversation from the other room.

'You got a name?' Dave asked.

'Yeah.'

'What is it then, a State secret?'

Roff was reluctant to reply. This, not because his name would expose him to ridicule, but because talking to this man, having a conversation with him, meant he had to look at him, acknowledge him, when all he wanted was for him to leave.

'Well?'

'Roff. My name's Roff.' He waited for Dave to laugh (as most people did), but Dave merely smiled.

'You're in good company,' he said. 'My middle name's Gillespie. I took a lot of teasing about it at school. You still there, at school?'

'Left.'

'When?'

'Last year.'

'Got a job?'

'Might get one,' Roff invented, 'on an oil-rig.' The brother of one of his friends worked on a rig, a mechanical engineer. Out in the North Sea, five hundred miles from shore, on top of an oil-field they called by a woman's name. Roff had often thought how exciting it would be, watching waves four hundred feet high, hearing all that ocean pound against the pipes of the rig, surrounded, by the devastating power of so much sea. That was how Roff felt the sea should be —powerful, violent, capable of killing.

Carefully Annie warmed the pot, made the tea. It was nice to hear them talking next door, Dave and Roff. To know they were getting along. It was nice to know, too, that a man in a pub, a man who travelled and who sold cement and who wore nice clothes, could find her attractive. Life, she reflected, was like Ernie, the fellow who ran the Premium Bonds – you never won a thing for years and then, when you were least expecting it, your number was read out on the telly.

This time, Dave laughed. The laughter was not intentionally malicious, though it sounded so to Roff. When Dave had finished laughing, he asked Roff if he was serious about working on an oil-rig.

'You'd have to fill in an application form,' he said. 'Have an interview.'

'So what?' asked Roff. 'I can read, write. I could train.'

'Oh certainly,' Dave told him. 'Certainly, you could train. And when you think about it, you must be just what they want, these huge oil companies. Exactly the sort of material they're after. They must be screaming out for people like you – a sixteen-year-old yobbo with a daft fucking name and hair sticking up in spikes. Just what they want.'

Roff did not react immediately; it took some minutes before he could make sense of Dave's words, before he understood. His mother came in, then, with the tea-things and when Roff offered to pour the tea, she was pleasantly surprised. 'He's a good lad,' she lied to Dave. 'Been having a nice chat, have you?'

The tea was hot and strong, scalding Roff's lips and tongue. He did not take his revenge immediately; he was prepared to bide his time. He listened while Dave told Annie about his recent week in Cardiff, selling cement for holiday flatlets. 'One thing the Welsh can't do right,' Dave said, 'and that's make tea.' He watched, while his

69

mother smiled at this remark, letting her skirt ride up her thighs, giggling as though Dave had said something funny. He heard a train passing, the sound of a car door slam, a woman's voice in the street outside. He saw Dave move his chair closer to Annie's, his eyes swivel towards her legs, his mother's almost imperceptible answering nod.

'Must go upstairs,' his mother said, sometime later. 'Have to spend a penny,' using a phrase Roff had not heard from her since he was very small.

Dave helped himself to the last biscuit. 'Sorry about that crack earlier,' he said, 'about the oil-rig. Only teasing.' Roff smiled, noticing the crumbs that dropped from the biscuit on to Dave's trousers, waiting until he heard the bathroom door click shut. 'Thinking of staying?' he asked, casually.

Dave smiled, complicit. *Women*, the smile said, *can't resist them*. 'I might,' he replied, meaning he was. 'I'd say your Mum was the hospitable type, wouldn't you?'

'Hospitable?' said Roff, as though the word was foreign to him, its meaning unclear. But he knew what Dave meant by it and he hated him.

In the bathroom, Annie flushed the toilet, brushed her hair, refreshed her lipstick, dabbed perfume between her breasts. So long had it been since she had felt the need for perfume that she was too liberal with it, and felt it necessary to rub off some of the scent with the damp corner of a bath-towel. Her neck was flushed, indicating sexual anticipation, a sensation she had not felt for years. Before Bob had walked out, they had been in the habit of making love three times a week; but after he left, she had been surprised at how little she had missed this aspect of their marriage. She thought that sex was like having a sweet tooth – something you enjoyed when you were young, but soon grew out of. It would still be nice, however, to sleep with a man instead of a Mills and Boon romance.

Downstairs, Roff smiled encouragingly at Dave and told him he looked like a decent sort of bloke. 'It's only 'cos I like you,' he said, 'that I'm telling you this. Just so as you know.'

Dave looked puzzled. 'Know what?'

Roff explained that his mother was in the habit of picking up men in pubs, that she often brought them home with her. 'My Dad's inside,' he plausibly explained. 'Manslaughter. Been in ages. She gets lonely, see, Annie does. That's why she does it. You're the fifth since Wednesday.'

Outside, Dave felt cold. Walking back to his hotel he noticed a frost had fallen, and he shook his head, knowing the arrival of the winter would mean people would be less willing to buy cement, to build, knowing his commission would fall accordingly. When he reached his hotel it was not yet midnight and he was able to buy himself a drink from the bar. The barmaid who served him was fatter than Annie, but younger, and she smelled of an expensive, faded perfume. Dave bought her a drink and himself a second, feeling in need of it. 'I'm just going off duty,' the barmaid told him, but instead of returning to her bedsit above a launderette she let herself be led up to Dave's bedroom on the third floor. They made love twice, the first time with their clothes on, the second naked. At about three A.M. they both fell asleep, and slept away their very slight sense of shame.

Annie drank four more cups of tea. She had been surprised when Roff had told her Dave had suddenly remembered an appointment in Carlisle the following morning; surprised, but less disappointed than she might have been. Roff turned on the television and together they watched a late-night horror film, one in which men and women returned from the dead as vampires. One of the vampires was particularly gruesome in appearance, horrific in white make-up, red-eyed, offensive to look at.

'That one', Roff remarked, 'looks like that Dave.'

Annie laughed. She didn't know what she'd been doing, she said, two rum and blacks and she was away. Going up the stairs while Annie washed the cups, Roff whistled to himself and thought he could still smell the odour of stale chicken fat from his mother's clothes.

During the night there was a storm. The wind pulled down wooden fences and ripped the last of the leaves from the trees. Slates were hurled from roofs and the sound of doors banging endlessly in empty, windswept houses punctuated the hours between three and seven. One middle-aged man, brooding upon his failed marriage in the solitude of the nearby golf course, was struck by lightning and taken, with severe burns, to the nearest casualty hospital; while a young couple narrowly escaped injury when their car was hit by a tree.

And nobody ventured near the sea. Beneath the clouds and a tiny, fragile moon, the landscape of the water terrified.

Throughout the storm, Roff slept.

He woke unusually early to hear his mother discuss the weather with the postman. Lying in bed, he scratched his chin, his chest, his genitals. He lifted an arm to pull back the curtains and heard Annie tell the postman winter had well and truly arrived. 'That storm last night', he heard her say, 'was what saw the end to autumn. It's all downhill from now on – frosts and snow and gales and rain.' The postman seemed to agree, Roff heard an answering grunt, then retreating footsteps. Annie closed the front door and Roff, leaning on his elbow, saw that the clouds were still, the storm had already died, there was no wind.

Below him, in the kitchen, the sounds his mother made were loud. They were the sounds those who are lonely make to reassure themselves that though their world is solitary, it is not silent; the clattering of tins, the rearranging of jars, the running of water, the drumming of fingers on the back of a chair. Roff found these sounds irritating and it seemed to him they had no sequence, no logic to them. He sighed, knowing that when he went downstairs, the water would still be running in the sink but the kettle not yet filled; that the shelf of tins would have been rearranged but no beans or jam would be available for breakfast. He knew his mother would smile and ask what he would like for breakfast; he knew she would point to the back yard, to some evidence of the storm – an upturned flower-pot, a broken gate hinge – and that she would talk, at length, of the weather, of her job as a waitress, of his sister's latest boyfriend, of the neighbours. He did not think he could bear this, and so he dressed quietly and when he reached the hall he opened the front door silently and let himself out.

The storm had left its smell – the stench of too much salt in the air, the rain-soaked earth, the rotting, drenched leaves, the stink of dustbins upturned by the wind. Roff passed a tree whose trunk was raw, its bark ripped from it by the storm, and he saw pieces of litter cluster together in a gutter by the kerbside. He remembered hearing storms as a child, the excitement of listening to the wind turn to disappointment when his mother would come into his bedroom and pretend to chase away the wind with a yellow duster. He felt peaceful now, surrounded by the storm's devastation, at ease in a world where nothing – not even houses – were safe, in a universe where nothing could be relied upon.

When Roff reached the promenade, it was sand-blown and empty. It pleased him to see the shutters of shops still down, the benches empty, the absence of traffic. Sometimes, he liked to pretend the town was his – the promenade, the sand, the sea – and this was hard to do when the sand was overcrowded with kids, the water's edge thick with paddlers, when deaf pensioners in thin overcoats took up all the bench space.

Roff stopped at the silver railings, swung himself under them, jumped on to the sand. Occasionally when he came to the beach in the winter he met a friend called Mick and together they would watch the sea and smoke cigs and wait for the arcade to open at eleven. Mick was all right; he had a tattoo on his arm, a swastika, and he'd been in a detention centre for a while during the summer for stealing. Roff supposed Mick was his only friend, the only person who really knew him.

On the sand, he waited to see if Mick would turn up. The sand was damp and coarse, and right in front of him lay the remnants of a sandcastle, damaged by the tide, the storm, by dogs. A herring-gull snarled at its edge and flapped its wings, seeing the stick Roff threw towards it.

The bird's panic made Roff smile. He thought that it was not just birds who were easily frightened, but people. On August Bank Holiday he had seen a man in the public lavatories at the end of the promenade expose himself to two small boys. The man had been dressed in a suit, a businessman, and Roff had seen him fondle his penis as though it were a priceless valuable, caress it with both hands. The boys were too frightened, too fascinated, to do anything but stare until Roff, coming upon the scene, had told them to bugger off. He had pushed the man against the tiles, the wash-basin digging into the man's back. 'Give us £50,' Roff had demanded, and the man had smiled, nervous and eager, as if expecting this punishment. He had given Roff the contents of his wallet – £75 in all – and run off. When Roff went up the steps again, the two boys were there, waiting. 'Thanks,' they said, 'thanks a million,' but they had not understood that Roff did not care about the man exposing himself, that it was the man's humiliation that was important. He had spent the money in an afternoon, on the Space Invaders.

'Hi,' said Mick.

'Thought you wasn't coming.'

'Been with someone,' boasted Mick. 'All night. She kept me busy.'

Roff nodded, pretending to understand. Mick had had more girls than hot dinners, he claimed, and they did things to him Roff had only seen in magazines. The sort of things, Roff thought, Dave might have done to his Mam. But he didn't like to think about that. He listened while Mick told him about the girl, and watched one of the fishing boats sail out of the harbour. The boat must once have been red, but the colour had been bleached now by the sun and the wind, and the boat looked shabby. The only red that Roff could see was the red bobble hat worn by one of the fishermen, the one who stood by the mast, looking back towards the harbour. Last year in school, Roff had written an essay about fishermen, thinking that he might one day become one, but the English teacher had returned it with a red pencil through it and a comment about bad spelling.

'Told me she loved me,' Mick was saying.

'Yeah?'

'Said she'd follow me to the ends of the earth. Shit, I said, didn't she know the earth was round? *I* know that, everyone knows that. Then I tell her to piss off and she cries. Stupid bitch. Left her tights behind.'

'That right?'

'Could of strangled her with them,' Mick said amiably. 'Saying she loved me. Stupid cow.'

'Yeah,' Roff said. Annie called him 'luv'. *'There's your breakfast, luv.' 'I've put your clothes in the washer, luv.'* On the telly, men and women sat on beds, or in planes or in restaurants and said they loved each other. Whenever they did this, Roff switched channels.

'You got a girl yet?' Mick inquired. On the promenade, a dog barked and Roff could hear the sound of traffic from the town.

'Naw.'

'Just as well,' Mick told him. 'Waste of time.'

'Yeah.' His mother wanted him to find a girl, to take her to discos, to go out and enjoy himself, but girls bored him. Groups of them came, now and then, into the amusement arcade, lipsticked and giggling. When they lost on the Invaders they shrieked and spoke in abnormally loud voices. Roff was glad Mick thought he was better off without one.

Mick sifted sand through his fingers; Roff watched the sea, thinking that when it was calm, as now, it looked like an expanse of lead. Somewhere, a school bell rang.

'Nine o'clock,' said Mick, and Roff said nothing. Speaking was an effort sometimes, people talked too much. Annie talked like she was addicted to it. When the telly was on, she talked over its volume; during tea, she talked. Sometimes Roff could even hear her talking in her sleep. 'Bob,' she would say, 'Bob. Don't go.' Talking too much, it got you nowhere.

When the woman walked carefully down the steps from the promenade to the beach, Roff and Mick remained on the sand, detained by inertia. They had, after all, nowhere to go. The arcade did not open for another two hours, they might as well sit on the damp beach as on a bench in the shopping centre or at home where the only telly on was for schools. The woman was on the sand now, stepping over the stones in sandals, wearing a beach-robe of bright blue, the kind advertised as super-luxurious in his mother's catalogue. Her back was slightly hunched, deformed, Roff thought, until he saw the woman was old, the hunched back due to age rather than malformation. When she came within ten feet of the water she bent to take off her sandals, and to place a striped towel on a pile of pebbles beside her. 'Some old bitch going swimming,' said Mick.

'Mmm.' Roff wasn't that interested. In his world, the old were irrelevant, they were like the places nobody ever bothered to visit any more – art galleries, ruined abbeys, old churches.

'That's what my Mam'll be like,' Mick predicted, as the woman took off her robe, stood in a black swimsuit skirted at the waist. 'She'll be old, like her, in twenty years. But she won't go swimming, she can't swim. She'll moan on about her age and want cups of tea made.' Roff nodded, not caring much about Mick's Mam, a woman he had never met, a woman who worked in a supermarket at the bacon counter. 'She'll drink tea and she'll want someone to read out her horoscope every fucking morning.'

The woman's hair was white; to Roff, its whiteness matched the colour of the sand, bleached by the sun in the summer's heatwave. But it was thin on top. 'She's going bald,' he said to Mick, but Mick told him all old people were bald, even old women.

'In them Homes,' he said, 'they wear wigs. When one of them dies, the next person on the waiting list for a wig gets it. Anyway,' Mick added, bored, 'you'll go bald, 'n all. That crap on your hair.'

Now, the woman was putting a swimming cap on her

head, fastening its strap under her chin, tucking her hair under the rim of the cap.

'She's really going in,' Mick said presently.

'What?'

'That old cow. She's going in for a dip. Water must be bollock-freezing.'

'Yeah.'

'Maybe,' Mick suggested, 'she's going to drown herself. That's what they do, old people. They kill themselves. I seen it in the paper. Last winter some old bloke walked into the water, all his clothes on. Shoes, socks, trousers, coat. Even his hat. The tide brought his hat back, and one shoe, the next morning. Took frogmen ages to find the body.'

Roff frowned, was silent for a minute. 'I never seen anyone drown themselves.' He thought it might be fun to stay where they were, just in case.

'Let's throw stones at her,' said Mick.

'Shout,' Roff replied. 'Tell her to fuck off.'

'She wouldn't hear,' Mick told him. 'Old people are deaf as well as bald. Anyway,' he continued, drawing shapes in the sand with a stick, 'you tell her to fuck off, she'd run a mile.'

Roff nodded, knowing this to be true, knowing old people feared bad language as much as they feared being mugged, knowing they were afraid both of life and of death. If he ever grew old, he'd hang himself. But perhaps this woman was different. If she was going to drown herself, she wouldn't care about someone shouting at her. If she were going to drown herself, she would turn a dreary morning into something special. 'I've never seen a dead person,' he confided. 'Only seen them on telly.'

'Me neither,' Mick replied. 'Seen me Dad beat up on me Mam, mind. Seen her half-dead. Not the same, though.'

'No.'

The water scarcely seemed to move as the woman waded in. But as she went further, a wave appeared suddenly, hitting her on the legs. Even from where they were sitting, forty yards away, Roff could hear the sound, like a smack. A second wave a few moments later slapped her across the middle.

'Must be crazy,' said Mick, losing interest. 'Old people are, you know. Stupid. They do daft things. My gran set fire to her bedclothes in the hospital. My Mam had to get her special clothes, fire-resistant. Cost a fucking fortune.'

In the water, the old woman dived beneath a wave. Roff held his breath, counted to ten, to fifteen. Later, in the arcade, he could tell everyone how he'd saw a woman drown herself.

'She's doing the breast-stroke,' he said, disappointed. He noticed the woman's arms move stiffly, the white cap, the water froth as she kicked her legs. 'She can't want to drown herself if she's doing the breast-stroke.'

Mick shrugged. He had written something in the sand, but Roff could not make out the words. 'When people drown, their bodies go all sort of bloated. Like inflatables.'

'Inflatables?'

'Or balloons. Blown up like balloons. Even their relatives can't recognize them. All the water gets in their bodies, see, through their mouths and ears.'

After a pause, Roff said, 'She might still drown herself. Or freeze to death in that water.' He remembered something his mother had once told him, how when a person kills himself God cries, sorry for the death, yet unable to forgive the person for taking his own life. But Roff knew this to be untrue. When Paul King had hung himself from the light fitting in the school cloakroom last year, the sun was shining. There had been no sign then of God's tears, of any rain. At the funeral, everyone was sweating, it was so hot. Sometimes Roff thought his mother was dead stupid, pretending God existed.

The woman was lying on her back now, floating, looking up at the sky. Roff watched as she flipped her body over, swam back towards the beach. 'She's coming out,' he told Mick.

'Oh yeah?'

Roff kicked viciously at the sand, cross as a child arbitrarily deprived of a promised sweet. When Mick suggested a few minutes later that they go and see if the arcade was open, he quickly agreed.

Sometimes looking at the sea was just about the most boring thing in the world.

7

I woke this morning, greedy for sensation.

I am normally quite moderate in my habits, eating frugally, drinking seldom and only occasionally am I profligate with the enormous amount of money George unintentionally left me. But last night I dreamed of George and the dream reminded me of my own mortality. I wished to do something I had not done for many, many years – drive a motor-car, consume too many sweet-centred chocolates, dance in the orchard. Upon opening my curtains, a calmness greeted me. Beyond the roofs of houses, beyond the trees of the municipal park, the sea appeared frozen, quite, quite motionless. It seemed to beckon me to swim in it.

Earlier, the storm had woken me. The wind, raucous and undisciplined; the slamming of a wooden gate; the cruel tearing of branches from trees; the hammering of rain. The prelude to winter. I imagined the sea slashing against the wall of the promenade, and I hoped nobody had been foolish enough to venture out in a boat. I ought, I suppose, to have prayed for those at sea, but I have never prayed and it is a habit I should prefer not to adopt, a smug little peccadillo which, unlike most peccadillos, has little reward in this life. When George returned from the Second War he took to praying for a time, to kneeling on the bath-mat beside the bath and loudly demanding bargains from God. Naturally enough, God paid scant attention to George's ceaseless demands and this indifference made George angry and more willing to cause me pain. I remember telling a friend at the time that I blamed George's unreasonable behaviour on God and the war, and my friend remarking that I was being far too charitable towards my husband.

When I woke again, the storm, nature's tantrum, was over, though fragments of my dream remained, embedded in my mind like shrapnel. 'I shall take a swim,' I announced to the world in general and to nobody in particular, 'I shall wash away my dream.'

I encountered the most astonishing difficulty when searching for my swimsuit, and for one alarming moment thought I must have given it to the woman from Oxfam who came all those years ago to relieve me of George's clothing. And when I did eventually come across the garment – in a drawer I thought I had reserved for the tablecloths I no longer use – it was stiff with salt, smelling of some long-forgotten beach. Nevertheless I put it on and it fitted, in a manner of speaking. The middle-aged claim the old shrink with the years, but they are mistaken. The proportions of the body simply realign themselves: the bosom drops, the stomach swells, the lower half of the body appears elongated. In my wardrobe mirror I saw that I looked unfashionable, but not ridiculous. Over my swimsuit I wore an old blue robe and by half-past eight o'clock I was trotting down the garden path with my swimming cap and a towel of generous proportions in my hand.

I felt adventurous, walking down the street. Like a child attending its first party, an adolescent discovering love. 'I am going for a swim,' I announced to the postman as I passed, and the look of horror he returned me was most rewarding. I walked on quickly, partly from anticipation, partly from a desire to keep the morning chill at bay. On my feet I wore sandals and beneath their cracked leather the leaves felt pleasantly moist, promisingly damp. I thought of Jean as I walked, imagining her carefully placing breakfast dishes into her dishwasher, surrounded by the humdrum gadgetry of her kitchen.

When I reached the beach, the water was grey, almost ashen in shade. Certainly it was less welcoming than I had assumed. Gulls pattered around the edge of the water, noisy and possessive, shrieking a warning to one another at my approach.

A few feet away from them, I took off my wrap, unbuckled my sandals, pulled on my swimming cap and strode towards the sea. For decades of summers I have watched bathers prepare themselves for a swim in this sea; seen the elaborate and unnecessary procrastinations people perform before finally succumbing to the water. The faltering steps, the coy retreats to the oasis of tartan rug and the beach towels, the small, involuntary shrieks as the water grazes their feet, the ritual splashing of water over legs and arms in the shallows in order to lessen the water's blow, the interminably slow immersion into the water. That is not the way to swim.

I walked into the water until it reached my waist, I dived, I swam. The cold was severely shocking to my system – my heart thumped, burned, leaped; my legs became numb, my teeth clamped defensively together. But the exhilaration I felt was immense and extraordinary. It was, quite simply, wonderful to swim in this empty sea, to be pushed about by the breakers, to move my arms and legs with the waves. It was wonderful to taste the water's salt on my lips and to see below me stones and pebbles and graceful lengths of green and brown seaweed.

It was wonderful to be eighty-four.

I swam for several minutes, while the clouds moved above me and the gulls flew warily past. The water's sounds echoed in my ears and the waves pulled at my bathing suit. I felt triumph and elation, and experienced a child's wonder at the world, and the sea applauded me, and accommodated me and treated me kindly.

The beach was deserted when I waded out and as I rubbed myself vigorously with my towel I sang, shrilly, to myself.

Of course, the doctor spoiled it all.

When I arrived home, he was waiting on the doorstep with the air of a man about to undertake a disagreeable and possibly tedious task. My recent experience in hospital had not endeared me to the medical profession and as an example of the general practitioner, Dr Grahame is unprepossessing. He was wearing a dreary suit; he was neatly, unmemorably attired, and when I approached his hand moved quickly to his tie, as though to confirm that he was properly dressed.

It was I who spoke first. 'Such a pleasant morning, Dr Grahame. Last night's storm seems to have quite exhausted itself.'

'Indeed.'

'You have come, I presume, to see me?'

'A chat.'

'Yes.'

'You've been down to the beach, Mrs Hopkins?'

'Swimming. The water was chilly, but pleasantly so.' I indicated my garb – my wet wrap, my damp towel, my cap. 'You find me', I said, 'confirmed in my eccentricities.'

Dr Grahame smiled. 'My wife enjoys a swim. She takes herself to the Baths every Wednesday morning.'

'I prefer the sea. I find the public baths offensive, reeking of chemical disinfectant. One swims in the urine of children and is made to wear a rubber band with a number on it around the wrist. The sea is cleaner.'

'Colder.'

84

'Fresher. You ought to recommend a swim in the sea for your more nervous patients. It would benefit them far more than swallowing all those dreadful pills you doctors are so addicted to prescribing.'

'If I were to recommend such a thing, half my patients would catch pneumonia. You yourself might catch a severe chill.'

'If I do,' I replied, 'you will be to blame. Perhaps we could continue this conversation inside, after I have changed and poured myself a rather large brandy?'

The doctor refused to drink brandy with me. It was only, he pointed out, nine-thirty. I knew that he had come to visit me solely at my daughter's insistence, that this mediocre man was Jean's emissary, her ally. In this sense, he was dangerous. He sat facing me in the breakfast-room, his legs neatly crossed, his fingers inter-laced, talking of the weather, scattering banalities like pennies. But I was not deceived. Doctors do not call on patients they rarely see at nine-thirty in the morning; they are not in the habit of waiting on doorsteps, nor are they desirous of a 'chat' with elderly women. No, Dr Grahame had called because he, like Jean, thought I ought to leave my home and live above her garage.

I ought to have been cautious. But I was cautious for more than forty years with George and I have outgrown caution, cast it aside like a pair of wellington boots that pinch at the toes. The brandy stimulated the circulation of my blood and brought a flush to my neck. 'You have had an unnecessary journey,' I pointed out. 'You find me in perfect health.'

'But you spent a day in hospital only last week. You fainted.'

'I feel quite well. Very well indeed.'

'Not ill in any way?'

'I daresay, doctor, you should like to find me ill in some way?'

'Not at all. But if you feel as well as you claim, you won't mind if I give you a small examination, will you?' He looked pleased with himself, as though scoring a point. He balanced his case on his lap in the eager manner of an insurance salesman and from the case pulled out a stethoscope.

'I do object,' I said, 'but I will permit you to examine me if only to prove that I *am* in perfect health.'

The examination was less perfunctory than I had hoped. Dr Grahame laid flaccid hands upon the beat of my pulse, wrapped black cotton around my upper arm to take my blood pressure, placed a wooden spatula tasting of disinfectant on my tongue. He asked me several impertinent questions and nodded at my answers. This will soon be over, I told myself, and I shall be rid of this disagreeable man with his clean fingernails and his patient smile.

'You haven't fainted since that day?'

'No.'

'Blackouts?'

'No.'

He put back his stethoscope, sat back, tenting his fingers. 'Your daughter,' he told me, 'is anxious about you. She wonders if you take proper care of yourself. The news that you spent a day in hospital distressed her greatly. Naturally, she got in touch with me. She is concerned for your welfare, your health, your happiness. She feels you lead a rather solitary and secluded life.'

'She is perfectly correct,' I retorted. 'I choose my seclusion. It has not been forced upon me.'

'Nevertheless, there are degrees of seclusion. She thinks this house is rather large for you, unmanageable, difficult to keep up.'

'My daughter,' I explained, 'is fastidious about cleanliness, a habit she inherited from my husband. When she claims my home is unmanageable, she means that I do not scour my sink as rigorously as she believes I ought. She feels uncomfortable in dirt – unwashed dishes disturb her, crumbs on the floor, a bed unmade until teatime. She thinks I ought to live as she does.'

'Yes, well.' Dr Grahame cleared his throat, and I imagined him doing this with his patients, prefacing the news of a terminal illness by this nervous habit. 'You eat properly, do you, Mrs Hopkins? There was some mention of a burnt egg.'

'I eat,' I said. 'Whether I eat properly or not is a matter for conjecture. Occasionally,' I teased, 'I use a spoon instead of a knife and fork.'

'It's not *how* you eat that concerns me, but *what* you eat.'

I sighed, remembering those interminable meals with George, remembering the engraved silver napkin rings and the bone china, remembering the roast pork and the gooseberry charlotte. Remembering the ease with which George shattered the china and with it the fabric of our life together.

'Mrs Hopkins? You were going to tell me what you eat.'

I paused. 'I was going to tell you to leave.'

Dr Grahame laughed, mistaking my rudeness for jest. He laughed uneasily, the laugh of an unhumorous man. I noticed several cavities as he opened his mouth.

For a minute I could not bring to mind what I ate; I felt only irritation at this man's questions, at his insistence, at his presence.

Eventually I told him I ate pasta.

'Ah,' he said, 'spaghetti? lasagne? That sort of thing?

My wife makes a marvellous cannelloni. She uses chicken livers in the recipe.'

'Pasta,' I said, 'out of tin.'

'A tin?'

'Squiggles of pasta. You buy them in tins at the supermarket. Pasta in tomato sauce. This really is the most ridiculous conversation I have had for some time, Dr Grahame. Must we proceed?'

He nodded. 'What else do you eat?'

'Cheese,' I said. 'The mice like cheese. And I drink sherry. Without fail I have a slice of toast in the morning, thinly spread with runny honey. I drink coffee, sometimes tea with lemon. Never with milk. One beverage I cannot abide is milk. Milk makes me bilious.'

'I see.'

For one frightful minute I thought Dr Grahame was going to invite me to his home to taste his wife's cannelloni, but he merely smiled, stood up and said, 'By all rights you ought to have died years ago of malnutrition. But you seem to be as strong as a horse.'

When he left, I did not hide my relief at his departure and he did not hide his disappointment in my good health. I knew, of course, what Jean intended to do. I knew the visit from Dr Grahame was the beginning of a long and extremely intensive campaign to wean me from my home, my seclusion and my independence.

I knew that eventually at the climax of the campaign I would be forced to take desperate measures, but I had prepared for this.

I shall enjoy the final battle and I will surprise Jean by the strength of my protest.

By noon Roff was bored again, having spent all the money he'd taken from his mother's purse on the Invaders. He'd shot down thirty enemy jets, twenty-four helicopters, bombed eight battleships, exterminated five space-monsters since five past eleven, and this made him not only bored but tired. He also had a headache and an unfamiliar whizzing sound in his brain, as though the noise of the machines was not in the arcade at all, but inside him. Mick had disappeared and the manager, sitting hunched in his plastic booth, kept staring at him as if waiting for an excuse to throw him out. He was hungry too, having left home without breakfast, and the smell of the previous night's dried glue on his jacket made him want to heave. He thought he might as well go home.

On his way back Roff made a detour via the shopping centre, sauntering into one of the town's larger department stores. He thought that the women behind the various counters did not look like real people at all; their eyes scarcely moved and their lips, artificially red, looked wounded. His sister Sheila had once worked in a department store like this, at the perfume counter, and on coming home from work in the evening Roff would be alerted not by the sound of her footsteps in the hall, but by the stench of several different perfumes. Sheila now worked for a mail-order company, sticking pins in shirts, wrapping the shirts in cellophane. She did a lot of overtime and they seldom saw each other. When they did, neither spoke. The other night Roff had heard her come in at four o'clock, spending a lot of time in the bathroom. He knew that meant she'd been at it with some man, maybe even a married man, and he had stored the knowledge up, knowing later it would come in handy.

The women in the department store all wore blue blouses and black skirts, and their names on small plastic labels right above their tits. One was called Marion, another Sylvia. Roff remembered what Mick had said about the girl he'd been with and thought of these women telling blokes they loved them and the blokes laughing.

He thought of Sheila, having it with some married man in his car, or on a bed in a borrowed room somewhere, and he wondered why she should do such a thing, why it was people thought sex was so special. When he masturbated, it was not the image of a girl that appeared before him, but the photographs of war atrocities that Mick had lent him.

Music was playing in the store and the women behind the counters smiled at the customers and rearranged bottles and tubes on the shelves behind them. Roff walked round the store quickly, as if in search of a friend, and when he went out through the glass doors at the side of the shop nobody noticed.

When Annie came in from serving lunches at the hotel, Roff gave her the rolled-gold bracelet he had stolen from the jewellery counter. He had thought at first of pawning it, but by the time he'd got to the pawnshop it was closed for lunch, and he thought he might as well give it to Annie as throw it off the end of the harbour into the sea. She held the bracelet up to the light, reminding him of the girls at the supermarket check-outs who did the same with a pound note or a fiver.

'It's real,' he said, as she placed the bracelet on her wrist. Roff gave her a smile, thinking of the woman at the jewellery counter, the one who had been examining her tights when he'd taken the bracelet. Annie smiled back, telling Roff she'd been on her feet since ten-thirty, setting cutlery, filling the cruets, making up the mustards, serving vegetable soup and braised steak and French beans. 'And chocolate puddings for desserts,' she said. 'Just like the sort I made you when you was a boy.'

Roff turned to stare out of the kitchen window. The dustbin was full again, its lid lopsided. A tin of peas had fallen out and lay on its side a few feet away, its jagged top rusting around the edge. Roff hated his mother when she reminded him of when he was younger, of when he was a boy. Yet he turned again to smile at her, thinking she had probably made the chocolate pudding up, thinking it unlikely she even knew how to make a pudding like that. His headache was less insistent, now reduced to a dull pain. If he took a swim later, the pain would disappear altogether.

Annie asked, 'Where'd you get it?'

Roff laughed, 'Stole it, didn't I? From that jeweller's in the High Street.'

'The one on the corner? That posh one with all the watches in the window and them engagement rings?'

'That's the one,' said Roff. 'I just wandered in, nicked it, wandered out again. Nobody saw me.'

A slight wind suddenly made the tin of peas in the yard roll towards the wall. '*Processed*,' Roff could make out on the label, '*sugar, salt added.*' He thought how stupid his mother was.

'You're having me on.' Annie said.

'Yeah.' Suddenly he couldn't be bothered saying any more; all he wanted was to get out of the house. He shrugged, knowing Annie was waiting. 'Saved up the money. Quid a week from my dole.' He watched Annie relax, hold the bracelet up to her cheek, feel its coldness.

'Here,' she said, reaching for her purse, pulling out a ten-pound note. 'You go out tonight. Treat yourself. Go to that new disco, meet a nice girl.'

Roff pushed the money into the back pocket of his black jeans. In the yard the can continued to roll gently in the wind.

8

Today is the anniversary of George's death.

Yesterday I swam in a sea chilled by the threat of winter and today I remember my husband's funeral. Such are the activities of batty old widows like myself.

The day of George's funeral was much as it was this morning when I began my customary walk to the sea. A frost, a wind, frozen threads of sleet in the sky. And while many of my memories of my life with him are mercifully dim, this morning I recalled that day with extraordinary clarity.

I must be quite frank with myself. I mimicked mourning. I wore the black theatrical costume of bereavement and I pantomimed grief. The house was filled with all kinds of the most ghastly people. Friends of George's, business acquaintances, peripheral relatives. They came to the house and the house seemed to accept them, all these people with their dark suits and ties, their low voices, their mute condolence, their communal grief. The house accepted them, but I did not. They cluttered up what was now my home, drank far too much sherry, spoke in voices too low. All the carbon dioxide in the air caused my geraniums to wilt and somebody managed to effect a blockage in the lavatory. People whom I hardly knew (and did not care to know) came up to me and spoke to me of a man who sounded like a stranger. 'Such a kind man,' they said. 'So entertaining in company.' 'A fine mind.'

'Nonsense,' I replied, but people did not acknowledge my reply.

'She's still in shock,' someone mistakenly assumed.

During the course of the early afternoon I slipped out of the house through the back door. George had always been an extravagant man – extravagant with his money, his temper, his gestures, and I assumed that his friends, these people cluttering up my home, would be too, and that they would only leave when the sherry had run out. I remember tying a scarf over my head and walking quickly down the road towards the shore. Although it was March and cold, an ice-cream van was parked by the promenade, and the man inside looked forlorn. He smiled rather sadly at me as I passed, an old woman in a headscarf, and I imagined him thinking, 'That woman, she'd be the last person to buy an ice-cream.' I felt immensely sorry for him, standing in his chilly prison waiting hopelessly for customers, and I stopped, walked back, took out my purse. He frowned as I gave my order, nodded as he opened the lid, peered inside, finally smiled.

My purchase was heavier than I had expected, and I had to remove the scarf from my head and use it to carry the ice-cream. By now the wind had died, the sleet diminished and a slab of sunlight hit the frost on the outside of the cartons, making it glisten. I felt immensely happy as I opened the back door, placed the ice-cream on the kitchen table, wiped the moisture from my hands. From the other rooms, from the drawing-room, the dining-room, the hall, the voices of George's friends and George's acquaintances and George's relations were low and cautious, colluding with grief.

I ate the ice-creams, I ate all of them. The ice-cream vendor with the forlorn face had particularly recommended the raspberry ripple – a preposterous name, but the flavour I found to my liking – so I began with that, before unwrapping a chocolate ice and the three tubs of something called mint delight.

When Jean walked into the kitchen with a tray of empty sherry glasses I offered her an ice, but she refused. She was rather cross, as I recall, and the expression on her face so reminiscent of her father's that I laughed aloud for several minutes, delighted in her displeasure. As I laughed, I watched Jean, and I waited.

'What', she presently asked, 'do you think you are doing, Mother?' I told her I was eating ice-cream, though it seemed hardly necessary to explain. The kitchen table was littered with ice-cream wrappings, damp, gaudy envelopes, silver, red, dark-brown. 'I am sitting in my own kitchen and eating ice-cream.'

'But where did you *buy* the ice-cream?'

'From an ice-cream vendor on the promenade. He particularly recommended the raspberry ripple.'

Jean looked puzzled, as though I had spoken to her in a foreign language.

'Raspberry ripple is a flavour of ice-cream,' I explained. 'Very sweet, red-veined, really rather delicious. I ought to have kept one for you, but I'm rather ashamed to say I have eaten them all. Your father's death has made me extraordinarily hungry. You could,' I offered, 'have a lolly. I bought three iced-lollies, too.'

Jean shook her head. No, she did not want a lolly.

'No, dear. Quite right. You've been drinking sherry all afternoon, haven't you. And sherry rather dims the palate for lollies.'

Jean sighed, as though suddenly quite exhausted. I wiped my hands on a towel and told her she looked most becoming in black. 'It suits you,' I said, but she did not acknowledge my compliment.

'All the guest have gone,' she said instead. 'Everyone has gone home.'

'Good. They were a tiresome bunch. Such mediocre people – dreary lawyers and their wives, middle-aged businessmen, dreary, dreary people. But then your father was so indiscriminate in his friendships – quantity mattered much more than quality. Promiscuous almost, one might say.'

'Father is dead, Mother. We cremated him not three hours ago. During the service,' she added, pointedly, 'people cried.'

'Only those who did not know your father well enough,' I said. 'Besides, people *do* cry at funerals. They cry because their wives have been unfaithful, or because their husbands have refused to buy them a new motor-car.'

'People cried,' Jean repeated, 'and you are eating ice-cream.'

I could not explain. I could not tell Jean of the immense relief I was feeling, of the pure joy of eating ice-cream. I could not then reveal to her that her father had been a bully and a tyrant and ought, if I am candid, to have been certified as insane.

Together we rinsed the sherry glasses, emptied the ashtrays, swept up the ice-cream wrappers. Later, as we listened to the six o'clock news, I thought of George's ashes, cowering from the breeze in a corner of the cemetery gardens.

I had been sitting for some twenty minutes on my promenade bench remembering the day of George's funeral when Jean appeared. Her appearance was so unwelcome that, had I been younger, I might have been tempted to run away. As it was, I concentrated on perusing the graffiti on the walls of a nearby shelter. '*Jack was here,*' had been scrawled on one of the walls in what seemed to be black paint. '*Pete . . .*' But I did not like to read the rest; the words were sexually explicit, and the grammar was quite atrocious.

Jean sat down beside me, resting a large shopping bag

at her feet. Each time I see my daughter, she is thus encumbered – shopping baskets crammed with frozen foods, bags of fruit, dry-cleaned articles sheathed in thin plastic, greengrocer's flowers damp at the stems, bound with tight circles of elastic. I sometimes feel these physical encumbrances are essential to her sense of well-being. Jean likes to feel she carries the burdens of the world upon her shoulders, she enjoys being weighed down by responsibility.

'What a surprise,' my daughter lies, 'to find you here.'

We sit uncompanionably together, sharing this wooden bench, and the clatter of the water on the pebbles punctuates our silence.

'I may be old,' I declare, 'but I am not a fool, Jean. You know my habits; you know I walk to the sea every day, that I sit here on this bench. Why have you come?'

'I've just been to the cemetery. I put some flowers on Father's grave. I thought I might have met you there.'

'No.'

The day is chill. The weather forecast predicted rain this morning, and I notice Jean has prepared herself for this eventuality; she wears a dun raincoat and sturdy boots. I find her presence irritating; I wish she would go away.

'I wish you would leave, Jean.'

'Why?'

'Because I know the reason you have come. You want to involve me in another tiresome discussion about my future; to cajole me into that slum for the elderly you call a granny extension.'

'It's not a slum. How can it be a slum, when it hasn't even been built?'

'Don't be pedantic, Jean.'

I sigh, telling Jean she is more like her father than she realizes. From her slight smile I see she takes this as a compliment. Below us, the incoming tide shifts the pebbles.

'Why,' I ask, 'did you visit the cemetery?'

'Because it's the anniversary of Father's death. I always go. Every year.'

'But why?'

'Because it's my duty. I buy flowers, I take them to the cemetery, it's my duty. Just as it's my duty to look after you.'

'I am perfectly capable of looking after myself.'

Jean laughs; it seems I have said something absurd, outrageous. If she would go away, I could read my library book.

'But you're so wrong, Mother. You don't look after yourself, you know yourself that you don't. Your eating habits, for a start. Well, they're . . . inappropriate. All this living out of tins. Tins of sardines and tins of spaghetti and cans of tinned tomatoes. Like a tramp. Junk food. And it's not just what you eat, it's that house you live in. Mould crawling up the walls of the bathroom – '

'Mould does not crawl.'

'And mice. You have mice. *They* crawl.'

'Mice do not crawl, Jean. It is quite obvious to me you have never taken the time to look properly at the motion of a mouse. Mice crawl only when they are dying. Normal, healthy mice scamper. Or scurry. Or even scuttle.'

'Whatever it is mice do, they do it in your house. Colonies of them in the kitchen. So unhygienic. Especially in the summer. Last summer I saw one, I saw a mouse in your kitchen, running across the floor. A *fat* mouse.'

'It wasn't fat, merely pregnant. It gave birth to six babies two days later. I saw them – pink and small, rather like those sugar mice we used to buy at Christmas.'

'Even worse,' shudders Jean. 'A pregnant mouse –

what sort of behaviour is that, Mother? Eating junk food, befriending vermin, living in a fossilized house? You don't behave as you should, like other women of your age – '

'Most other women of my age are dead.'

'Any other person with your wealth and your intelligence would see the benefits of moving out of a house like that. Living with us, with me and Alan. You know, Mother, if I live to be your age I shall be a perfectly ordinary octogenarian. I'll wear thick, sensible stockings and woollen suits and I'll knit sweaters for my grandchildren.'

'But you can't knit.'

'I can't knit because you never taught me. You taught me to play cards instead – solo and canasta, cribbage, bridge.'

'Your father taught you.'

The water heaves itself up the shore, marooning a paper cup on the pebbles. Jean lights a cigarette. She is thinking of her father, but our memories of him are not the same. I think the only thing George ever taught me was unhappiness.

Jean say, 'You never loved him, did you?'

I have to smile. My daughter's generation need so many certainties from life – confirmation from the past, reassurance from the future; safe memories and a building-society book. 'I loved him,' I reply, knowing this is not what she wishes to hear.

At the back of the town, a train leaves the station and I hear it pass, an express sardonically bound for some distant city. I think George proposed to me on a train, yes, I am quite certain he did. 'Do marry me,' he said in the first-class compartment, reaching out to take my hand. My hand lay in his and I looked out of the window, permitting several miles of dun countryside to pass –

fields, a village, a church – before giving him my answer. 'Yes,' said George, nodding. 'You will be a good wife,' but it sounded like a warning. When I finally disentangled my hand, red marks lay on it and it ached ever so slightly.

'Don't you ever get tired of staring at the sea, day after day?'

'What a preposterous question.'

'The sea bores me.'

'Yes, dear,' I say, 'I know.'

'And I'll have to go soon. A hairdresser's appointment. Alan and I are going out to dinner tonight. We'll go for a cup of coffee and I'll walk you home.'

The restaurant is on the fifth floor of a department store and the table at which we sit looks complacently out towards the harbour. At other tables like ours other women sit, talking, smoking, drinking coffee. The waitresses who clear away the empty cups are dressed in flowered overalls, and yellow caps sit awkwardly upon their heads. I tell Jean with some petulance that I do not care for the habit of drinking coffee in the afternoon in an over-heated restaurant, but she laughs as she always does when I speak my mind. I did not dare speak my mind to George when he was alive; but might not he too have laughed?

Jean drinks her coffee slowly, telling me how delightful I would find life, sharing it with her and her husband. 'If you take no interest in your own comfort or in good food, think at least of the companionship,' she urges.

'Ah yes,' I say. 'The companionship.'

'You say it as though it were a dirty word.'

'Possibly I do. I prefer privacy. It's one of the few privileges available to the old and the healthy and the relatively well-off.'

'Don't be ridiculous, Mother. I honestly believe you say these things for effect. You don't really mean them.'

Music plays unmemorably and my daughter looks at her watch. I imagine her at her dinner parties, speaking of me with a frown. 'Mother is immensely trying,' I hear her say. 'She simply will not do as she is told.' I leave my coffee half-drunk because I know to do so will cause her some mild irritation. Then I turn to look out upon the harbour, waiting for a boat to enter, to leave, imagining the thick smell of fish lining the harbour walls.

'If you refuse to move in with us, I might think of less pleasant alternatives. You will not always be able to look after yourself.'

'Alternatives?'

'There are always Homes,' Jean warns. 'Geriatric homes.'

'I am merely old. Old, not geriatric. I could not abide to live in such a place, I would find it perfectly unbearable,' I say, 'quite intolerable. All those women wearing faded cottons, smelling of stale lavender water bought for them too many years ago, sitting in a circle in a draughty room, collectively knitting. And the men – unshaven, wearing obtrusive hearing aids, ill-fitting dentures, frayed collars, trousers either too short or too long, never quite fitting . . .'

'Do be quieter, Mother,' Jean warns. 'People can hear.'

'But I *want* people to hear. And I am ashamed and appalled that you should even make such a suggestion to me, that you should even contemplate such a place. I have no wish to shuffle from one dreary room to another in fluffy slippers, staring at linoleum floors, watching television before noon. Besides,' I claim, 'the food would be disgusting. Scrambled eggs, dumplings, meat, custard. And prunes; there would naturally be prunes for breakfast.'

'Please, Mother, don't make a scene,' Jean is pale, frightened by the vehemence of my reaction to her threat.

Of course it is nothing but a threat. 'Let's go. I'll be late for my appointment.'

George carried out his threats. His mind was maimed and his threats were carried out. And they had an ineluctable logic about them, an inevitability, like the ebb and flow of the tide.

For my tea I eat a tin of spaghetti letters – a child's food, I am informed by advertisements on television, but one that was unavailable to me in my own childhood. The fork clinks engagingly against the sides of the tin as I eat, but otherwise the house is silent; the mice must be sleeping. I must remember to buy some milk chocolate for them tomorrow; they are fond of a little grated chocolate, scattered behind the refrigerator and beside the sink.

After tea, I switch on the television set and watch, with the sound turned down, a comedy series of astounding mediocrity. And I imagine the Home where my daughter threatens to send me if I do not comply with her wishes. I imagine the sort of conversations I would be subjected to – talk of the past, of other people's lives, the interminable reminiscences about dead husbands, wives who are long since buried. I imagine sharing a room with a view of a tree, possibly two; a single bed, a bland, white central heating radiator, a chest of drawers made badly from plywood.

I turn up the sound on the comedy series, but I cannot laugh.

Sheila was watching television when Roff returned home. She was sitting in the chair he usually sat in, her legs curled beneath her, picking at her toes through her tights. The dress she wore was pink, the same shade as the candy-floss kids stuffed their faces with on the prom, and she had pink stuff round her eyes. Mick had once told him that all the girls who worked in the mail-order firm knocked clothes off, and Roff remembered this, thinking of Sheila maybe stuffing the dress into her bag some dinner-time when nobody else was about.

The telly she was watching was some play; two people stood about in a posh room, talking about not loving each other any more. Roff thought it stupid, he preferred films where something happened, old cowboy films, movies about the war, films in which blood was shed and you could see the wounds in close-up and where people died. Them, and horror films. Come to think of it, he was sure there was a horror movie on the other channel.

'You watching this?' he asked.

Sheila didn't even turn to look at him. 'What's it to you?'

'Just asked,' he said. Sheila was a real pain in the arse. Once, when he was four and had pissed in his pants, Sheila had pointed to the stain and laughed.

'It's all about love,' she said. 'Something you don't know nothing about.'

He noticed, as he sat down, that Sheila was holding the bracelet he had given Annie. She knew he was watching her, so he pretended to be interested in the telly. 'You betrayed me,' the woman was saying, and she slapped the man's face. The man looked surprised and rubbed his cheek and then laughed. 'That's the worst thing you could possibly do to me,' said the woman, 'to laugh at me.'

Roff thought it all stupid. Out of the corner of his eye, he could see that Sheila was still fingering the bracelet, letting it slide from one hand to the other, then clasping it on to her wrist.

'Nice bracelet, that,' she said.

'Give it here,' he said. 'It's not yours.'

'Not yours, neither. Nicked it, didn't you? Stupid little bastard. Nicked it and then gave it Mum. Stupid prick.'

Roff didn't answer. He thought if his Dad was still about, he wouldn't of let Sheila speak to him like that, calling him a stupid bastard. If his Dad was still around, he'd be on Roff's side. On the telly, music was playing, old-fashioned music, the kind that was played in the pubs he and Mick was banned from. Sheila was still picking her feet and the sound of it set his teeth on edge. 'Steal that dress, did ya?'

'It was give me. The manager give it me.'

'So was the bracelet,' he told her. 'That was give me, 'n all. Some woman in the department store just put it in my hands.'

'You'll get done,' Sheila said, 'one of these days you'll get caught. Locked up. It's where you should be anyway.'

'You piss off.'

Sheila threw the bracelet on the floor and lit a cigarette. Her nails were painted green, but there were stains of nicotine on her fingers. Roff couldn't think how any man could fancy her.

'I seen you,' she said presently. 'The other night. Down the beach, sniffing that glue. You wanna grow up.'

Roff told her to shut up. He wished his Dad hadn't gone. If it wasn't Annie getting at him, it was Sheila. 'If Dad – '

'Dad!' scoffed Sheila. 'He's never coming back, Dad isn't. He went off and he'll not be back, not ever. He went before you was even born. He doesn't,' she said, emphatic, 'even know you're alive, that you exist.'

'You're lying,' he told her. 'You're lying because you're jealous. When he comes back, me and him, well, we're going places together.'

'What places?'

But he didn't tell her how he had it all planned, how

103

they'd go to London, find themselves a flat. How they'd sit in pubs and talk about football together. Or save up, buy themselves a little boat, take it out weekends, just the two of them. 'It doesn't matter what places,' he replied, defiant. 'It's none of your business.'

Sheila's laugh made him even angrier. 'The only places you're going is the dole queue and prison if they find out about that bracelet. Anyway, he's never coming back, never.'

'How do you know?'

'I know.'

'How?'

'Because he's dead, that's how I know. He died in a car crash and when they pulled him out, his body was all burned. Burnt to a crisp.'

Roff waited. He was good at waiting. He waited that night and the following morning, until Sheila had eaten her breakfast and gone to work, and Annie was out shopping. He found Sheila's clothes in her wardrobe and in her chest of drawers and he threw them all on to her unmade bed. The room smelled of perfume and unwashed tights, and the house was silent as the scissors in his hand snarled their way through his sister's dresses, and her jumpers, and her jeans, and her fake-fur coat.

9

The woman at the Job Centre asked Roff what skills he had.

Her arms were fat and the earrings that dangled from her ears were long exclamation marks of sterling silver. Roff thought his own earrings – abrasive gold studs – far superior. He noticed, looking around him, that many of the men – and the women – in the Job Centre were dressed neatly in suits and dowdily in dresses; this was, he presumed, because they were either working there or else looking for a job and wishing to appear smart in order to be offered one. That, of course, was the difference between them and him. He didn't want a job. Even if there hadn't been however many millions unemployed, he still wouldn't have wanted a job. Annie had made him come down here, and he hated her for it. Annie had found Sheila's clothes and had ordered him to pay to have them replaced. Annie had been angrier than he'd ever seen her before and had even slapped him across the face. 'You get yourself a bleedin' job,' she had screamed, 'and you pay our Sheila back the money for all them clothes.' Annie had said other things, too. Called him an idle bugger and a slob and a layabout. She had said it was time he started making some sort of contribution to the running of the house. Roff did not know what exactly contribution meant, but he did know, whatever its meaning, that it was unpleasant and would involve effort. Sometimes he felt like throttling her, even though he knew he'd never get away with it. It just went to show you couldn't rely on nobody. Only on yourself.

'Skills?' the woman asked again. Roff crossed his legs and rubbed at an invisible mark on his black boots. The woman was writing something down in a notebook but he couldn't see what it was. The glass front of the Job Centre made the place hot and his leather waistcoat sticky.

The heat made it harder to bring to mind any skills he possessed. 'I can swim,' he presently volunteered. 'And dive off the top of the harbour wall. Not belly-flop neither. I can do the crawl all the way to Whitby and back,' he lied immoderately. 'Twice.'

The woman, whose name was Moira Canning, wrote again in her notebook. '*Spaghetti,*' she wrote. '*Filter coffee, fruit juice, two tins of Italian canned tomatoes.*' As an afterthought she added, '*green peppers,*' remembering that her lover enjoyed eating them raw with his meal. She looked up at Roff, scratching the back of her ear with her pen, wondering how this boy could think swimming a skill. 'When we have our next vacancy in for a cross-Channel swimmer, you'll be the first to know.'

'That's right,' said Roff, adding that he could have been an Olympic swimmer but for the fact that his uncle, with whom he lived, had forbidden it. 'His wife drowned,' he embellished, 'while she were out swimming one day. Caught by the current, see. Put him off swimming for life. Dead against me swimming, Uncle is. Dead against.'

'Yes,' Moira sighed. 'I see.' In her notebook she added several more items to her shopping list and hoped that by the time she reached the supermarket after work button mushrooms would still be available at the fresh vegetable counter.

She said, 'What sort of a job did you have in mind?'

'I dunno.'

'*Any* job?'

106

'I won't do nothing boring,' Roff said, with a certain firmness.

Before walking into the Job Centre, he had studied the white cards in the window. He had seen jobs for panel-beaters and for painters, vacancies for typists and for computer operators. The last struck Roff as the sort of job he would be good at. After all, computers were like Space Invaders, all you had to do was twiddle a few knobs. But by and large the jobs on offer were tedious and boring and included working on Saturdays. Saturdays was the day the arcade opened an hour earlier, on account of the manager expecting visitors to the town for the day. Roff wasn't going to work Saturdays for nobody.

He told the woman he'd take any job that wasn't boring and left his Saturdays free. 'My aunt likes me around, Saturdays,' he explained, 'helping her in the garden.'

'But I thought your aunt was dead? You told me she drowned.'

'That was my proper aunt. This is my uncle's second wife. I suppose,' Roff added helpfully, 'she's my step-aunt.'

He smiled. The only person who knew he lived with his mum and his sister was Mick, who'd told him he ought to leave home, doss out somewhere, squat. 'No telly', Roff had grumbled, 'if I squatted.' He'd been with Mick last night and he was still excited by the memory of what they'd got up to. Together they'd got arseholed drinking scrumpy in a pub in an alley off the harbour, shouting and spilling people's drinks until they'd got chucked out. 'Child's play, that,' Mick had said with some contempt afterwards. 'Let's have ourselves some real fun.'

At first Roff hadn't understood what Mick meant. 'The arcade?' he had asked, 'The disco?'

But Mick had shaken his head again. 'You'll see,' he had promised, leading Roff towards the bus station. 'Just wait and see.'

As a place in which fun could be sought, the bus station appeared unpromising. The poor lighting made Mick's face look green, the café was closed, and Roff almost stepped into a puddle of vomit. The buses were empty and their windows grimy, and there was nobody about. Mick kicked a Coke tin around, scoring a goal at the entrance to the café. 'No point staying here,' Roff said, not telling Mick that between the ages of six and eight he had come here every afternoon after school, watched the arrival of every bus between the hours of three and five-thirty, waiting for his father to come back. 'Let's go.'

But Mick had insisted. And when the old drunk had appeared, slurring his steps between the entrance to the station and the bogs inside it, muttering into his beard, Mick had said, 'Right,' and Roff had followed him into the bogs.

Putting the boot in had given Roff immense satisfaction, endowed him with a moment of sheer, rewarding joy. Too drunk to be frightened, the old man had lain on the tiled floor and babbled at them with his eyes closed. The bogs had smelled of piss and the wash-basins were clogged up with toilet paper. As soon as the old man lost consciousness, Roff had told Mick to lay off. 'Don't go killing him,' he'd said. Afterwards, Mick had laughed, telling Roff nobody'd notice anyway, a bloke like that. Mick was angry, because all they had found in the pockets of the man's stinking coat was a packet of smokes with one cigarette in them and a foreign coin that looked like a ten-pence piece until you held it up close.

'Have you any CSEs?'

'What?'

'CSEs. How many?'

'Hot,' said Roff, 'innit.'

'The glass,' Moira explained. 'Like working in the botanical gardens.'

'Yeah.' Roff took off his jacket and thought how he'd like a smoke.

Moira fanned herself with her notebook. She had to remind herself on days such as this that it was almost the end of October, that in a few days the clocks would be turned back. She attempted, with the aid of a sketchy diagram of a clock, to determine whether this arbitrary interference with Greenwich meantime would allow her an extra hour in bed with her lover or not, and calculated that time was on her side. She scrutinized Roff's hairstyle, his clothes, his manner, and thus rapidly assessed his educational qualifications, a gauge which rarely failed her. She bet herself a glass of dry white wine at lunchtime that the answer to her question would be two CSEs, one of them in woodwork.

'Your educational qualifications?' she prompted.

'A CSE,' said Roff. 'English.'

Moira frowned, and added a bottle of supermarket wine to her shopping list, having deprived herself of a drink at lunchtime. 'You could always put your name down for one of these courses,' she said. 'You could learn a skill.'

Roff shook his head negligently. He didn't much fancy learning a skill, he said. 'My aunt wants me to have a proper job,' he explained.

'Let's get this straight,' began Moira. 'You've absolutely no skills whatsoever – '

'Swimming – ' Roff reminded her.

'No skills, and only one CSE. And you want a job.'

'Well,' said Roff.

'Do you, or do you not, want a job?'

'Suppose,' said Roff. 'Yeah.' He thought he might as

109

well ask about jobs on the rigs. He knew there was jobs going, and what Dave had said about him not having a chance all that time ago mightn't of been right. In the paper jobs was already being advertised on the rigs. And the thought had occurred to him since last night that the police might be after him and Mick for putting the boot in that old man. The police, he was reasonably confident, could never find him in the middle of the North sea.

'Is there any job,' asked Moira, cautious, 'that you think you might have a special aptitude for? One you feel you might be good at?'

'Yeah.'

'Ah. Now we're getting somewhere. What sort of job had you in mind?'

'On a rig.'

'A rig?'

'One of them oil-rigs in Scotland. In the North Sea.'

'I see.'

'Bringing up the oil,' said Roff. 'I'd be good at that.'

Moira smiled, as was her custom under stress. Her lover, with whom she often discussed her work, believed that most of what she told him about her interviewees was too extraordinary to be true. Between dinner and lovemaking she would tell him about this boy, this thick sixteen-year-old who had the grandiose idea of working on an oil-rig. He would laugh immoderately and, as a reward to her for making him laugh, would be more considerate towards her in between the flannelette sheets.

'Let me explain,' she told Roff. 'We only cater for jobs here, in this town. Not for jobs in Leeds or Birmingham or Glasgow, or even in the North Sea. If you really wanted a job on an oil-rig, you'd have to go to one of the recruiting agencies. And if you *were* to go to an agency, I really feel you would rather be wasting your time and everybody else's. The sort of work you're talking about is

110

highly skilled. And you couldn't get that sort of work because not only are you patently *not* highly skilled, having only one CSE to your name, but you aren't old enough. You have to be eighteen.'

Roff said 'Oh,' and waited.

'You're not by any chance a piping engineer,' Moira asked, 'are you?'

'Naw.'

'Or a mechanical fitter?'

'Uh-uh.'

'Or an experienced diver?'

'Only', said Roff, 'off the harbour wall.'

'Yes. That's rather what I suspected.'

'Someone told me, see,' Roff said forgetting who, 'that there was jobs going for people like me on the rigs.'

'That someone must have been pulling your leg.'

'Yeah.'

'Take my word for it,' said Moira, after a pause, 'it's dreary working on oil-rigs. Sixteen, eighteen hours a day, fourteen days at a stretch. No company but that of other men. No girls. Sharing a cabin, no drink. Really very dreary.'

People were walking past the Job Centre. Roff watched them. Most of them walked quickly, as though going somewhere important. He saw a woman pushing a baby in a buggy, smacking the child when it kicked off its shoe and it landed by the kerb. The baby cried so loudly that even through the glass the sound made his ears hurt. 'My Dad works there, see,' he said presently. 'Off-shore. Been there years. One of the bosses, he is, supervisor. Ten thousand barrels a day.'

'Really?'

'Yeah.'

'Is that why you live with your uncle? Because your father's away?'

111

'That's it.'

'Well, I'm surprised your father didn't write and explain that you'd need skills for a job like that. I imagine *he* has skills. You must miss him a lot.'

Roff shrugged.

'So,' said Moira briskly, 'let's lower our expectations a little, shall we?' She sighed. For weeks her lover had been trying to persuade her to give up her job and emigrate with him to New Zealand, where together they would open up a wholefood restaurant. The idea was crazy, they didn't even eat wholefood; but this morning the scheme was tempting to her for the first time. She picked up a sheet of paper and began to read through it.

Roff whistled and drummed his fingers against the sole of his boot. In ten minutes the arcade would open.

'Have you ever worked with animals at all?'

Frowning, Roff considered the question. Once his mother had bought a cat, a grey tabby that had eaten its way through eleven tins of tuna fish a week and had slept right in front of the electric fire, blocking its heat from everyone in the room. The cat had been with them for a year until one day it had disappeared. Annie had cried, thinking the tabby run over; Roff reckoned at the time it had just got pissed off with tuna fish.

'We had a cat. Got run over.'

'You've no experience with, well larger animals? Cows, sheep, pigs?'

'Naw.'

'But you've seen such animals?'

'Seen donkeys,' said Roff, 'on the beach. Ten pence a ride.' He didn't think that, on the whole, he was that struck on animals. 'I'm not bothered about cows and them,' he said.

'No,' Moira replied, 'but that doesn't matter. I'm not asking you to *like* animals. The job I have in mind

112

. . .well, whether you actually like them or not is imma-
terial.' Moira laughed. 'The vacancy I'm thinking of isn't
in a zoo.'

'Yeah,' said Roff, not caring much.

'Not in a zoo. But in the abattoir.'

The sun had been sliced off by a cloud and the Job
Centre began imperceptibly to cool down. The presence
of so much glass sometimes made Moira feel uneasy; the
whole town, as it passed by, could look in and see her at
her desk, and the window-cleaners who spent every
alternate Tuesday afternoon cleaning the salt and grime
from the glass frontage would smile at her too much
and make offensive suggestions that she could lip-read
through the glass with ease. Moira often wished some
unemployed yobbo would chuck a brick through the
glass, thus relieving her from the lewd mouthings of
the window cleaners, from the offensive heat, from the
exasperating curiosity of passers-by. She would much
prefer to work in privacy and in the cool behind a large
sheet of hardboard. This Jenkins lad looked the type to
heave a brick through the windows of her place of
employment. He did not, she was certain, look the type
to take a job in the town's abattoir. She said, 'it sounds
right up your street, this vacancy.'

'Oh yeah?'

'They want someone to start on Monday week. A
school-leaver it says. And you wouldn't have to work on
Saturdays.'

'I wouldn't?'

'And the money's not too bad. With four weeks' paid
holidays a year.'

Eleven o'clock. Moira thought longingly of morning
coffee, waiting for the tea-trolley. Roff realized the arcade
would now be opened.

If he took the job, he'd only get to the arcade after

113

work. If he didn't take it, Annie wouldn't cook his meals and she would nag him about paying Sheila back for the clothes he'd cut up. If he took it, he could give Sheila the money, tell her where to shove it, and piss off. Get a flat. Even share with Mick.

'What's the job, anyway? In the abattoir?'

'Maintenance,' Moira said firmly.

'Maintenance?' asked Roff. 'What's that?'

'Well,' Moira hedged. Was that the tea-trolley or was it simply the rumble of bus wheels outside in the street? 'I'm glad you asked me that.'

'So?'

'Maintenance,' she explained, 'is keeping the place clean. Well, spotless, actually. And tidy. The abattoir has exacting health regulations.'

'Keeping the place clean.'

'Yes, that's right. Sweeping up. Hosing down the yard after the animals have, well, after they've been slaughtered. It might be rather a *messy* job, if you see what I mean. You'd need a strong stomach. They wouldn't want someone who fainted at the sight of a spot of blood.'

'Oh well,' said Roff, 'that's okay then. I don't mind blood.'

After the boy had left, Moira drank two cups of coffee and thought she might renege on her bet and have a lunchtime drink after all. She found the idea of working in an abattoir nauseating. But then school-leavers were so desperate for jobs, they would work anywhere.

The abattoir was on the outskirts of the town, conveniently hidden from the public gaze by a copse of strategically place imported Japanese trees, which had been planted twenty years before, in the same month as the abattoir had been moved from the centre of town to its new resting-place. Those well-versed in slaughterhouses claimed this one to be the most modern in Europe, the most efficient in the Western world, the best, in fact, of its kind. By this it was meant that the turnover of slaughtered animals per week was higher than that of slaughterhouses in West Germany, France, North America and even, it was claimed, Argentina.

Roff thought it clean. The cleanest place he had ever set foot in. When you spoke, your words bounced back at you from the tiles, like in the swimming baths. But this place was not like the swimming baths, it was not like anywhere Roff had seen. The men who worked there wore white smocks and white caps; they were all of them big men, their hands huge and red, their faces large, their backs wide. They did not pay much heed to Roff and he was not included in the rounds of jokes they exchanged, the jokes about women and about Micks and about blacks that they threw at each other and at the tiled walls, their laughter echoing, bouncing, tumbling through the building.

Roff did not know why they laughed so much at jokes he did not find funny. On his first day, the manager said they were all a bunch of psychopaths. 'Gets to them in the end,' he said, 'working here, killing animals.' He looked at Roff for a long time and sniffed. 'They're psychopaths, and you're a punk. I'm not going to ask you to get that hair chopped off, because I don't reckon you'll be here long enough to make it worth the bother. But I *am* going to tell you to keep it clean. We don't want germs here. Nits, lice, that kind of thing.' He told Roff he would be working in the cleanest abattoir in the whole country and he tapped his foot against the floor. 'Spotless, see,' he indicated. 'You could eat your dinner off that.'

Roff, however, ate his dinner in the yard, squatting in a corner, his back leaning against the brickwork. His arms ached, for he had spent his morning hosing down the pens where the slaughtered sheep had been kept. The hose was heavy and the jets of water so strong they pushed everything out of the way towards the gutter. One of the men walked past in a bloodied apron as Roff was chewing an iced doughnut. He told Roff that if his work turned out to be half-way decent, he might get promoted after a few months. 'Promoted?' asked Roff. The doughnut was hard and without the mouthful of raspberry jam at its centre that he'd expected.

The man smiled, adjusting the strings of his apron. 'You might get to be a stunner.' He told Roff a stunner was someone who stunned the animals before they were killed. 'Good job,' he said. 'Overtime, too. Better than hosing down sheep-shit all day.'

'Yeah,' said Roff. His doughnut was finished and he was still hungry. Working in the abattoir was giving him an appetite. As the man walked away, Roff thought of the old man he and Mick had given a going over the other night. He'd been stunned good and proper.

It rained on Saturday, the Saturday after Roff's first week at work, but he still went to meet Mick in the arcade where the smell was of wet rubber boots and drying leather. He'd lost a fiver on the Invaders by the time he spotted Mick standing in a corner talking to a girl with thin blonde hair and eyes dark and muddy with make-up.

He watched Mick lean earnestly towards the girl, smile, say something that made her laugh. Annie was always on at him to get himself a girl but Roff didn't like to admit girls didn't interest him. Girls wanted babies and getting married and a nice council house with a garden, and when they weren't talking about one or all of these things, they went on about how nice it would be to have a job at

116

the cheese counter of Tesco's and wear one of those red and blue striped hats.

'I'm all set up for tonight,' said Mick as they left the arcade later. 'That Sandra. She's okay. She'll do.'

The rain escorted them to the harbour, where they sat on the harbour wall letting their legs dangle towards the water. The sea was a bleak shade of pale grey and each wave left a froth of yellowed foam on the sand as the tide ebbed. The beach was empty, the way Roff liked it to be, and he could see the rain falling on the water and the sand and the pebbles. Roff thought that while Mick was giving Sandra one tonight, he would be stuck at home watching telly with Annie. During the evening she would make tea and maybe a couple of corned-beef sandwiches and she would talk too much about too little. If there was anything good on telly she would ask him about his new job, out of boredom, but when he'd start to tell her she would pretend to shudder and say how sorry she felt for all those poor animals. She might even say – she had already said it every night since Monday – that the thought of working in a place like that turned her guts and made her think people who was vegetarian weren't as daft as they looked.

'Saw that old fucker,' said Mick. 'The one we done over the other night. Saw him yesterday along the pier. He was sat on a bench, pissed as a fart. Wasn't even dinner-time.'

'Thought he might of died,' remarked Roff, without much interest. The harbour wall smelled of fish and when he kicked at it with the backs of his feet, pieces of rock and stone fell off with gratifying ease. He kept promising himself that one of these nights he'd come down alone to the harbour with a can of red aerosol paint-spray and paint all over the walls, but it was hard thinking up what words he would write. Mick pulled the hood of his jacket over his head and asked him why he'd gone and got himself a job.

'Something to do,' Roff replied.

'Yeah.' The way Mick said this indicated that there were better things to do than working. 'You oughta of went in the Army,' he suggested. 'That way you get to kill people, not just a bunch of stupid animals.'

'Don't kill animals,' Roff said, sulky. 'Not yet. Got to train for that.'

Mick laughed, and the sound of his laugh dripped towards Roff like the rain. Sometimes Mick pissed him off something terrible. 'What do you do then? What sort of job you got there?'

Roff shrugged. 'Just a job.'

But Mick persisted. 'Boring, is it? I reckon, see, that job is boring. All jobs. My Dad, he's got a job. Bus-driver. Works nights. Had this job seventeen years. And he's boring, my Dad. Job makes him boring, talks about it all the time. When I go out, he doesn't ask me where I'm going. He just says, "What bus you taking?" That way he knows where I'm going, see. Or he thinks he does. So what's your job?'

'Maintenance,' said Roff.

'What's maintenance when it's at home?'

'Sort of cleaning up. Yeah, cleaning up, hosing down. There's this huge hose they give you, see, the water that comes out, it's so strong you could knock a man off his feet with it. And the – '

'Hosing down what?'

'Well, shit, mostly. Guts sometimes. And blood. There's a lot of blood.'

'Shit,' said Mick thoughtfully, 'and blood.' He shook his head and Roff could see he wasn't impressed. The rain was softer now, almost tickling his face as it fell. He told Mick what one of the men had said, about how he

118

might get to be a stunner. He explained how they killed the cattle, how each bull was herded into a frame, open at one end, narrowing down to a blank wall with a shutter in it. 'The stunner's standing behind this shutter, see, waiting till the bull's right in front of it. He opens the shutter, fires a metal bolt through the bull's head. Right between the eyes, straight into the brain. The stun-gun's on a spring, see, so it comes out again.'

Mick asked him why.

'So they can use it again. They get through thousands of cattle just in a week. You never seen so many dead animals,' Roff added, proud. 'Just thousands of dead cattle and dead sheep and dead pigs. Anyway,' he went on, 'after the bull's been stunned the floor revolves below them and the bull's tipped out underneath. Tied to the floor like, chains round its legs, so it can't move. They cut its throat then, before it goes on the conveyor.'

He watched Mick light a fag, chuck the match into the harbour. 'So,' Mick said, 'go on.'

'Well, the sheep. They kill them differently. Electrocute them. They do that in the yard, more room, see. All them sheep, just standing about in bunches, and there's two men. One of them grabs the sheep, holds it beween his legs while the other puts the electrodes on its head. Zap, and they're dead. And if they do it in the wet, the men get a shock too. It's funny to watch.'

'Mmm.' Mick looked at his watch and said he'd better be going soon.

'The chickens get gassed,' Roff said quickly. 'In chambers. And they boil the hair off the pigs.' He sensed he was losing Mick's interest, but he continued to talk. The rain didn't bother him, in a way it was comforting, though he couldn't have explained how. He smiled to himself, remembering how he had watched Arthur, the bloke with the electrodes, jump six inches into the air when he'd

119

zapped the sheep. Everyone had laughed out there in the yard, with the smell of greasy sheep's wool clinging to their overalls and the sky dark and heavy. For a minute out there Roff, laughing with the rest of the men, had felt like he belonged somewhere. Mick looked at his watch again, so Roff began to tell him about the kosher section of the abattoir, the place where they kept the Jewish cattle. 'The rabbi comes in twice a week to kill the animals,' he explained. 'He's wearing all his gear, see, and he hog-ties them and then slits them right down the middle. He's got this set of ceremonial knives, like, sharp as razors. And – '

But Mick interrupted him. Mick said, 'You mean you're sweeping up shit all fucking day?'

'Well, I'm not trained yet. In a couple of months – '

'I reckon', Mick said casually, 'that you don't have the guts to kill anything. I reckon you haven't got the guts to do anything except clear up shit. You was scared the other night when we duffed up that old bugger in the bus station. I could tell you was dead scared. The look on your face. You're too scared to do anything. You're too scared,' finished Mick, 'to even fuck a girl. That's how scared you are.'

The rain had left a legacy of mist behind it, which hung over the harbour and along the beach. But even through the mist Roff could see the man walking slowly along the sand towards the steps to the promenade. A small black dog barked at the man's feet, the kind of dog Roff couldn't stand. Glancing around him, Roff could see nobody else about but the man and the dog.

'I'll show you,' he told Mick, 'just how scared I am.'

I was witness this afternoon to a most horrific incident, an incident of such brutality that it has left me shaken, bewildered and appalled.

120

My day began inauspiciously, with the shriek of the telephone. I was taking my bath at the time, so naturally I let it ring. But it continued to ring as I soaped my body and prevented me from hearing the gulls which so often perch and squawk on the roof and whose noise never fails to remind me the sea is but a brisk walk away. Usually I linger in the bath, listening to the gulls, letting the bath-tap run until the water gently scolds my feet and the pipes begin to complain. But this morning the telephone curtailed this small pleasure of mine; it was still ringing as I dried myself scrupulously with my bath-towel.

My irritation, when I answered, must have been obvious, but Jean swept it aside. 'Mother,' she began. I can always tell that my daughter is about to give me unpleasant news by the manner in which she prefaces that news with the word 'Mother'.

'I was in the bath,' I said, but Jean cut short my words.

'You have all day in which to bath,' she said. 'My time is rather more precious. I have simply rung to say that the builders have begun work on the extension and that I very much hope they will be finished by Christmas. We expect you to move in shortly after then.'

I put down the receiver – hung up, I believe, is the correct expression – but not before using a phrase that I have seen written down and even, once or twice, heard on television, but never before used myself. Not before I told Jean to bugger off.

The anger that swamped me after speaking to Jean ruined my breakfast; I quite simply could not swallow my toast and the tea I made tasted bizarrely of custard. (I realized later the tea's unusual flavour was not caused by anger at Jean, but was due to an oversight on my part; I had added custard powder to the tea-pot instead of Earl Grey.) I pulled up the window sash and broke my toast into tiny fragments for the birds, while consigning the tea to the sink-tidy.

As I closed the window, raindrops were beginning to settle on the rotting wood of the window frame. Generally I delight in the rain – its constant movement, its rainbow of sound – but I had taken my macintosh to the cleaners' the previous day and I knew that in my mink I would be uncomfortable on my daily walk to the sea. I was listening to the rain and I plugged the kettle in again for my tea, and as I switched the kettle on I heard a sizzle, a popping noise and saw steam unaccountably swoon from the spout. 'How silly,' I said to the birds on the windowsill, 'I have forgotten to refill the kettle.' The birds took no notice of this act of absentmindedness and continued to chew my toast, but the smell of the burning element reproached me, seeming, as it did, to confirm my daughter's conviction that I was becoming forgetful.

For the first time in my life, doubts besieged me. *Was* I becoming forgetful? Was my omission to refill the kettle just that, or a preface to more incidents of similar absent-mindedness? (I had not yet discovered my substitution of custard powder for Earl Grey; I did not notice the open tin of custard powder until much later, after returning from my walk, and by then it seemed too trivial to claim my attention.) Ought I, after all, to move in with Jean? Allow myself to be consigned to her purpose-built out-house? Permit her to cook my meals, invade my privacy, arrange my life?

I boiled water in a saucepan and wisely made myself a cup of coffee. (The coffee jar is clearly marked; it cannot be mistaken for anything but coffee.) Carrying my coffee upstairs, I went into the bedroom to air my bed, only to find the rain had somehow insinuated itself into my bedroom and was dripping on to the carpet from a damp oval in the ceiling. The raindrops clung for a few seconds to the ceiling, as though reluctant to fall, postponing the moment when they would release themselves and gently plip on to the carpet beneath.

I had the absurdly fanciful idea that the house, with its leaking roof and its rotting windowsills, was, like Jean, conspiring against me.

My morning was spent on the telephone, and I cannot recall ever having spent so many arduous hours over such a small matter. The firms which I telephoned seemed to shirk from my leaking roof. One man claimed he would be unable to pay me a visit until a week next Friday; another was booked for the next month; the third resented my ringing on a Saturday and suggested I buy a plastic bucket until Monday and then ring him again; and a fourth said he no longer undertook roof-repair work as it was far too dangerous. The fifth man to whom I spoke was sympathetic and promised to come next week, but it remains to be seen whether he will. In the meantime I can only hope the weather will turn dry. I left a saucepan in a strategic spot to catch the raindrops and poured myself a soothingly large schooner of sherry before lunch.

When I left the house after lunch I was drenched almost before I had reached my garden gate. My shoes slapped on the path and the sensation of wet fur around my neck and wrists was both unpleasant and undignified; I wished for the relative dryness of my macintosh. But I did not turn back. I have often told Jean my daily walk is a celebration, a regular affirmation that my body still continues to function. 'I feel an enormous gratitude to my organs, my limbs,' I have said, 'for allowing me to walk to the sea and back.' Jean affects to scoff at this, but she has no imagination. She is unable to understand what it is like to be eighty-four.

I walked. During the months from October to April, a seaside town takes upon itself a neglected air, a carapace of disrepair. Many people believe that to be confronted by an empty promenade, by unpainted railings, by a rain-sodden pier, is to be reminded of their own misguided aspirations, of opportunities wasted, of mediocrity. This consensus of opinion is reinforced by all those television dramas which use empty beaches and the rotting canvases of piled deckchairs as a backdrop for tales of lost souls and dispirited lovers. People see a hotel occupied only by a middle-aged waitress, cafés with their shutters down, a dog on a lonely stretch of sand, and they say, 'This is how I feel – empty as the hotel, neglected as the beach. Out of season.'

Jean tells me I am unique in preferring the town's winter landscape, in finding serenity among the pebbles of a silent beach, constancy in the deserted hotels. Perhaps it is because, I, too, am out of season.

I ought not to have worn my stilettos, it was the most frightful foolishness on my part. By the time I passed the first promenade hotel, the rain had made my stockings sodden and my calves were aching. It would serve me right, I chastised myself, if I caught a chill. The hotel as I passed it looked quite inviting – pretty curtains framed the dining-room windows and the lights had been turned on in deference to – or defiance against – the dark skies. I shall treat myself, I promised, to afternoon tea after my walk. To warmed scones and a piece of Battenberg cake.

The wooden bench on which I usually sit was much too wet to even contemplate sitting on it, so I chose instead a seat in one of the shelters facing the beach, a few hundred yards from the harbour. The tankers which I was used to seeing queuing on the horizon were absent, making the horizon look not only infinite, but bereft. The tide was out and the pebbles on the beach too far away for me to see them with any clarity, but I imagined them cold to the touch, round and damp and smooth, a memory of prehistory. Behind me, the present asserted itself with the hooting of a car, the sound of bus tyres on the wet road, the noises of shoppers. I felt snug in my concrete porch, closeted against the elements, and I thought again how deeply I would miss walks such as these were I to move to Jean's home on the outskirts of the town. I confess I wished she had moved away when she had married and my only contact with my daughter was a weekly telephone call, a monthly letter, an annual visit. Duty for her would then have been nothing more than an intellectual exercise, not an act of invasion.

I was thinking of Jean when I chanced to see the old man. The way he walked – and the presence of the dog in the tartan coat – made me feel certain it was the same person I had seen a few weeks before, the man who had shared my bench, spoken to me of the weather, the man who had called himself Henry Jones. I remembered his name precisely because of its ordinariness, as one recalls the brand name of a particularly ordinary household cleaner.

I watched the dog sniff at the sand, while its master, several yards behind, prodded the pebbles with his walking stick. I imagined him a solitary man, one who lived in an inadequately heated flat, and who shared dreary meals of sausages and cabbage with the small dog.

The dog alerted me to the danger; its barking snapped through the misty afternoon, its ears rose, premonitionary, warning. The youth was walking quickly towards Mr Jones from the direction of the harbour with the careless, powerful strides only the young possess and only the young take for granted. He was dressed in a green jacket and tight trousers and his hair rose from his head in spikes. 'Mr Jones,' I called out, but as I rose from the seat Mr Jones fell.

He fell awkwardly, flopping on to the pebbles and I

heard the smack of a stone against his head. The boy spoke then, but his words were indistinct, muzzled by the mist. I could hear only the gulls call, the dog's agitated bark, the boy's arrogant laughter.

My voice, as I reached the promenade railings, was shrill, like the gulls. 'What have you done? How dare you harm an old man. How dare you!'

The boy looked up towards me and it seemed for a moment he would speak. 'I shall report you to the police. I have never seen such behaviour before on a public beach. You have rendered that poor man unconscious,' I shouted. 'How dare you hurt an old man. How dare you!'

The youth looked at me. His green jacket was damp and his face wet. The rain had made his black boots sleek, and his hairstyle sleeker. Behind him the small dog yelped and the sea slouched towards the beach. The boy shrugged, as though my words, like the dog's yelps, were irrelevant and by the time I had negotiated the steps that led to the beach, he had gone.

Mr Jones was unconscious and blood from a wound in his forehead leaked softly into the damp sand.

I called an ambulance from a public telephone box on the promenade. There was some irony in the recollection that the last time an ambulance had been summoned to the promenade, the day I had fainted, had also been the day Mr Jones and I had sat briefly together on a wooden bench. 'We are unlucky for each other, this stranger and myself,' I said, and I hoped he would not die.

The ambulancemen were efficient and arrived within four minutes of my telephone call. I pointed to Mr Jones, to the small semi-circle of curious and helpful and anxious and ghoulish passers-by which had appeared, and I explained what had happened. I felt exhausted and sat upon the steps as the men placed Mr Jones on a stretcher, lifted him from the sand, carried him towards the ambulance.

'Will he die?' I asked, once, on the journey, but the ambulanceman said he was not qualified to say. I remembered the dog only as we turned into the hospital gates, a silly black terrier yapping at the chilling, indifferent water.

The dog followed him, whining. Roff stopped to light a fag and the animal bit him on the ankle. He kicked at it and the dog snarled. 'Stupid mutt,' said Roff, telling the animal to bugger off. His heart was beating fast, thumping away, working on overtime, like it had done the first time he'd ever shoplifted. A bag of peaches he'd stole, from outside a greengrocer's shop. He'd never eaten a peach before, and for some reason the fuzziness of the fruit's skin made him shiver. He'd taken the bag to the park, sat on the grass, bitten into the peaches. Later, when he was boasting about it to Mick, Mick had laughed. 'You don't want to go nicking peaches,' he'd scoffed, 'that's kids' stuff.' Roff hadn't told Mick that at the centre of four of the six peaches he had found a small white worm curled against the ridges of the stone. If he'd of told Mick that, Mick would of said it served him right.

Well, it wasn't kids' stuff, what he'd just done. Mick had been watching it all. Mick had seen the way he threw that stone, the way the old bugger had fallen so easily like he wasn't a person at all, only a large empty cardboard box. That had showed Mick. He looked towards the harbour, lifting his hand to wave to him, but the harbour was deserted. Nobody was about. Mick had gone. He couldn't believe it. He couldn't believe that Mick had pissed off, that he hadn't stayed to hear Roff tell him all about it. He just couldn't believe it. Mick hadn't even asked to see the ceremonial knife Roff had knocked off from the rabbi, the long thin one he'd took when nobody was about. Mick had said he had no guts, and hadn't even hung around to see that he had.

The knife was in his inside pocket, wrapped in a sheet of newspaper. He took it out gently, carefully, knowing how sharp it was. He felt sad and angry and a lot of other things he didn't know the words for. He threw his butt into the water, watching it float, and he dug the knife deep, deep into the damp sand.

The dog came along then, nuzzling against his thighs, and the knife went in easy, as easily as it had when he'd watched the rabbi slaughter the lamb the other day.

On his way home, Roff thought about the old woman. But he doubted she would go to the police as she had threatened. That was the thing about old people, they was frightened. Too frightened to live, too frightened to die. Like zombies, they was, hanging about the seaside, watching other people live their lives. No, she wouldn't report it. She'd be home now, making herself a cup of tea, pretending her hands wasn't shaking. By teatime, she'd have made herself forget the whole thing, forget she'd even been on the beach. People like her, Roff knew they had no guts.

10

The signs which ambushed me as I followed the nurse down a windowless corridor were printed in alarmingly large bold letters. Pathology said one; Artificial limbs another; Mortuary the third. I walked slowly past these signs, hampered by the tight leather of my still-wet stilettos and the heaviness of my damp mink. We turned a corner into another corridor and as we did so, we passed by a door marked Mortuary, a brown door, with a square of plain glass above the door handle. I stopped, peered curiously through the glass, but death was not visible. Only a small and chubby man in a white coat who stood in the centre of a bare room, polishing his spectacles with a handkerchief. As we passed he looked up, saw me, waggled a finger in my direction. 'Your time will come soon enough,' the look said. 'You may well end up here.'

'Come along,' said the nurse. Peering into the mortuary was something visitors were not encouraged to do, she said with some severity. But that afternoon I felt immense curiosity about my death, about when it would arrive, how, where. The assault I had witnessed on the beach, the hospital, the possibility that Mr Jones would not survive – all this conspired to fuel my curiosity. I should so hate to die of a long and unspectacular illness, I thought as we turned into yet another corridor. To die of cancer or angina or Parkinson's disease. If I am not to be allowed to die quickly in privacy, I said to myself, I shall die quickly in public. Be run over by a bus. Or, better still, an ambulance.

Mr Jones lay marooned in a narrow bed in a small room. Rain tumbled against the window beside the bed, and the hospital trees beyond the gravel path appeared dismally bare. The room itself was scarcely less dismal – confining, claustrophobic, overheated, speaking to me of human frailty. 'Mr Jones is tired,' the nurse said, 'so you mustn't stay long.'

But I had no wish to stay long. The events of the afternoon had left me enervated and shocked. The horror of the boy's assault remained with me. What sort of boy, I asked myself, could strike an old man with a stone and then walk away, as though the consequences of his actions had no relevance for him? As though suddenly losing interest in something which did not concern him? I wanted only to go home, to return to my large and grubby house where crises were measured by raindrops spilling from a saucepan on to a bedroom carpet. Where a leaking roof was the sum of my problems. I could not breathe in this small, cramped room; I was damp and uncomfortable and my feet ached dreadfully. I did not know this man, this Mr Jones, who was smiling gratefully at me from his narrow bed, this bandaged stranger. Violence had brought us together, and brutality. An anonymous youth on a rainy beach, a stone thrown in anger or hate, a shared ride in an ambulance.

I sat down in a chair beside the window, a few feet from the bed. The bandage which slanted across Mr Jones's forehead and which covered one eyebrow gave him a jaunty appearance. It seemed to decorate his head rather than to cover a deep wound. From the rest of his face – large, surprised eyes, a non-committal nose, a flat mouth – I tried to guess his age. He was a man of seventy, perhaps more, possibly less, and the eyes betrayed disappointments in life, regrets, small failures that to anyone but him would seem meaningless.

It was he who spoke first, and in the quiet and melancholy tones of one accustomed to conversing alone. 'I thought it was a cricket ball,' he said. 'When something struck me on the head I don't know why, but I presumed I'd been hit by a cricket ball. I remember falling and I remember the sand, the smell of the sand. Someone laughed and Trixie barked. And that's all I can remember.'

'The boy, the youth who threw the stone. You don't remember him?'

'A boy, you say?' He spoke vaguely, slowly shaking his head.

'The boy meant to harm you. He might have killed you.'

'Yes, Well.' He shrugged. Mine has been an insignificant life, the shrug said, to die on the wet shingle of a Saturday beach might be appropriate. 'When I was a boy, my mother used to bring me here for the summer holidays. We stayed in a small boarding-house and every night for tea we were served ham salad. After breakfast we would come to sit on the beach, even if the day was dull. I spent my time building sandcastles. Ambitious, crenellated, turreted affairs, decorated with shells and the feathers of gulls. When I retired, I suggested to my wife that we move here. I had always been happy here, you see, as a child. I thought I, we, could be happy again.'

He adjusted his bandage, sighed, looked down towards the impeccable sheets. The rain dripped from the trees and I wished it would stop. The intimacies of strangers have always embarrassed me and I hoped Mr Jones was not about to be indiscreet, to confess past unhappinesses to me, to admit to pain, to disclose frailties. Solitude makes one selfish, I thought, and in old age many emotions become inadmissible.

'We bought a bungalow, but we were not happy. My wife missed the city, she missed her friends, her drama group, her shopping trips. She hated living by the sea. She claimed the salt in the air made cleaning the windows impossible; she did not like to walk by the sea, the landscape was unfamiliar to her. She felt ill at ease. And she blamed me for uprooting her, for wrenching her from the city, from shops and offices and industrial chimneys and multi-storey car-parks. We squabbled most of the time and I thought, well, she'll get over it, she'll soon grow to like living here, she'll make new friends. But she didn't. About two years ago she fell ill. The doctor told me it was cancer, but we agreed not to tell my wife. She died last year.'

'I'm sorry.'

'I felt it was my fault, you see. That I was to blame. For her death, for the suffering. And it was too late to make amends, far too late. All I could do was to bury her where she would have wanted to be buried. In the city. The cemetery where she lies is overlooked by a large housing estate, and a petro-chemical factory lies to the left.' Again he shrugged. 'It was all I could do.' He smiled briefly. 'You were very kind to help me. The nurse told me it was you who called the ambulance. It was most kind.'

'Nonsense,' I said. 'I am not a kind person. I am simply an old busybody.' I felt relief that his intimacies had ceased and I spoke brusquely. I had no wish to dwell on Mr Jones' story, to think of his wife's suffering. Most of all, I did not want to feel sorry for this man. Pity is a useless emotion and anger was what I had been feeling all afternoon. I did not want pity to dispossess me of my anger. I thought: if I can retain this anger, if I can let my anger take me to the police station to report this incident, if I am brave enough to protest about the boy's assault, then perhaps I can be brave enough to protest about what Jean is doing. But the youth had shrugged when I spoke and walked away, and I knew that Jean would not give in so easily.

'Trixie,' said Mr Jones. 'What has happened to Trixie?'

'She is being looked after,' I lied, and only then did I remember that I had left the dog on the beach. 'The ambulancemen are taking care of her.'

And I thought, how lucky you are, Mr Jones, how enviable to be alone in the world, to be without a daughter clamouring to take over your life, to have only the minimal emotional claims of a small dog with an absurd name.

'The ambulancemen, you say?'

'Yes.' My lie appeased him, he lay back against the pillows and smiled. He was markedly more concerned for his pet's welfare than for his own, a folly I have often remarked in pet owners. Damnation, I thought, now I shall have to go in search of the dog when all I seek is the warmth of my sitting-room and the comfort of my solitude.

I looked towards the window. Under the dripping trees the hospital grounds were drab – a gravel path, a few cars, a bench nobody would sit on until the arrival of spring. 'We must tell the police about what happened. The boy will have to be caught. Charges will be made.' I spoke vaguely, unsure as to what charges would be made, not knowing whether the boy would even be caught.

'The police? Do we have to tell them?'

'Of course.'

'But it might have been an accident. A boy throwing a stone on an almost empty beach? Boys throw stones all the time. He might have intended the stone to land in the water.'

'Hardly. The water was in the opposite direction. And

it was not an accident. I saw the boy, he meant to hurt you.'

'I was lucky. A few stitches, a bandage. The nurse told me I can leave tomorrow. I wasn't badly hurt.'

I rather bullied poor Mr Jones, lying captive in his narrow bed. I was earnest and persuasive and possibly he was a little frightened when I raised my voice and spoke determinedly of justice. 'By not reporting this, you put in jeopardy the lives of other old men and women,' I claimed. 'If that boy is permitted to go scot-free he will only assault someone else.'

Mr Jones looked thoughtful. 'You seem to have a bit of a bee in your bonnet about this boy.'

'The youth was a bully.'

But I did not say that I had spent all my married life with a bully and neither did I explain that the look on the boy's face as he threw the stone reminded me of my husband's: a look from which all compassion had been erased.

The walk from the hospital to the police station was long and the concrete of the pavements pitiless to my already aching feet. An exhaustion of the spirit chaperoned me, like a sour-faced duenna dressed in black. The streets seemed peopled by umbrellas and the matt grey sky cast sullen shadows on the shops, the cars, the road. All testified to the arrival of winter – the trees plundered of their leaves, the barren beach, the plethora of colourless umbrellas. But one does not live to reach my age without a certain tenacity, and it was this tenacity that drove me to the station, up the steps, into a large room marked Inquiries.

'I am terribly sorry to disturb you, but I wonder if you could help me.'

'Madam?' The policeman who rose from his seat was large. A comforting sort of person, I thought, who watches sport on television and who allows his wife to make him a bedtime drink.

'I wish to report a crime.'

'You do, madam?' He spoke loudly, startling me.

'I am not deaf,' I said. 'I may be old, but my hearing is unimpaired. This afternoon I was sitting in a concrete shelter on the promenade – '

'Yes, madam?'

' – and I was witness to a serious crime. Attempted murder, if I am not overstating the facts. I saw a youth attack an old man on the beach. He threw a stone at him, a large, round stone, which struck the old man on the forehead, causing him to fall heavily. I was the only witness to this. The beach was almost deserted at the time, people were at home, it was raining heavily. Because I am the only witness, I have come here. You will wish me to make a statement. You will require my description of this youth, and despite the mist I will be able to give you one. You will doubtless find flaws in my statement – I am not accustomed to this sort of thing. You will find irrelevant details inserted, essential information left out. My eyes are still excellent but my age precludes me from remembering everything that I ought. Occasionally I am prey to mild amnesia – I forget to buy bread, or tea – but this is a condition no more irritating than a head-cold and one which ought not to prevent you from catching the youth.

'You look at me with some scepticism, I see, officer, and I wonder if you believe me to be one of those melancholy widows who seek to occupy their time by visiting their local police station to complain of assaults that have never taken place, of non-existent belongings stolen, of invisible men who follow them down darkened streets. Let me assure you that I am not one of those women, that the attack I saw actually took place and that

Mr Jones – the victim – is now lying in a hospital bed in an overheated room with only a bandage and the sound of the rain for company. When I have given you my description of the boy, I would be extremely grateful if you could call a taxi for me. My home is more than a mile away and I have had rather a trying day.'

The officer smiled, and led me into a small, comfortless room off a wood-panelled corridor. He offered me tea, but I refused. I have absolute faith in the police force to perform their duties assiduously and competently, but I doubted whether the same could be said for their brewing of tea.

My description of the youth was lamentably insufficient, but the police officer was generous enough not to call attention to its deficiencies. I could describe neither his footwear nor the colour of his eyes. I had omitted to take note of his build, beyond a youthful slenderness. I had thought his jacket to be green, but now I could not be sure. And his age remained unclear. 'He was between the age of sixteen and nineteen,' I said, apologizing for my unreliability. 'He had a most singular hairstyle. Quite extraordinary. The hair rose from the centre of his scalp in what I can only describe as spikes. The yellow of rapeseed. A very rich hue.'

'Hugh?'

'Shade.'

'Yellow, you say.'

'Yellow. Spiked. Like the spine of a prehistoric animal. He should be easy to recognize,' I said, 'by the colour of his hair.'

'A lot of lads in this town have hair like you've just described.'

'You astonish me, officer. I thought it most uncommon.'

'It's the fashion.'

'Is it really?'

'A kind of uniform, you might say. Dozens of them wear it. Hundreds, when we get an influx of yahoos during the summer months. Of course, we'll do our best to find this one but if I were you I wouldn't expect too much.'

'I see.'

'Sorry.'

'The boy was wearing dark trousers,' I said, presently, 'if that is any help.'

'Nope,' the officer replied, with conviction. 'That's not much help at all.'

I was about to leave the police station when I realized I had forgotten the dog. 'A small black terrier,' I explained. 'I believe it answers to the name of Trixie. It was wearing one of those ridiculous little tartan coats. Mr Jones was most concerned about the dog. The blame is mine. Once the ambulance arrived, I forgot completely about it. You see, officer, I care very little for pets. I am not an animal-lover.'

I am not an animal-lover, but when I saw the dog's corpse I was appalled. 'One of the weekend fishermen brought it in about an hour ago,' the officer said. 'He noticed this bundle lying by the edge of the water. Went to have a look, saw the blood, carried it in to us in his waterproof cape. Been beaten here, you see, and there. Kicked, most likely, if you want my opinion. The throat's been cut, too, you'll notice. Almost sliced the head in two. The knife must have been razor-sharp.'

A young policeman drove me home in a police car and escorted me to my door. The whisky I drank immediately I was inside diminished my nausea, but only a little.

So. I married George. I married a bully. I was young and rather frivolous and I mistook passion for love. George

137

was a handsome man and it was not difficult to feel that in that hearty moustache, in those ash-grey eyes, in that rather large and lazy mouth, lay the promise of endearment. The staccato of my heart when I saw him did not alert me; it was a comfort. And when George held my hand, the world was crammed with endless possibilities.

Yes, I was young. And when I remember myself then I remember a stranger – a girl unschooled in life, closeted from reality, a piece of insubstantial driftwood floating towards a dangerous harbour.

We became engaged in the autumn of my twenty-second year, and the party we held to celebrate our betrothal took place in one of the hotels George had inherited from his father. (The hotel still stands, and stands still, a rather tawdry monument to a forgotten past. These days it is frequented by businessmen in grey suits and weekend couples committing adultery.) Needless to say, George's wealth, his several properties, delighted my aunt. 'It is much easier,' she used to say, 'to marry a rich man and be happy than it is to marry a poor man.' During the party – attended by perhaps fifty people – I slipped out of the ballroom into the garden, and sat for a while under a poplar tree. Autumn did not seem to me then a season of decay, but one of infinite promise. 'I shall love George for ever,' I told the poplar, and my pledge gave me a sense of peace. I so desperately wished to belong to somebody, I who belonged only to a generation of spiritual orphans, those who had grown up during the Great War, those who had seen the results of that war, those who had lost faith. My mother was dead, and my father, and God who had caused so much damage to humanity. I had no allegiances, except to George.

When we married, I was three-and-twenty and emerging from my girlhood, George four years my elder. The church in which we were wed was both sufficiently ancient and sufficiently damp to meet my aunt's requirements of propriety. 'Marriage requires a firm foundation,' she told me, tapping her feet on the stone floor of the church the day before the wedding. The fact that George was a free-thinker and I a non-believer, were to her only trivial heresies, akin to forgetting to put on gloves before leaving the house. Our lack of faith was an irrelevancy that could be overlooked. What was relevant and important – and proper – was that we be married in a church. And, after all, the vows we were to make would be sacred, permanent, enduring; we believed in each other even if we did not believe in God.

It rained the day of our wedding and the rain caused my aunt much distress. She, who had planned everything, who had schemed the day so perfectly, had forgotten to allow for the contrariness of English weather. But I did not mind the rain; it did not seem to matter that my dress was a little wet, my hair damp. I remember only hearing its beat on the roof of the church orchestrating the ceremony of our marriage, gently applauding our future together.

The church had been decorated with so many flowers that upon first entering it I was momentarily unable to breathe. But perhaps I am being fanciful, perhaps nervousness took away my breath, or the sight of George's energetically erect back as I walked up the aisle. Or the prospect, the promise of passion.

A reception was held in the ballroom of one of George's hotels. It was a grand affair – the women were elegantly dressed, the men splendid in morning suits, champagne tickled the roof of the mouth. More flowers decorated the ballroom, a band played discreetly, waitresses moved skilfully between the groups with glasses of champagne and mouthfuls of delicacies. Shortly before George and I were to leave to catch the boat-train to Paris, my aunt took me aside. 'You have never quite belonged,' she said, resting a gloved hand upon my wrist. 'Your mother never seemed to care for you a great deal and your father died too young to be of any good to you. I have done my best, but we have never been close. George seems to be a kind enough man, and perhaps now that you are married you will find a person and a place to belong to.' I smiled with some relief; I had been afraid she might have wished to speak of honeymoon matters, of physical love, but I ought to have known she was far too circumspect for that.

So long is it since I have felt passion, that to try to remember it is like trying to remember a country one has never visited. One knows where the country is situated, what rivers run through its cities, which mountains mark its frontiers; but the country itself remains vague and undefined, teasing but not satisfying the imagination. I see George undressing in the dark of a Parisian hotel, a young man with a fine body, speaking softly to me, gently, knowing that though unafraid I am nevertheless nervous. I see him walk towards me, skilfully unbuttoning my dress, removing it from my shoulders, kissing my flushed neck. I see us perform the physical act of love; I watch my surprise as I discover pain is absent; I hear the laughter of a man and a woman outside our window. I feel as though I could climb a mountain or compose a symphony. I feel, finally and irrevocably, that I belong to George.

'You were nervous,' said George.

'A little.'

'But not frightened?'

'Not frightened, no.'

'And it pleased you?'

'Yes.'

George laughed. 'You are wicked,' he told me. 'Women are not expected to enjoy the carnal side of marriage. But passion is an opium, one becomes addicted. I see you are already addicted to me.'

Later, we went out to eat. I do not recall the meal that was set down before us, but I know I ate a great deal and that my appetite caused George much merriment.

Passion has its rewards and its consequences, and when we returned from our honeymoon I was already expecting George's child. My state caused me some physical distress and more emotional anguish. I did not want to share George, I did not want our marriage to have to accommodate another human being. As we were, we were entire. I told George my secret one evening early in June, as we sat outside in the garden overlooking the orchard. I had not seen George all day, for he had been occupied with his hotels – in those days the resort was at its most popular – and the chef from one hotel had given notice at the same time as the manager of another. When he returned, half an hour before dinner, he was not in the best of tempers. He forgot to kiss me and claimed his drink had not been properly mixed.

I said, 'I have a surprise to tell you, George.'

'A surprise, my dear?'

'I am expecting a child.'

'Is that so?'

'Yes, George. I have not been feeling well for some weeks.'

I do not know now what I expected from George – approbation, congratulation, a kiss, a gruff word of approval, a gesture dismissive of the haste with which the child had been conceived. 'The child will make no difference,' I wanted to say. 'We shall love each other as passionately as we do now.' But George was silent, and looked moodily towards the damson trees, and so I remained silent.

'Let us hope', he said presently, 'that the child will be a boy.'

The summer that followed was hot, uncongenial to pregnancy. The heat was everywhere, thumping down upon the trees of the orchard, scalding the pavements, scorching the sea, stifling the house. Only the scullery with its stone floor and its meshed window was cool. Though pregnancy was as unfamiliar to me as passion had been before meeting George, it made me afraid as passion had not. At night I dreamed the child would be born with a ghastly deformity; during the day my body was so heavy it seemed filled not with blood, but with mercury.

'All women have children,' said my aunt, who had not. 'All women find the state of pregnancy alarming.' When the child was born, she claimed, I would forget the discomfort; I would be a mother, the child would adore me, George would love me more.

These words, intended to comfort, seemed only the thoughtless truisms of a spinster. 'George is determined upon the child being a boy,' I said, but she laughed.

'All men want boys,' she said, 'until they see their daughters.'

I carried the child for almost ten months and the night it was born the first snow of that winter grazed the ground. From my bed I watched the snowflakes flicker past the window, counting them to divert my mind from the pain which punished my body. 'How trying you are, pain,' I remember muttering, 'how immensely trying.'

But the pain did not go away; its power astounded me, preventing me from rational thought, from conversation with the doctor, even from opening the new Trollope which lay, uncut, on the counterpane. During the course of my labour, perspiring in the chill of the room, I prayed to the God in whom I had no faith, but the prayer was cut short by the merciful administration of the ether.

I awoke some time later to the sound of an immense silence, as though all noise had been snuffed out by the snow. The embers of the fire were hot and red and still, and at the other end of the bedroom sat the doctor, his eyes closed. When I spoke my voice was unfamiliar, made hoarse by the ether.

'The child?' I said. 'Why is it not crying? All babies cry when they are born. Why does mine stay silent?'

'The baby is dead,' said the doctor, rising from his chair. 'The boy never learned to breathe.'

After the doctor had left the room, I began again to count the snowflakes. They fell randomly, some with infinite reluctance, others skidding so rapidly past the window that I could not keep count. I imagined the trees of the orchard, leaf-bare, snow-heavy; the path which led to them white and treacherous; the roads and pavements undefined; the landscape of the town oppressed by the tyrannies of winter.

I counted flakes of snow. And George, once told of the child's death, left the house and stayed away from home that night and did not return until the following evening. That night George took the first of his mistresses. That night his passion for me died.

When I look at the photographs of George and myself taken after that winter, I notice that we do not stand close together and nor do we touch. We smile, of course, yet we do not appear to be smiling at the same things, or even in the same direction. We do not seem to belong to each other any more.

11

The policeman who called at Roff's house was young and nervous and ill-suited to the job. Some months before he had applied to train as a fireman and had been put on a short-list of three. He had failed the final interview because, though tall, he had not appeared sufficiently well-built to be able to carry distressed women from fire-enraged tower-blocks. 'Try the police,' the Fire Superintendant had kindly suggested, and Mills had taken the advice.

The door at which he would knock – when he got the nerve – was painted brown, and a free news-sheet poked out of the letter-box. Mills, though inexperienced, possessed a certain astuteness and took the news-sheet to indicate one of two things – either the occupants of the house were out, or they were too lazy to remove the paper from the letter-box. If they were out, he could allow himself a quick coffee in the Snac-Box café at the corner before getting back to the station. If they were lazy, they were probably hostile to the police (laziness and hostility to authority going hand in hand), and might refuse to answer his questions, making an already difficult job impossible. Mills knocked softly and hoped nobody would answer. Asking questions of strangers did not come easily to him, and he had a great many questions to ask. A dead dog and an old man with stitches in his head. He frowned, not knowing which questions to ask first, how to ask them, even whom he should ask them of. He didn't even know which crime was the more serious – killing a dog or injuring an old man. He was extremely fond of dogs himself, and thought if he managed to stay in the force he might apply to become a dog-handler. He knocked again, thinking wistfully of the motorist he had caught that morning for doing thirty-three miles an hour in the High Street.

Annie didn't hear the knock at first, absorbed as she was in the hospital serial on telly. The fifteen-year-old girl who'd just been admitted with a suspected appendix was sitting up in bed, listening to Dr Grant – the hospital's best-looking registrar – explain that she was in labour and might give birth at any minute. Dr Grant didn't know – though Annie did – that when he came off duty in half an hour and drove home, he would surprise his wife in bed with another man. Annie couldn't wait to see the look on his face. Nobody knew what would happen when Dr Grant found them together, but Annie thought it unlikely he would hit his wife. What he'd do would be to pour himself a drink, because Dr Grant was an alcoholic and everyone knew his days at the hospital were numbered. It was only a matter of time before the knife would slip in his unsteady hands during a crucial operation.

The main reason Annie had for keeping on her job as a waitress was afternoon telly. Between the hours of two and five-thirty, she was off work and used this free time to put her feet up, brew a large pot of tea, watch television. The old black and white films, the serials, even the children's programmes, took her mind off filling the salt-cellars, laying the tables, serving all those portions of chicken and French beans and sauté potatoes. Sometimes just looking at a sauté potato made her want to heave. The hotel where she worked had once been posh, but now they only changed the tablecloths once a week and the gravy stains were hidden by vases of plastic flowers.

The ads were on when she heard the knock on the

front door, and she waited until the advertisement had finished – she wanted to see the cornflakes trampoline in the air – before getting up to answer it.

Her first thought when she saw the policeman standing there was that he'd come about her Bob. Even though Bob had buggered off more than sixteen years ago, he was still in her mind. Sometimes, in bed at night, she'd put down her Mills and Boon and go off into a day-dream about him. He'd send a letter, asking her to join him in Majorca; he'd appear at the hotel one dinner-time with a huge bunch of roses; he'd ring up and say he was on his way home. Sheila said she was pissing in the wind, hoping for Bob to come back, but girls these days weren't romantic, not like she'd been when she'd met Bob. Sheila wanted a good time and no strings and – eventually – a house on a modern estate. Sheila didn't believe in love.

Bob might be dead. The policeman looked serious, like he had bad news. If he was dead, she'd put flowers on his grave, just to show there was no bad feeling. And if, by any chance, he'd left her some money in his will, for old time's sake, well, she'd not go daft with it, like some women. She'd get the bathroom redone and get a new cooker on instalments, one of them with a clock on it, so the kidneys wouldn't burn.

'About Bob, is it?' she asked. 'Only if he's died, you'd better tell me quick, because I'm missing the serial and I'm on dinners in three-quarters of an hour.'

But the policeman knew nothing about Bob, didn't even know he existed, and she was disappointed to learn he was interested only in her son.

'Oh, him,' she said, not inviting the policeman in. 'Nobody cares', she told him, 'when a man walks out on his missus and a baby and another on the way without a by-your-leave and isn't heard of for sixteen years. He'll come running home when he gets in trouble, mark my

146

words. Always knew what side his bread was buttered on.'

PC Mills said, 'Yes, I expect so,' and looked sympathetic. From the front room Annie could hear raised voices and the sound of breaking glass. That would be Dr Grant finding his wife in bed with that no-good lawyer, the one who'd beaten up his girlfriend.

'Fighting,' she explained. 'He's just got home and found them. Just so long as that lawyer gets what he deserves.'

Annie shook her head, as if to stop the policeman from speaking. She didn't want to hear what Mikey had been up to. He'd never been the same since he'd changed his name to Roff and started messing about with his hair. When he was a baby he'd had lovely hair, soft and sort of blond, with little curls at the back. She thought what a shame it was that kids grew up and became surly and used up all the tomato sauce.

She said Michael wasn't in. 'He's at work till six. Got himself a job. In the abattoir it is, looking after the animals. Steady work.' She couldn't say what time he'd be home, not exactly, she never knew herself. 'I'm usually out, see. Shifts at the hotel. Lamb cutlets it is tonight, and butter beans. Chocolate pudding for afters, with that cream on top, the stuff you squirt from the can. Gets his own tea, Michael does. Leaves his dishes for me to wash. Doesn't know how to wash a dish, thinks they wash themselves.' The other waitresses at the hotel sympathized with her, saying it must be hell trying to bring up a son and a daughter on her own. Sometimes when she got up in the morning and came downstairs to make breakfast, she hoped she might find a note on the kitchen table. '*Gone to London, Roff*.' Something like that. If he went, she'd put an advertisement in the paper for a lodger. A nice, quiet businessman. In the evenings they could watch the telly together and during News at Ten she'd slip out into the kitchen and make supper – sliced pork pie, some scones from the supermarket, a pot of tea.

'Michael's not in,' she repeated, listening for the sound of an argument on the telly. 'You want to try the arcade later on. Goes there sometimes after work. Waste of time, if you ask me, them machines.' The policeman nodded, thanking her for her time. When Annie got back to the front room, the lawyer and Dr Grant were still shouting at each other, while Dr Grant's wife was getting dressed, pulling on a pink lacy slip. She ought to have tried wearing sexy underwear sixteen years ago, and maybe Bob wouldn't of walked out.

In the Snac-Box café, PC Mills ate a stale iced bun and drank a cup of luke-warm coffee. On his next day off he thought he might find out whether any vacancies were going for milkmen. He didn't hold out much hope for his career in the police force.

The lamb cutlets were gristly and two guests complained, demanding chicken instead. Annie smiled and said, 'Certainly,' and blamed the chef for doing her out of a tip from table four. All evening she was busy and all evening the commercial traveller in bathroom accessories sitting at a corner table kept giving her the glad eye. He was a squat man who read his newspaper during the meal, and when Annie brought his coffee he pointed to the paper and began to read out the weather forecast. 'Dry tomorrow,' he said in a low voice, 'so you and me, we could take a dander somewhere.' He reached out his hand, grabbing her by the arm, almost making her spill the coffee. 'A walk,' he said, winking, 'in the hills.'

Annie carefully put down the coffee, noting the traveller's bad breath, his dirty fingernails. She asked him what sort of a girl did he think she was, and walked quickly away when he replied that he didn't think she was a girl at all. 'Been a long time', he shouted across the dining-room, 'since you were a girl.'

The chef, to make amends for the gristle on the chops, told her to help herself to a chocolate éclair from the freezer, and said once upon a time a man making indecent suggestions like that in a hotel like this would have been asked, firmly and politely, to leave. 'Times have changed,' he said, and Annie – remembering Michael as a baby, thinking of him as he was now – had to agree. By nine o'clock the last diner had left, and she sat down with the other waitresses to finish off the chocolate pudding. While the other waitresses talked about the chambermaid who had found one of the male guests in bed with two girls that morning, Annie thought that there must be more to life than eating other people's left-overs. The trouble was, she couldn't think what.

'There was a policeman here,' she told Roff when she got home. She waited for him to look frightened or worried but he continued to stare at the telly, without even bothering to look up.

'You making tea?' he asked.

'Came this afternoon. Young lad, tall. You was out.'

'Yeah.'

'Asked questions, so he did.'

'Lost his way to the beach, had he?'

'Asked after you.'

'Tell him I was all right, did you?'

'I told him,' said Annie, 'that you was out. Working.'

'I am back now. What about that cup of tea?'

'I said he might find you at the arcade after work.'

'I never went to the arcade. Worked late. Rush order for back bacon. Pigs, see.'

149

Annie said she knew bacon came from pigs, she wasn't daft. She also knew he was lying, but she didn't say so. She lit a cigarette and read the warning on the side of the packet: *Cigarettes can seriously damage your health*. You couldn't turn on the telly these days without seeing photographs of diseased lungs, all black and shrivelled. Fair turned her stomach. The cigarette tasted funny after all that chocolate pudding. Maisie, one of the other waitresses, had given up smoking and bought herself a rabbit fur with the money she'd saved, but the coat only made her look fat.

'You been nicking things?' she asked.

Roff told her he'd robbed a bank in the High Street. 'Me and my mates. Shot the security guard with an AK 4, raped the tellers, tied up the bank manager, made off with forty thousand.'

'Cheeky bugger,' she said. And then, just to make sure, 'You never.'

'You're right. I never.'

'What'd he want, then, the copper?' she asked. The smoke from her cigarette hung around the room. One of these days, she promised herself, she'd get the house decorated. Paint, new curtains, one of them furry white rugs for in front of the gas fire.

'I dunno what he wanted, do I? You was here when he came, you saw him.'

'Came in the middle of the telly,' she said, pointedly. 'Made me miss half of it. Just so long as you haven't been getting in trouble.'

'Naw.'

'You sure?'

'Yeah.'

'Well, that's all right then.'

Roff smiled at her. 'You making that tea now?'

While waiting for the kettle to boil, Annie put some

150

cake out on a plate. It had probably been a mistake, that copper coming. He'd got her Michael mixed up with some other lad. Anyone could tell, just by looking at him, that he'd never do anything bad, not really bad. Yes, that was it. A mistake.

The last person Roff wanted coming to court with him was Annie.

On the bus they sat on the top deck so they could smoke, but they didn't speak to each other. They lit up their cigs and smoked and stared out of the windows. Roff's breakfast lay in his stomach and every time the bus turned a corner too sharply he wanted to heave it up again. Annie had made him wear his suit, the one she'd bought him when he left school when he was four inches shorter and half a stone heavier. When the bus jerked to a stop at the traffic lights, ash spilled on to his trousers, but he didn't bother to brush it off. 'You needn't of come,' he said, but she pretended not to hear, to be looking down at shop windows – fur coats, sheepskin jackets, leather waistcoats. 'Nice, them,' she muttered.

Sometimes he really hated Annie.

The police had come back. Two of them had arrived at the abattoir Monday morning, first thing. They'd interviewed him in the supervisor's office, asked questions. The office was small, with a pin-up on the wall and dead butts in the ashtray. One of them said he'd already spoken to the supervisor. 'Stole one of the rabbi's ceremonial knives, did you, boy?' He hated the way they had called him boy. The knife had been so sharp it had sliced a hole in his jeans that afternoon at the beach. So sharp. Roff couldn't understand why people used guns to kill when knives were so much better. He'd never forget the way the knife had slid into the dog's throat, so quickly, so easily. 'I dunno about any knife,' he'd said, pretending not to care. He knew that would make them angry. He seen it on telly.

'The rabbi reported it, you see. The missing knife. Part of a set. He can't kill those animals without all his ceremonial knives. It's not sacred, you see.' The copper turned to look out of the window, and Roff heard the squeal of pigs in their pens. 'So what'd you do with the knife? Throw it in the sea?'

Annie was wearing too much make-up and Roff walked a few paces behind her, not wanting to be seen with her. He thought she looked like a scrubber with her purple eyeshadow, that red blouse, those tarty earrings. Yet she seemed proud of her appearance, and as they walked from the bus station to the court house he caught her glancing at her reflection in shop windows. A taxi drove slowly past and when the driver whistled, Annie giggled and pretended to be embarrassed. 'You want to show them you come from a nice home,' she said. 'A respectable place. Then they'll see they've made a mistake.'

'Yeah,' Roff replied.

The police had asked him about the dead dog. Roff still thought it funny, the two of them standing in the supervisor's office in the middle of the abattoir, going on about a fucking dead dog. 'I dunno about no dead dog,' he'd said, and told them how many cattle were slaughtered every day, how many sheep. 'They sling them up on hooks,' he'd told them, 'and you've got to use a special chemical to get the blood off the floor. Gets in your eyes, this chemical, makes them sting.'

'A dog,' they'd repeated. 'Slit from ear to ear. An old man's pet murdered.' They'd been more interested in the dog than the old man, asking him was that how he got his kicks, murdering animals.

'You got proof?' he had asked, listening to the pigs screech.

The court was chilly as they went in and they were asked to wait in the corridor. Annie moaned about the cold. 'What you need,' she told an usher, 'is central heating put in.' But nobody paid her any attention. Benches lined the corridor and Roff noticed marks on the walls behind these benches, head-high greasy marks where people had sat waiting for hours, waiting to go into court. They squeezed on to the end of a bench, beside a man smelling of vomit, and Roff was about to light a cigarette when his mother pointed to the No Smoking sign in red letters on a door and made him put the packet away. On the floor by his feet lay several dimps, some plastic cups, cracked and crushed, a chocolate wrapper. 'Crowded,' Annie remarked, like they was sitting in the cinema. The clock on the wall said ten past eleven. 'They'll be getting dinners ready now,' Annie told him in a loud voice. 'Chicken fricassee,' she said, though he wasn't interested, 'sprouts and carrots and sauté potatoes.' She crossed her legs, pulled her skirt up, and her knees were ugly and dimpled. Roff looked away.

'Enough proof,' one of the policemen had told him with a smile. 'We've got enough proof to pin this one on you.' After they had gone, the supervisor had called Roff to one side. 'If you ever steal meat from here,' he'd said, 'you're out on your ear. Got that?'

In the corridor men coughed and a woman sniffed and a girl cried. The crying was so loud, Annie raised her voice to be heard over it. 'Puddings, see,' Roff heard her say. 'People don't go in for them like they used to. Cheese and buscuits they want, or fresh fruit salad.' She talked about puddings while Roff watched the second hand on the clock move round. She said she'd be losing a day's pay, coming to court with him. 'Told the manager, like, and he said he understood. He's two kids of his own, he knows what tricks kids get up to. I didn't say,' she said in a loud voice, 'that you'd done what you did. I said it was for driving a car without a licence.'

While she was still speaking, Roff got up and went to the toilet. He washed his hands slowly, keeping one hand on the knob that released the soap until it had spilled over the wash-basin, dripped on to the floor. In the mirror he noticed a new spot on the side of his nose. He thought about writing on the bog doors but he couldn't think what to write and he didn't have a pen, anyway.

His mother was standing up by the bench, looking worried, when he came out. 'Five minutes,' she told him, adjusting his tie, making the knot even smaller and tighter. 'They thought you'd scarpered, but I told them you wouldn't do nothing like that. Said you'd been brought up proper, a good home.' He noticed now that one of the buttons on her red blouse was missing and revealed an inch of grey underwear, but he didn't think it worth it, telling her. He supposed the old man would be in court, but he was surprised, when he and Annie were ushered inside the courtroom, to see the old woman there, too. She was wearing a fur coat, the same one she'd worn that day on the beach, and her hair was white, dappled in parts with grey. Under the bright lights she blinked and when she caught sight of him instead of looking away she studied him, a distant inspection that made him feel uneasy.

The lawyer had told him to plead guilty. 'You might get off with a suspended sentence,' he had claimed, 'because this is your first offence. And the evidence is pretty circumstantial – the knife hasn't yet been found, the old man never saw you, the woman probably can't identify you. You plead guilty, and they'll let you off easily.'

'Not guilty,' said Roff, standing up, and in the court people muttered, coughed and shifted position; stretching their legs, crossing their arms, settling themselves in for the morning. The judge, ensconced upon his judicial throne, gently patted the warm wooden bench in front of him, finding its warmth reassuring, fancying he could detect a slight scent of beeswax rise from its surface. He looked at the defendant, deciding that on the grounds of his anarchic hairstyle alone the jury would find him guilty, and was silently grateful for the fact he had sired only daughters.

Below him, shuffling papers, the clerk of the court felt the first pangs of indigestion cut across his guts. During the recess he would drink milk and crunch three antacid tablets, and think longingly of the holiday he and his wife had planned touring Scotland in a luxury coach.

At the back of the court, Annie noticed a hole in her tights, and bent to inspect it. The hole was the size of an old penny, just below and to the right of her knee. At the hotel, the manager had pulled her up once or twice in the past – not for holes in her tights, but for what he called 'sloppy appearance'. When she thought about it, her uniform appeared less clean than those the other waitresses wore, and her shoes gathered dirt from the streets, dust from the dining-room carpet. Once, she had been attractive, attractive enough for Bob to fall in love with her and to agree to marry her when she'd told him about Sheila being on the way. 'A nice looker,' he'd said once, when he'd had a few pints inside him. But she knew she was attractive no longer and would never be smart. Not like the women she saw on telly. Oh, she knew they had piled on the make-up, could pick and choose their clothes, that their hairdressers were always on hand. But she suspected that even without those props, such women would always look elegant, appear smart. Like that old woman sitting near the front. She was bobbing on in years, but she was still smart, with her fur coat and her polished shoes and a good head of hair, despite her age. Annie sighed to herself, thinking that smartness, like happiness, had eluded her in life.

Henry Jones sat near Grace Hopkins and wished himself anywhere but in the courtroom. A man who had assiduously avoided conflict throughout his life, he felt discomfort, knowing the young man had pleaded not guilty, knowing he would be called to the witness box, knowing voices would be raised, knowing the job of the police was to ensure the youth be found guilty. Knowing he was the cause of all this. The sight of the youth frightened him, the stitches in his head hurt, he could not get Trixie out of his mind. He had not even been given the chance to bury Trixie; at the police station a sergeant had explained that the dog's body had already been disposed of. In his small and damp and gloomy flat, the rooms smelled of Trixie and of the companionship that had been so brutally stolen from him. The dog's hairs were embedded in the weave of the rug that lay beside the hearth; the chewed rubber ball was still in the basket in the kitchen; when he opened cupboards in search of tinned steak for supper, he was transfixed by the sight of endless tins of dog food, by the picture on each of a healthy, white-toothed labrador. His neighbour had suggested he buy another pet and had been puzzled and embarrassed by his answering tears. He was sixty-nine and all his life he had wished only for peace – peace at work, at home, simple peace. It had not seemed too excessive a request to ask from God that he be permitted to lead a quiet and uncomplicated and uncontroversial life, but the request had either been ignored or dismissed – as he suspected – as unworthy of God's attention. 'You are a dreary man,' he could almost hear God say sadly, 'a dreary, suburban man with few capabilities and a limited

156

imagination, and your request for peace does not interest me.'

In retirement, he had expected a measure of tranquillity – walks by an autumn sea, the potting out of geraniums, a round of Scrabble with Marjorie. But his wife, unhappy in their new home, had engineered domestic rows, forced upon him trivial confrontations, nagged him and squabbled with him and been querulous and argumentative and ill-tempered. Out of spite she had cooked meals he did not enjoy, placed before him plates of highly spiced foods which damaged the lining of his stomach, had cooked him indigestible meats, served up puddings which smelled uneasily of too much nutmeg. Even after her death, peace had eluded him – or become an illusion, he was not sure which. The young couple who shared the flat above him seemed to pace the floors of an evening in heavy boots, to play music too loudly, to make love with an excess of enthusiasm. When he took Trixie for walks, cars hooted as he crossed the road and pedestrians growled as Trixie snapped at their ankles.

He envied women like Mrs Hopkins who had bullied him into letting her report the incident on the beach to the police. He envied her tenacity, her arrogant way of speaking, the outrageous things she said. She would not feel bereft at the death of a pet; she was not afraid to be sitting in this courtroom, about to give evidence; she did not dream at night of the past or think, during the day, of the wasteland of the future. She did not look at the youth, at the judge, at the wood-panelled walls, at the congenial faces of the jury, and wish herself elsewhere.

When Grace Hopkins was called to the witness stand, she caused mild confusion by refusing to swear on the Bible. She held her head erect and her hands by her side and she shook her head firmly.

'I prefer to take the affirmation,' she said, and her

157

clear, authoritative voice alarmed the defence, woke the judge, and alienated the two Methodist and one practicising Catholic on the jury bench.

'Such a spurious document,' she said, referring to the Bible which the clerk now held in one hand. 'Besides,' she added, 'I always tell the truth. One does when one is old, when one is no longer afraid. The affirmation will suit me nicely.' The lawyer for the defence rose first and the questions he put to Mrs Hopkins were straightforward and routine, and were answered in confident tones. Occasionally the noise of a scuffle in the corridor, or the thrum of a bus passing outside, entered the courtroom, but Mrs Hopkins simply raised her voice during these intrusions and it is perfectly possible that even in the tiled sanctity of the court's ladies' room her evidence could be heard.

'You claim you saw a youth pick up a stone, and throw it at Mr Jones, striking him on the forehead,' said the barrister. 'But was it not raining at the time?'

'Drizzling. Drizzle is not the same as rain.'

'I would have thought,' said the barrister, turning towards the jury, 'that the two were indistinguishable.'

'You are mistaken,' said Mrs Hopkins. 'It is obvious to me that you spend much of your time indoors, and that when you do venture out it is under the protection of one of those ridiculously large black umbrellas that your profession is so fond of.' Some members of the public and one or two of the jury smiled at this statement, thinking the witness was intending to amuse. Henry Jones cast his mind back and found he could recall little of that afternoon but the smell of sand in his nostrils and the distant barking of Trixie.

'It is difficult, if not impossible, to be aware of the difference between rain and drizzle under a black umbrella,' continued Mrs Hopkins. 'I, who do not possess such an article, am well aware of the gradations of rain, of the difference between a light, intermittent drizzle and a heavy downpour. And I know why you are so insistent in your questioning. I have watched serials about the police and the courts on my television, and I know you are trying to intimidate me. You are trying to force from me the admission that because it was drizzling I could not see the youth clearly. But I saw him. I see him now.'

'You are absolutely certain.'

'I could not be more certain.'

'Thank you,' the defence lawyer said hopelessly. 'You may step down now.'

It was agreed, while the jury was out, that if the youth were convicted, it would be only because of the old woman's evidence. Counsel realized this, as did the judge and the clerk of the court. Annie knew it, sitting at the back worrying about the loss of a day's pay, picking distractedly at the hole in her tights. Henry Jones knew it, thinking of Trixie, wondering if he dared return the dozens of tins of dog food to the supermarket where he had bought them and ask for a refund.

Roff knew it. He knew the jury would believe every word a woman like that said; that people trusted an old woman in a fur coat who talked like an old-fashioned actress, the kind his mother watched perform in old films on Saturday afternoons. He knew that if he got sent off somewhere *she* would be to blame. He thought how unfair life was, that a woman like that was still alive and kicking and allowed to give evidence in a courtroom against him when she ought to have died years ago. He hated her more than the old man he'd hit, more than the police, more than the jury, more than Annie.

The jury was out for forty-five minutes. When it returned, the foreman stood at the end of the jury bench

159

with a solemn and rather smug expression on his face, the expression of a man charged with making an important and just decision, the expression of one who has done his duty and who can sleep well at nights and whose moral world is intact and inviolable. He hesitated for a few seconds before reading out the verdict, savouring the court's attention, the momentary power the actor has on a solitary stage. When the judge cleared his throat, he began to speak.

Annie made a scene and the judge had to order her to be quiet. Roff could not see her, but he knew her face would be loose and red and distorted as she swore at the jury and then began to sob. Later, she would go back to work and she would tell the other waitresses that her only son had been unjustly put away, sent to a detention centre for two months for assaulting an old man on a beach. She would serve dinners in the apron that was never quite clean enough and during courses would escape to the cloakroom for a five-minute weep.

When Annie had stopped crying, she called out her son's name across the courtroom, but Roff didn't bother to turn round.

12

I insisted Mr Jones allow me to buy him afternoon tea at the Grand after the trial. He looked dismayed at my request, as do those people who receive invitations rarely and who feel more obligation than pleasure in accepting them.

'Standing in the witness box,' I admitted, 'has given me the most frightful thirst. And neither of us has eaten lunch. It is all very well seeing justice done, but one does not expect to have to see it being done for quite such an interminable length of time. We shall gorge ourselves on crustless hotel sandwiches.'

Mr Jones smiled as we walked down the steps. 'I have never taken tea at the Grand,' he confessed.

'We must celebrate. Treat ourselves.'

'Well,' he said, 'yes.' He wore a suit of synthetic material and his shoes had been highly polished. I judged him to be a neat man, fastidious in his personal and domestic habits, paying his bills regularly. I imagined the kind of home he would inhabit – somewhere small, unobtrusive, inexpensive. He would fret over the price of fresh fruit, worry about the tardy arrival of refuse collectors, reread favourite books. I did not know him well enough to envisage the kind of books he would prefer, but thrillers came to mind, detective stories, histories of the Second World War. When he was not reading he would try to keep his home scrupulously clean and never quite succeed. He might occasionally visit a public house, but seldom for the space of more than one drink. His wife, I already knew, had died, and his children (if, indeed, any existed) would live far away. Their visits would be infrequent and unregarding and grudgingly made. 'You should look after yourself properly,' they would say, not caring whether he did or not.

'I found the trial an ordeal,' he acknowledged. 'And I'm greatly relieved it's over. I felt intimidated, you see. By the judge, so still and stern – '

'And somnolent,' I added. 'He dozed. I am quite convinced of the fact. I distinctly heard a snore.'

'And the lawyers. All those questions. But you were splendid. It was your evidence, you know, that led to the boy's conviction. I would never have dared to speak as you did.'

'I have rather a loud voice,' I said. 'And besides, the defence lawyer mumbled.'

'You seemed so, well, so sure of yourself.'

'Quite so.'

But I did not feel sure of myself. To be perfectly candid, I felt that all the certainties in my life had been erased. In the witness box I had told the truth. I had explained all I had seen, admitted what I had not, answered each mumbled question with as much accuracy as I could. My memory of that afternoon had not been impaired by time, but as we walked towards the hotel I began to ask myself whether my motivation had been at fault. Whether the reason I had reported the crime, agreed to be a witness at the trial, identified the youth in court was not – as I had believed – owing to a concern for justice, but simply to divert myself from my own problems. To cause a youth to be incarcerated simply because I did not wish to live with my daughter seemed unfair and unworthy. 'He will think me a vindictive old woman,' I told Mr Jones, but he did not appear to hear me. Doubtless his mind was on his dog.

Even before we had ordered our tea Mr Jones said, 'You must let me pay.'

'Nonsense,' I replied. 'I would not think of it. I have a great deal of money and very little to spend it on.'

We positioned ourselves at a corner table in the lounge, a room oddly proportioned, the shape of a lozenge. The wallpaper which covered each of the curved walls was a vivid, unrestful orange, wearisome to the eye, and flimsy net curtains obscured our view of the sea. But it was nevertheless pleasant to be sitting in a hotel lounge about to partake of afternoon tea. This, I thought, will be one of the pleasures denied to me when I am living with my daughter; when the sea and the hotels and the promenade will be several miles away; when privacy will be as inaccessible to me as youth; when I am my daughter's keeper.

Our tea arrived, and we spoke of trivia as befits the eating of delicate sandwiches and the company of a near-stranger. The tea was strong and served by a young waitress, and the cakes home-made. Mr Jones proved himself to have a poor appetite, eating with small, nervous bites, holding firmly on to his teacup lest it might drop and stain the brown carpet.

'You have children?' I asked, pouring a second cup.

'A son and a daughter. My son lives in Melbourne, he works as an electrical engineer. My daughter has a flat in London. Neither', he said, sadly, 'has married. I visit my daughter three times a year. I take the coach and she meets me at the other end, at Victoria Station. We go to shows and sometimes we feed the ducks in Richmond Park. She says I should get myself another pet. Not a dog, though, a cat. They're less trouble, she claims. She wants me to move to London to be closer to her, but I'm too old now to move again and London tubes are so confusing. You have children?'

'A daughter. She lives on the outskirts of town.'

I cannot think why, but as we drank our second cup of tea and politely offered each other the last cake, I told Mr Jones of my dilemma. 'My daughter wishes me to live with her,' I said, and the inaccuracy of the phrase struck me deeply. 'She claims I am too old, too feeble, to live alone in my large house. She has plans to put me in an extension.'

'Really?' said Mr Jones, as though the scheme had some appeal.

'An annex. She will place me in this annex, with a few of my most cherished possessions. She will provide me with a large colour television which I shall not watch. She will ensure my refrigerator is always well stocked with sensible foods, with unappealing items like yoghurt and cottage cheese and cooked meats. She will provide me with a key to this prison, thus giving me the illusion of freedom, and pot plants will be strategically placed on windowsills where it will be impossible for me to forget to water them. She will invite me, once or twice or even thrice weekly, to eat dinner with her and her husband, and during the meal we will politely discuss the weather or the state of her garden or the programmes they have watched the previous night on their television. She will monitor my health, comment upon my mode of dress, ensure I bath sufficiently. She will accompany me on my daily walks, ensuring they are not too exacting; she will buy me sensible footwear and confiscate my stilettos; she will harass me with her kindnesses and irritate me with her concern. She will,' I concluded, 'probably make me ill, and inevitably hasten my death.'

'I'm sorry,' said Mr Jones, and I regretted having subjected him to such sudden intimacy. He was embarrassed; the sort of man who holds so dear the companionship of a dog in a ridiculous tartan coat is not the sort to welcome intimacies from an old woman. He removed a handkerchief from his pocket and blew his nose cautiously, and as he did so I was filled with the most alarming thought. That this revelation of mine, this unburdening of my soul to a stranger in a polyester suit, might be another of the eccentricities my daughter found so distasteful. It will not be long, I thought, before I begin to accost shopkeepers and park-attendants and postmen with details of my private life. Or forget to wash or brush my hair. Or wear inappropriate clothes – cotton in midwinter, my mink in a heat-wave. Or eat damson jam with tomatoes (already my eating habits were idiosyncratic). Or leave the fire on all night.

Or become incontinent. One day, I thought, I shall be walking damp-knickered in the street, smelling heavily of yesterday's urine, and my daughter will see me and be vindicated. She will triumph.

'Another cake, Mr Jones?' But there remained on the plate only crumbs.

'I expect things will work out,' he said. 'Your daughter sounds as though she means well.' But his words were unconvincing and I sensed he wished only to leave as soon as possible.

'You think me foolish, doubtless, and ungrateful?' I asked.

'You seem to me a most remarkable woman,' he answered, shyly, 'and you know your own mind. Why have you not told your daughter you want to stay in your own home?'

'But I have,' I said. 'Endlessly. She has unfortunately inherited both my determination and my stubbornness. She will not give up. One day, when I am least expecting it, she will arrive on my doorstep and remove me. But I shan't give in without a protest.'

Mr Jones spoke dubiously. 'A protest, Mrs Hopkins?'

'You think because we are old, you and I, we are past protesting? I assure you *I* am not. I have a plan.'

'A plan?'

'One that will prevent her from carrying out her wishes, of course. A plan,' I emphasized, 'that will ensure I never have to live above my daughter's garage. Oh, it is the most marvellous thing. Quite, quite *perfect* in its simplicity.'

Mr Jones looked at me with interest. I sensed he was not curious by nature, but that curiosity had overtaken his earlier embarrassment.

'More tea?' I offered.

'Oh no, thank you. Tea makes me wakeful.'

'Really?' I smiled. 'I have always found it the most restorative of all non-alcoholic drinks. At the bridge club where I play, the tea comes from tea-bags and does not have the same effect at all.' I lifted the net curtain beside me in order to inspect the outdoors. The railings at the front of the hotel were painted black and they glistened a little; a child's lost mitten had been placed on one of the black spikes.

'Well,' said Mr Jones,'I hope your plan is successful.'

'I have not yet worked out the finer details, but I fancy that, yes, it will succeed.' I did not reveal it to him, though I had no doubt its boldness would have fascinated him.

'Not *dangerous*, is it?'

'Goodness gracious, no. Illegal, possibly, but certainly not dangerous. I have no intention of harming my daughter, if that is what you mean.'

Mr Jones laughed. I, too, laughed. Life seemed, suddenly, perfectly amusing.

We parted at the entrance to the hotel. With over-exaggerated courtesy, Mr Jones thanked me for the tea and shook my hand. I watched him walk towards the town, scarcely lifting his feet from the pavement, his head bent down, his arms by his side like a mourner at a stranger's funeral.

For some minutes I stood by the railings in front of the hotel. The sea had a hopeless grey look to it, reflecting a dead winter sky. People passed me, striding purposefully towards late appointments, meetings with friends, dinner at seven-thirty. I cannot think why, but I found myself following some of these people, walking behind them, pausing at a bus-stop outside a shop selling badly made novelties. When a bus pulled up, I ascended the stairs and positioned myself at the front.

The conductor was most amenable when he discovered I had no money for my fare. 'I am unaccustomed to travelling on municipal transport,' I explained, 'and I have only just emptied my purse of coppers in order to furnish a hotel waitress with a tip.' I offered to supply my name and address but he indicated that it was not necessary. 'Going far?' he asked, but I told him I was only there for the view.

And indeed, the view was spectacular, panoramic. One could see for several miles – the sea, the pier, even the fishermen. The roofs of office buildings, the tips of trees, the railway-line. I have always eschewed the omnibus, preferring the comfort of the town's black taxicabs or the exercise of limbs in walking, but I felt quite privileged to be sitting on the top of a red double-decker, watching the town splayed beneath me. 'What an exciting day I have had,' I said to myself, cataloguing my visit to the court-house, the afternoon tea, this ride on the omnibus.

When we reached the suburbs, the view, however, became rather dull. The houses on each side of the road wore a uniform of white paint and red brick. All, without exception, were ugly and all looked the same. How ghastly, I thought, to live in houses like these, in charmless homes with television aerials pointing towards the sky and garages painted blue and tidy lawns. And I thought with much affection of my own home – of its uncertain stone, its sturdy ivy, its irregular, rotting sills.

The bus drew itself to a standstill and it was then, as I pressed my face to the window to watch people get on and off the bus, that I realized we were but a few yards from Jean's house. I saw the cement-mixer standing in the driveway and the hideously large pile of bricks that lay beside the front gate. The two men who were squatting on top of my daughter's garage wore dark-blue overalls and were in the process of erecting what appeared to be tubular steel poles at each corner of the garage roof.

I did not wish to look further. The bus moved on and when we reached the terminus, the conductor was kind enough to direct me towards the bus which would take me home. He called me 'luv' and suggested, with an amused grin, that I try to remember to carry my purse with me next time I travelled on public transport.

The barman in the Fox and Grapes attempted to draw him into conversation, but Henry indicated that he preferred to sit in a corner and read the evening paper while drinking his half of lager. The pub was ill lit and Henry had some difficulty in finding a corner which would allow him relief enough from the gloom to peruse his paper without causing him eye-strain. He sat, eventually, by an unwashed window, placing his glass on a stained beer-mat that warned jocosely of the dangers of drinking and driving.

The lager was cold, and by sifting it between his teeth and swilling it cautiously around his mouth he was able to remove the few persistent cake crumbs that still adhered to his teeth. The cakes had been rich, full of unaccustomed delicacies like cherries and walnuts, and he realized he ought not to have allowed Mrs Hopkins to have forced a fourth upon him. The trouble with him, he reflected with only a little bitterness, was that he was a coward. He allowed other people to make his decisions for him, he let himself be persuaded into actions he did not wish to pursue. The only decision he had taken on his own was to retire here to the coast, and it was the one he most regretted, because the move had hastened his wife's death.

The evening newspaper told him of the decisions of others – of politicians and of leaders of industry – and it was some comfort to know that others, too, could make mistakes and be guilty of cowardice. He read the front page, the weather report, the late news bulletins printed in red at the side of the page. He perused the television column, learned of an imminent strike, squinted at the classified advertisements. He realized that this unaccountable interest in second-hand three-piece suites and reconditioned vacuum-cleaners was merely a delaying tactic, that he was reluctant to return to his flat. He knew this reluctance was owing to the absence of Trixie and he wondered how long the unacceptable grief at her death would last. He thought – though he was not absolutely certain – that it might possibly last longer than had the grief after the departure of his wife. Trixie had always provided more companionship than Marjorie – he could throw a ball to Trixie for hours in a park and she would never become bored or disconsolate or irritable. He was immensely saddened by the fact that in court little mention had been made of Trixie's murder, that a small cut on his head from a wayward stone requiring fewer than twenty stitches had seemed – to everyone but him – of infinitely greater gravity.

He folded the newspaper, placed it on the table beside his glass. He would not finish the lager, its bitterness was unpleasant. Cider was preferable, but cider was an ambiguous drink; people in public houses sniggered at him when he ordered it. Once a man sitting nearby had made an unpleasant aside, connecting the drinking of cider with homosexual habits, and he had not drunk it in public since.

The barman had turned on the lights, revealing, as Henry had feared they might, the dust on the windowsills and the ash on the carpet. He would have to leave soon if he were to catch the corner shop still open. He would not require much for his evening meal – a quarter of cooked ham, a tin of potatoes, some frozen vegetables. The afternoon tea had been more than adequate. Over the years his appetite, like his wardrobe and his acquaintances, had diminished. Half the tin of potatoes would suffice; the remainder could be heated up for lunch tomorrow. He reflected that he had enjoyed not only the tea, but the grand surroundings in which it had been consumed: the soft, accommodating armchairs, the expensive wallpaper, the thick carpeting. He was not quite so sure about the company, about Mrs Hopkins. He had taken her for a very old and quite rich and slightly odd woman, but her extraordinary outburst about the business of moving in with her daughter had astounded him. It was not just that she resented her daughter asking her to live with her – resentment at such a generous offer was bewildering enough – but that she should appear to resent it so thoroughly that she had formulated some scheme to prevent its execution. At the mention of her plan, she had become positively manic, waving her arms about and banging for emphasis –

without herself realizing it – on the table. And then had offered him more tea, as if she had forgoten her outburst. At one moment, Henry had been sure he had glimpsed madness in her eyes. Of course, there was little to choose between eccentricity and madness, often the two were indistinguishable, but even so . . . Henry shivered a little. He had not dared to mention that he was waiting for a place in a sheltered-housing unit, where he would be given a small bungalow, would eat communal meals, and where a warden would patrol the grounds around his bungalow at night to ensure his safety during the hours of darkness.

Henry shook his head, picked up his newspaper and walked out of the pub. He would have an early night and when he woke in the morning would be relieved this day was over.

13

The bars on the windows of the detention centre were thick and uncompromising, and the forty acres of ground around the building were surrounded by a wire fence eighteen feet high. Beyond the fence the moors lay, where the gorse was dead and the sheep-shit hard with frost, and where even fell-walkers were aware of a sense of desolation.

The centre was called Blackthorn Grange, and Roff arrived in time for tea.

The journey, under police escort, had taken almost three hours. In the front seats the two policemen had talked about football, argued over politics, grumbled about their wives, boasted of their children. They had laughed and joked and smiled and shouted and when, half-way through the journey, Roff had indicated his urgent need to visit a lavatory, they had ignored him.

Crossing his legs in the back of the car, Roff stared out of the window. He saw the sea disappear as they turned a corner, and empty fields take its place. He saw blighted hedgerows and small, dying villages and a muddy river bed. He saw the hard shoulder of a motorway and fast lorries and several electricity pylons. Soon, the landscape bored him and he turned his attention to the inside of the car. For ten minutes he watched the speedometer waver between seventy and eighty, the backs of the policemen's heads, the broad hands that lay on the steering-wheel. He listened to the talk of football clubs he did not support, of women he did not know, of politicans he had never heard of. He thought of the old woman standing up in court, of the judge telling him he would benefit from the disciplined environment of a detention centre, of his mother screaming and crying and telling everyone in the courtroom that her boy had never done any harm to nobody never.

With the heater on full, the interior of the car had been warm, and Roff, bored by everything around him, had had little difficulty in falling asleep.

Blackthorn Grange had accommodation for a hundred and fifty young offenders and ten prison officers, five of whom were expert in the skills of humiliation. One of these five, an officer called Jordan, made Roff strip upon his arrival, bent him over like a willow and made a thorough investigation of his rectum with plastic-gloved hands. 'Got a razor up there, have you?' he asked, probing Roff's sphincteral muscles. He had known boys bring razors or drugs into the centre by this method, and though his search of every new arrival was not always quite so meticulous, he thought he saw in Roff's eyes the look of one who exulted in damaging the centre's clean record.

During the search, Roff looked at the floor, noticing the linoleum was scored in several places as though someone had skated on it. He did not think it likely that skating on the linoleum was allowed in a place like this, or even possible, but he kept his mind fixed on the marks that criss-crossed the floor because that way he wouldn't think about being sick.

'Two months,' said Jordan, peeling off the plastic glove. Roff nodded. The room was cold and his skin looked sallow. During the summer when he'd swum every day, he'd been sunburnt; the sun had helped his spots clear up. He put on his underpants thinking he wouldn't want to crap for weeks. He might even be bleeding.

Jordan spoke again. 'Two months,' he said and Roff realized he was supposed to answer.

'Eight weeks,' he replied, for he'd worked that out in the car. Two months was eight weeks.

'Wrong. Not eight. Not eight fucking weeks. Nine.'

'Yeah. Nine.'

'Not nine either.'

Roff shrugged. Eight weeks, nine. Did it matter?

'Nine weeks, *sir*.'

'Nine weeks,' said Roff. 'Sir.'

Jordan threw him a regulation shirt. With clothes on, Roff felt a bit better, but not much. He shivered, thinking how cold the room was, not realizing he was frightened.

'By that time, your hair'll have grown.'

'What?'

'Your hair. In nine weeks it'll have grown again.'

'It doesn't need to grow.'

Roff watched Jordan laugh. At the abattoir there had been this psycho, a bloke the others had warned Roff to steer clear of, who used to get a real kick out of gassing the chickens. Who laughed like he was demented when he locked five hundred chickens in and turned on the gas. Jordan's laugh was like that.

'You're getting it all chopped off. Right now. Regulations. Get a bloody move on.'

He followed Jordan. Through a large room with a billiard table and a small television, along a corridor, up some stairs, past two closed doors, into another room.

The barber had two cold sores on his mouth and his breath smelled of mustard. He didn't use scissors but a razor. Jordan watched and smiled as the razor screamed through Roff's hair and lopped off his spikes. Roff was reminded again of the abattoir by the noise of the razor, for it sounded like the electric clippers the men used when shearing the sheep before they were electrocuted.

Roff had always reckoned sheep were pretty stupid animals until he'd worked at the abattoir, but he found out they wasn't that stupid at all. Mostly, when they heard the sound of the clippers they'd panic and run around in circles, looking for a way out, like they knew what was going to happen to them. He, too, thought of running, but the barber was a big man and Jordan was right beside him, and he knew that if he ran all that would happen would be that he'd get the shit beaten out of him and that it wouldn't be just nine weeks, it would be twelve or eighteen or even longer.

He watched the spikes fall on to the floor. One of them landed on Jordan's foot and he kicked it away, like it was dog-shit. He knew it wasn't right, wasn't fair, what they were doing to him, but he couldn't protest about it. And when he tried to think of all the people he could blame for it – people apart from Jordan and the barber – people like Mick or the old woman or Annie – it seemed to him that when it came down to it, it was his Dad's fault. If his Dad hadn't of pissed off before he was even born, he mightn't be here at all, he mightn't be watching his hair falling to the floor in big clumps, feeling the razor graze his scalp. But thinking this didn't make him feel angry, only sad.

The barber turned off the razor. 'Nice job,' Jordan told him and motioned Roff to follow him. 'Time you saw the Governor.'

The Governor asked Roff why he thought he had been sent to the Grange. Roff replied that it was because he had hit an old bloke with a stone and killed a dog. The Governor, a keen Baptist, shook his head at the reply. 'You sinned against society,' he informed him.

Roff hesitated. He was not sure what the word sin meant, not exactly. 'It's a sin,' Annie would sometimes say on mornings when she was tired, 'it's a sin I've to go to work today.' He remembered the phrase, but it failed to enlighten him. At school, the religious instruction he had received had been sporadic, concentrated on the theologically abstruse. Zoroastrianism had been studied briefly and mention made of somebody called Joe Smith. Roff thought he could recall something about reincarnation – being born again as an ant or a dragonfly. At the time he couldn't see the point of wanting a rebirth only to spend years buzzing around a fruit shop or in a back yard. But sin had not been mentioned during these classes. If he had sinned against society, then so had thousands of motorists. They, too, killed animals, ran over them in cars with large wheels, left them squashed in the middle of the road. Every day at the abattoir more than ten thousand cows and sheep and pigs and chickens were killed. Nobody had ever said that was a sin, nobody. In fact, everyone had been proud of these figures, of managing to slaughter so many head of cattle in a day. The supervisor had a chart in his office and would point to it when visitors came, claiming it proved how efficient and streamlined the abattoir was. Nevertheless, Roff now wished he hadn't killed the dog; it had been a pretty stupid thing to do. But the dog had been getting on his nerves, running at his heels, yapping.

'Wanted to find out if the knife was really sharp, see,' he explained.

The Governor shook his head, wondering whether he was dealing with a psychopath or a simpleton. Sometimes the difference between the two was barely distinguishable.

'All knives are sharp,' he said, 'Except in here, where they are made of plastic.'

'Yeah.'

Another bell rang. 'Tea,' said the Governor, asking Roff whether he was a church-goer. In his experience, young offenders did not go to church, did not even believe, and it was this widespread lack of faith that led to moral laxity among the young, to pregnant schoolgirls and petty theft and streets unsafe to walk in after dark.

'While you are with us,' he told Roff, 'you will go to church every Sunday morning. You will learn to pray and to sing "Jerusalem". All our boys go to church. It is not compulsory, but those boys who refuse to attend are given unsavoury tasks to do instead. Those boys who refuse are given a mop and a bucket and a bottle of disinfectant and a lavatory brush, and are told to clean the lavatories. It is not a task I myself am familiar with. At home my wife sees to the cleaning of the bathroom. But you might prefer to clean lavatories than sing "Jerusalem"?'

Roff didn't know what Jerusalem was, but replied that he wouldn't mind singing it.

The Governor smiled. 'You see,' he said, 'we are fair in here. Like God.'

The chair Roff was sitting on was hard and his arse ached. The abattoir would be closed now and the animals they hadn't managed to kill would be shuffling about in their pens. Annie would be at work, telling anyone who would listen that her lad had been taken away, sent to some place miles from home where a visit would take a train journey and two bus rides. Mick would be in the arcade, or shagging some girl. Roff thought that the only reason he'd thrown the stone at the old bloke was to show off to Mick, and Mick hadn't even bothered to stay to see him do it. The trouble was, you couldn't trust nobody.

The Governor said, 'Can you read?'

'Yeah.'

'And write?'

'If I want.'

'Splendid. And hobbies, what about hobbies? Football, woodwork, weight-training, that kind of thing?'

Roff said he liked Space Invaders, and the Governor said he was sorry to hear it. 'We pride ourselves on our physical education unit. We have one hour in the gymnasium every day. All fit boys take part. Vigorous activity in the pursuit of skill.'

Roff nodded and said he was a good swimmer.

'No swimming baths here. Just the gymnasium. We monitor your progress in the gym for two weeks. See how you get on. If you try hard, and if your conduct in the workshop and in classes and in the centre generally is good, you become a grade two. You get to wear a red tie instead of the green one.'

Roff said he'd never worn a tie in his life, which the Governor took as another indication of moral laxity. 'I am never without a tie,' he said, 'I have several in my wardrobe at home. But you will like wearing a red tie. Red is my favourite colour. And by the time you leave here, you will find, I have no doubt, that you have become accustomed to wearing a tie, and to going regularly to church and to running on the spot in our splendid gymnasium. You will find yourself despising the person you once were and avoiding your former friends. You will, in a word, have reformed.'

For ten minutes, the Governor spoke. He talked in an earnest and slightly bombastic manner, as if used to speaking publicly to an audience less intellectually equipped than he. The vestiges of a public-school education were apparent in the almost continuous twitch in his left eyebrow and in the clear enunciation of his prepositions. He explained the rules of the centre, emphasizing the fact that in every field – in work, at play, in the gym, at meals – boys were expected to conform to a high standard of behaviour. 'Politeness,' he assured

Roff, 'will equip you better for the world outside.' He allocated work in the kitchen to Roff, and praised the discipline of potato-peeling. He made reference to the television in the activities room, stressing the fact that watching the six o'clock news after tea was a privilege and not a right. He informed Roff that he would be expected to attend at least one evening-class a week and that he might be lucky enough to learn to make soft toys or how to weave a basket or be introduced to the joys of orienteering. He boasted of the centre's kitchen garden, claiming that during the summer its vegetables had fed every single prisoner in the nearest high-security jail for two months. He talked of discipline and of motivation and of the learning of life skills; he told Roff about the visiting hours and the number of letters he would be allowed to write each week. And he made frequent and firm reference to the perimeter fence, to the alsatians that patrolled the grounds, to the impossibility of Roff's ever managing to leave the centre except by the conventional method.

'Any questions?' he asked, hopeful, but Roff had only one.

'Can I go for tea now?'

The food was better than Roff had been accustomed to at home; the portions larger, the meat more cheerful, the plates less cracked. The clumsy plastic knife and fork made eating a slow and difficult process and the trestle table at which he sat, with twenty-three other boys, wobbled and smelled thickly of cheap bleach. Roff sat between a boy of fifteen who had been found guilty on thirty-seven counts of shoplifting, and a seventeen-year-old who had murdered his step-father. He faced a boy who had sexually assaulted his six-year-old sister and another who had all but blinded a woman with a poker. Hearing of these crimes, Roff felt his to be paltry by comparison. Listening to these boys, he wondered if it had been a mistake, his being sent to this place. He did not think it fair that a man called Jordan should have poked a finger cruelly up his arse and mocked the size of his dick; nor that another man in a posh office should have ordered him to go to church and to peel potatoes and to spend his evenings making soft toys. It did not seem right that he was now having trouble eating his meat because of the plastic cutlery when he could be spending Annie's money in the amusement arcade. He wanted to throw a chair through the window, but the window had bars on it and there were no chairs, only benches nailed firmly into the floor. He felt like crying, but crying was what Annie did when she read the last page of a Mills and Boon. And besides, he did not know how to cry. Like square roots, it was something he had never learned how to do.

So when, that night, Roff was dragged from his bed by two of the other inmates, pulled towards the bathroom, flung across the bathroom floor, stripped, spat on and sexually humiliated, he did not cry. He pretended he was somewhere else, that he was swimming in a cold November sea, swimming underwater for as long as he could hold his breath.

14

Jean said, 'Many happy returns. Very many happy returns. We hope you have many more.' She spoke with the air of one bestowing an inestimable favour.

'Yes,' said Alan, 'our best wishes.'

I found their smiles treacherous and benign, yet I, too, smiled. It was, after all, my eighty-fifth birthday.

I had intended to spend the day usefully rather than in frivolous celebration. To return my library books, to take my customary walk, a rubber or two at my club. But Jean disrupted my plans, ringing me on the telephone on the eve of my birthday, announcing her intention to have a small family celebration. 'A bottle of champagne,' she said, laughing when I protested that champagne made me bilious, when I said I was unaccustomed to eating in company. 'Don't make excuses,' she said. She had spent a great deal of time and effort on the occasion, she claimed. She had concocted a wonderful dessert, prepared a rich main course, bought some linen napkins specially for the occasion, a tablecloth that matched, new champagne glasses. It would be inconsiderate of me to disappoint her, she would not hear of it.

'I must return my books to the library,' I said, to Jean's answering laugh. How could I return books to the library, she demanded to know, how could I? Was I not aware that tomorrow was Sunday, that my birthday fell on Sunday, and that on Sundays the library was closed?

'Tomorrow is Wednesday,' I said. 'And today is Tuesday.'

'Today is Saturday,' she replied. 'Tomorrow is Sunday.'

Her words – and the firmness she used to accompany them – disconcerted me. I held the receiver of the telephone away from my ear in a state of mild agitation. I could not understand where Wednesday had gone, if today was Saturday. Nor the manner in which I had passed Thursday. Nor indeed, how Friday had slipped past me. I had often mislaid things, I thought – small trinkets, jewellery, pens, books, even items of food – but I had never before mislaid a day, two, three. 'My mother is going senile,' I could almost hear Jean say. 'She has mislaid Wednesday, Thursday *and* Friday. Lost them. The grossest carelessness.'

But Jean had said none of these things. 'We'll come and collect you tomorrow at noon,' she said before hanging up the telephone. It seemed my bout of temporary amnesia had not surprised her at all, but confirmed something she already knew.

'Quite an occasion,' Alan remarked. He was a man socially at ease, scattering tritenesses. He wore a lounge suit and smoked a cigar whose smoke I found mild and inoffensive. Through the windows of Jean's living-room I could see the garden, a cat stalk a blackbird, a stray leaf catch in the hedge. On the greenhouse shelves presumptuous winter blooms stood in clay pots.

'Eighty-five,' said Jean.

I sipped my sherry, and heard church bells. I thought of my bridge partners, returning from church, looking devout in their drab coats and their felt hats. And of Mr Jones, spending his day in faded slippers by a mean electric fire, mourning the death of a pet. I saw him tell his neighbours of the trial, making light of his injuries, stepping carefully through life.

'Yes,' said Alan, refilling my glass. 'Eighty-five.'

'Quite,' I replied, adding that I had never found any especial merit in adding another year to one's life. Alan laughed, as though I had said something amusing, some-thing controversial, and I held my glass up, intending to get rather drunk.

'You must be relieved,' said Alan, 'that the trial is over and the young man put away.'

'I must be,' I said. The sherry was very dry; dry enough for me to drink it quickly.

'You'll be drunk, Mother,' warned Jean.

'After the trial we had tea,' I said, 'Mr Jones and I. We ate sandwiches of brown bread, and cakes. Mr Jones ate four.'

'How odd,' said Jean, 'entertaining a complete stranger to tea. Allowing yourself to become involved in the whole business. You should never have permitted the police to put you in the witness box. Your name was in the local paper, Mother, and your address. My friends saw it, and several of them asked me if you were quite right in your mind. People will have read the report and seen your address. Burglars will know you are an old woman living on your own. You could be robbed. You ought to have walked away when you saw what was happening on the beach. You should simply have minded your own business.'

'I mind my own business all the time. To mind some-body else's for a while made a pleasant change. And if you think you can frighten me with talk of robbers, you should know there is very little worth stealing in my house. I cannot think it would be worth a burglar's time to break in. What, after all, would he steal? My galoshes? My reading glasses? My bridge card?'

Jean looked grim. 'You're being silly now, Mother. You know perfectly well you have valuable things in that old house. Precious old tea-sets, silver cutlery, the television. They could take the television.'

'They could take the television,' I said, 'and indeed,

183

were they to do so, I would be eternally grateful. I have never taken to television, never. I watch it only when I find myself between library books. When I do watch it, the newscasters mumble and the serials are dislocated and the channels change arbitrarily every time I switch on the kitchen light to make myself a cup of tea. And as for the tea-sets and the cutlery, I no longer have any need for them. These days I please myself in the business of table manners; I eat with my fingers. I find the food tastes better that way, without the intermediary of knife and fork. I use my fingers as a trowel, digging them into the tin. I have decided it is the only way to eat baked beans.'

Jean said, 'You're drunk, Mother.'

'Quite possibly I am about to get drunk. The sensation of two sherries drunk in quick succession is not an unpleasant one. Yes, thank you, Alan. I would like another.'

'Are you sure?' asked Jean.

'A small one,' said Alan.

'Sure?' I asked Jean. 'A large one, if you please,' I said to Alan.

'Sure you ought to drink another. I mean, is it wise?'

'Wise? You expect me to be wise as well as eighty-five? Of course it is not wise. I leave wisdom to the middle-aged, I leave it to you.'

'I wonder, Mother,' said Jean, 'whether you are trying to deliberately make me lose my temper, or whether you simply cannot help infuriating me.'

'You yourself can be infuriating, Jean,' I retorted.

'Me?'

'You.'

'Jean,' said Alan, 'Grace. Please.'

'You see how she treats me?' said Jean, turning to

184

Alan. 'You see how she talks, after all I have done for her?'

'What have you done?' I asked, but Jean did not see fit, then, to tell me.

'Lunch,' she said, and we rose to follow her.

I cannot recall what we ate, the food Jean spent so much time preparing. 'Such a hearty meal,' I said at some point, 'it can only be for a person condemned.' I ate. The food passed down into my stomach. When Jean talked again of my moving in I interrupted her, preposterously praising my own home, telling her – untruthfully – that the roof had been mended by two very pleasant workmen who had drunk too much tea, exaggerating its comforts. 'I am a cantankerous old woman,' I said, 'and you could not bear to live with me.'

I thought the battle won, but it had not even begun.

After our meal we drank the champagne and it made me drowsy.

I am told that wild animals seldom sleep when they sense imminent danger. That their ears prick up, that they are alert to the slightest sound. We humans are too civilized to retain this ability; we feel it as redundant as an appendix. So, unaware of danger, I slept. I have no idea how long I slept – fifteen minutes, perhaps twenty, possibly much longer – but I woke to the sound of urgent whispers. I did not immediately open my eyes, but sat in the armchair, my head propped back on a cushion, listening as the whispers became more urgent and less cautious.

'She is,' I heard Jean say.

'Is what?'

'A cantankerous old woman.'

There was a pause, the sound of a newspaper's pages turning, a slight sigh. Alan said, 'It says here that there are only fifteen more shopping days to Christmas. Have you bought my present yet?'

'You don't want to talk about it,' said Jean, 'do you?'

'Christmas? Oh, I don't know. I think – '

'You don't want to discuss Mother, do you? Maybe you don't even find her cantankerous. Maybe you think she's charming when she's rude to me.'

'It's amusing. You rise to the bait. You can tell she enjoys making you angry. Was she like that with your father?'

'Never. She never fought back, even when he was unkind to her. Even after the war, she . . . Well, she was never argumentative. Not like she is now. She's changed; widowhood has changed her. Sometimes I don't even recognize her memories, things she says about my father, stories about when I was young. She inhabits this twilight world where eccentricity is normal and where she alters the past and the present at will.'

There was a pause, during which I snored ostentatiously to give veracity to my sleeping state. Alan must have picked up the newspaper again, for I heard him audibly scanning the television column. I listened while Alan and Jean argued amiably over which television programmes they would watch after my departure. My eyes were shut, my mouth slightly, comically open, my head slipped a little on the cushion. I shall sit here, I told myself, in the manner of the aged asleep, in this ludicrous posture of the eavesdropper, until the question of television programmes has been amicably settled and the conversation returns to me. I heard Jean get up to pour more coffee, the sound of a telephone ring in the house next door, the rustle of a newspaper being discarded. Presently Alan spoke again.

'What I don't understand,' he remarked, 'is why you want her to live with us at all. When you're together you bicker constantly. I mean, you don't even like each other, for God's sake, do you?'

Jean sounded puzzled by the question. 'Like?' she replied. 'It hardly matters, surely, whether we *like* each other.'

'You never have liked each other,' Alan pursued. 'The first time I ever met your mother, you and she squabbled. We ate duck and cherries and you and she sniped at each other across the dining-table.'

'I was nervous. I didn't know whether you and she would get on.'

'We got on. After the meal she offered me a large brandy.'

'Three large brandies. You drank them too quickly and then you threw up.'

'Did I?'

'You threw up, yes. And when you emerged from the bathroom, Mother offered you another brandy. Out of perversity. She enjoys being perverse, she always has.'

'And you want her to live with us?'

'Of course I don't. But it's my duty.'

'Couldn't we just ask her over for Sunday lunch instead? We could do that, surely? Have her over on Sundays. Every bloody Sunday, if you want. That ought to be enough to exorcize your sense of duty.'

Jean sighed, and said it was too late for that, far too late now and at that point I opened my eyes and yawned and smiled pleasantly and asked sweetly why it was too late.

'Mother, you're awake.'

'You have a guilty look about you,' I said, 'You are wearing exactly the same expression on your face that you wore the day you were six and swallowed several of my loose pearls, mistaking them for mints.'

Jean said, 'We have a surprise for you, Mother. Another birthday present.'

'The gloves,' I assured her, 'were quite sufficient.'

Nevertheless, Jean's insistence and my own curiosity led me out of the room, past the neat arrangement of dried grasses in the hall, past the framed pictures of English cathedrals that hung by the stairs. It led me to a door off the landing which I at first mistook for a hot-press, but which when Jean opened it and led me inside I discovered to be, not a hot-press at all, but a self-contained flat. 'This is it, Mother. This is your surprise present. The granny extension. This is your future home.'

Most of the guests who had booked a table for Sunday lunch at the hotel had finished their roast beef, disposed of the roast potatoes, chewed the overdone, over-processed peas and were now deciding upon dessert. Parents with young children inquired of the waitresses whether ice-cream was available and if the sherry trifle would be suitable for a toddler and where the nearest lavatories were. A young couple, away for a dirty weekend and sitting at a secluded corner table, decided (while waiting for the Black Forest gâteau and without each other's knowledge) never to see the partner again. Near the kitchens, where the smell of food was overpowering and might soon become intolerable, a middle-aged couple stared at the walls and the tablecloth and the waitresses, and wished themselves at home in their four-bedroomed Neo-Georgian home on the outskirts of London.

The customer at table five, with a view over the promenade, waited until Annie passed him the sweet menu before speaking.

'You and me,' he said in a low voice, 'we might have a drink together. Tomorrow night suit?' He had been watching her over lunch, he said, watching the way she

188

managed to carry five plates of roast beef in one hand, the way she smiled at everyone, the way she had said it didn't matter when the little boy at table seven had dropped his potatoes on the carpet and spilled the gravy on the cloth. On the basis of this, he said, he had decided that Annie was a nice woman, a kind and pleasant person, the sort of person, if she didn't mind him saying so, that he might like to get to know better. 'I'm in stretch covers,' he said, asking whether she would recommend the trifle. 'I got in yesterday.'

Annie smiled, but only a little. She'd been on her feet since ten-thirty and she was tired. She wasn't used to men asking her out, and the mustard pots still had to be filled before the next meal. Unexpectedly, her period had started an hour ago and she had slight abdominal cramps. She had hoped to finish early and get home in time to watch Joan Crawford in *Mildred Pearce* – a film she had seen six times already but which always made her cry. But the manager had asked her to serve coffees and afternoon teas in the lounge as one of the other waitresses was sick. She'd had to say yes because she needed the overtime and the tips.

The man said he'd try the trifle, and if tomorrow night didn't suit, what about the night after? 'Tuesday. We could find a nice quiet pub and have a few drinks.'

'I'm busy Tuesday,' she said, knowing she wasn't. She didn't trust travellers. Some of the other waitresses who went out with them confided that the drink that was offered was usually in a plastic tooth-glass in the traveller's hotel bedroom, and that if you said no after two drinks they brought out pictures of their wives and their children and their pets and talked about how lonely it was on the road. If, on the other hand, you said yes and went to bed with a salesman, you still had to look at the photographs of their wives and their children and their pets and listen to how lonely it was on the road. Only they waited until you were getting dressed again before pulling the photos out of their wallets. Annie had heard all this from the other waitresses, and one thing she knew for certain was that she had better things to do than look at photos of women she would never meet and never want to meet.

'Tuesdays,' she said firmly, 'I'm always busy.'

'That's a pity.' He sounded as though he meant it. Annie relented, explaining that she didn't mean to be unkind, but she didn't make a habit of going out with strangers. 'I wouldn't have the trifle, if I was you,' she added. 'Chef made the custard with water 'cos we run out of milk, see.' The Black Forest gâteau was the best bet, she said, because it came straight out of the freezer. 'Real tinned cherries,' she told him. 'And proper cream.'

'I'll get fat,' said the customer, patting his stomach.

Annie liked that, a man who worried about putting on weight. Bob had been slim, and all the men in her Mills and Boons were slim as well. Tall and dark and slim. Or tall and fair and slim. She'd been reading a lot of romances lately, ever since they'd took her Michael away to that detention centre place. It kept her mind off thinking about him. She had cried a great deal at first, and the other waitresses had been sympathetic, giving her hankies to dry her eyes, taking her into a corner of the kitchen for cups of tea, offering her éclairs from the freezer. 'Awful,' they agreed, when she said Michael would be homesick in a place like that, it didn't seem fair, locking up a sixteen-year-old, sending him miles from home. 'Two buses and a train and another bus,' she had explained, 'and I'm not allowed to visit him for three weeks.' They had nodded, Gladys and Sylvia and Sally, and been kind. But one day she'd heard them, heard them talking about her in the cloakroom while she was round the corner, unseen, combing her hair. 'Poor

Annie,' they'd said, ' a psycho of a son like that. Better off without him, if she only knew it.' She knew what a psycho was, she'd seen the film. Anthony Perkins all thin and demented and that awful twitch in his eye. 'Killed a dog, her son did. Read it in the paper. Not right that, is it. Not normal, going about killing dogs. Best place for him, locked up.'

She'd thought about Michael all the rest of that day. About whether they had been right, that he wasn't normal. 'A misfit,' the judge had called him, and she'd seen that film, *The Misfits,* too. When she got home, she went into his room, coming across a dirty magazine and a stiff pile of grubby socks and a book on Olympic swimmers. She didn't think any of these things – not even the dirty magazine – meant that her son was a misfit. A misfit was a tramp who wore no socks and tied his overcoat at the waist with string. Or a person who talked loudly to himself in the middle of a crowd. Or that Mr Freely, the one in the afternoon TV serial, the one who was forever trying to do himself in and who would have surely died had it not been for the dedication of Dr Grant. Nevertheless, she had to admit that without Michael around, life was . . . well, tidier.

'Des,' said the man, when she returned with the gâteau. 'That's me. Des. Short for Desmond.'

'Annie,' she replied, 'I'm Annie.'

'Pretty name. You worked here long?'

She tried to think of something funny to say, but she wasn't used to being chatted up and the mustard pots still had to be done. 'Years,' she replied, adding that the hours suited her. But the truth was that the hours no longer suited her, that she walked from her house to the hotel and back three times a day, that her legs ached more and more, and that sometimes the smell and sight of so much food made her want to heave. 'Monday night,' she said, 'I'm not doing anything.'

Des took her to a steak-house, where the waitresses all wore red dresses with blue frilled aprons and red and blue hats. The lights, too, were red and blue, as were the tablecloths and the napkins and the curtains. Des suggested they have the prawn cocktail followed by a rump steak with all the trimmings. The waitress poured the red wine, and Des raised his glass to Annie and toasted their friendship. Annie felt special.

She had dressed with particular care and borrowed Sheila's musk perfume to dab behind her ears. The dress she wore was blue with tiny white flowers, and her tights were only out of the packet that day. 'I can see we're going to get on,' said Des, pouring more wine. 'I can always tell.' He told her she was a nice person, someone whom he'd very much like to get to know better, the sort of woman he felt comfortable with. In his job, he explained, he met a lot of women. 'Stretch covers,' he reminded her. 'Men aren't struck on stretch covers; it's the women who are interested.' He told her she was different from all the women he met, that he could tell she cared about other things in life. 'Most women, you see,' he went on, 'only care about recovering their three-piece and shampooing their carpet. But there's more to you. I can tell you want more from life than that.' He said they had an affinity, a statement she made no reply to, not knowing whether he was being fresh or not.

Over their steaks he talked about his job, mentioning the fact that he was staying in the area for six months, hoping to find himself a flat. 'You get sick of travelling,' he said, 'of hotel rooms with breakfast television and automatic coffee-makers and the sound of the man in the next room opening and closing drawers and cupboards in the morning to make sure he hasn't forgotten anything. You get sick,' he said, 'of fruit compote for breakfast, and all that tea.'

'The steak's nice,' Annie said. She couldn't see how anyone could get tired of hotel rooms, but she agreed about the compote. She smiled, knowing the dim lighting made her teeth appear less yellow. 'The thing I get sick of,' she admitted, 'is when people complain about the food. Or even send it back. Makes me furious.'

Des smiled back, sympathetic, and said he guessed she had experienced sadness in her life. 'It's in your eyes,' he told her.

She hadn't meant to talk about Bob, but she did. 'Waltzed off one day,' she said. 'Never heard a word from him since. It's hard, bringing up kiddies on your own, nobody to help you.' She explained that she'd always done her best for them, that it was a job you never got thanks for. 'Things are better now, mind,' she said quickly, not wanting Des to think her the complaining type. 'My Sheila, she's got a job and a boyfriend and she's thinking of getting her own flat. Michael – he's sixteen – he's away. Working in London.'

Des listened, and appeared interested when she said it was a stroke of luck them meeting, and while they were waiting for their coffee he reached his hand over and touched her gently on the wrist. 'Yes,' he said, 'Fate's on our side,' and when he said these words, Annie felt happy. She was glad that although he told her about his work and his travelling he did not mention a wife or children. She thought it best not to know whether he was married or not. Knowing would spoil things. Over coffee they held hands, and Annie knew that the other customers in the steak-house thought them a couple in love. Nobody had held her hand before – no man, that was, not even Bob. Bob used to say that holding hands was for the

193

birds, soft; but times had changed since then. And Des had soft hands and clean fingernails and twice remarked on the delicate shade of her skin. If he offered to walk her home, she'd say yes and maybe even ask him in for a cup of tea.

15

'Your future home,' said Jean and led me inside.

This, then, was the place that would be my prison; these the rooms in which I would be detained until my death. The smell of plaster freshly applied was strong and I guessed the builders had not long completed their task. It was then – and only then – that I recalled my trip on the bus, the sight that had met me then of bricks piled outside the house, the huge steel tubes erected on top of the garage, the cement-mixer on the front path. I imagined how Jean must have bullied the builders into finishing their work in time, how urgently she must have explained to them the extension had to be completed. 'A birthday present', I imagined her saying, 'for my mother.' 'Nice,' I imagined the builders replying, working with extra zeal at the thought of the bonus Jean would give them.

'This is the living-room, Mother. You'll notice it faces south. I chose the wallpaper, Alan did the decorating.'

But the room was not only decorated; it was carpeted, completely furnished, ready for immediate occupancy. Curtains the shade of porridge hung from the windows and a beige carpet covered the floor. A gas fire had been installed – modern and new and brightly chrome – and facing the fire squatted a chair, a fireside chair, the sort of chair generally regarded as suitable for the elderly. The sort of chair one sees in old people's homes.

'You'll find it very comfortable,' Jean said. 'But just in case you don't, I've kept the receipt.'

The chair was green, and against its back lay a matching

green cushion, and I thought, this will be my grave, this comfortable green moquette fireside chair with its pertly matching cushion. This will be where my daughter expects me to die quietly one evening.

I walked past the chair, towards the window. There was a view and I did not wish to see it. But I looked, nevertheless, as a child will look upon a dead bird, unable to help himself. I looked, and I saw the back garden and beyond it a small park – some trees, a pond, two ducks, a long rectangle of grass that would be used in the summer months as a putting green.

'The view is better in the summer,' Jean said.

'Yes.'

'In May, when the cherry blossom is out – '

'Yes.'

So, I could see grass and trees and two ducks upon a pond; nature at its most confined. But I could not see the sea, not could I hear it, and it would have taken a more determined imagination than mine to believe oneself only four miles from the water.

'The kitchen,' said Jean, leading me gently from the window as though the view from it was matchless, as though to spy suburban trees from a window was the sum of human achievement.

'It's very compact,' she explained, 'functional. Small and clean and bright. I told the architect exactly what I wanted. Once you've settled in, you can invite us up for a meal.' She laughed, and the kitchen absorbed the sound and did not expect me to reply.

The bedroom was not yet furnished and the window had been left open to release the smell of plaster. From it came the shouts of children in the park. I moved through the room, my heels noisy on the wooden floorboards while Jean talked of bedroom furniture, of the possibility of built-in wardrobes, of a ceiling that would be painted magnolia and walls Alan would paper in pink. 'You might want to bring you own bed,' she said, 'or your dressing-table. A few bits and pieces.'

Yes, I thought, I have lived on this earth for eighty-five years and I am to move in here and all I am permitted to bring are a few bits and pieces, the fragments of a life. I am to sleep here in this bedroom – which will be pink – and I am to watch and listen and wait. I am to observe back gardens from this window and hear the shouts of strangers' children and wait for the cherry blossom to bloom and eventually, eventually, life will be something I watch and hear and occasionally smell but never, never participate in.

Downstairs, Alan poured me a brandy. He smiled but he did not speak. Had he spoken he might have said, 'I'm sorry. I know this is not what you want; I can imagine how you must feel, but I do not want to interfere.' But he did not speak. I felt the brandy hit my stomach and I sat down.

'We wanted it to be a complete surprise,' said Jean. 'A birthday present right out of the blue. Though God knows the builders were unaccommodating, to say the least. Making all sorts of excuses not to have it finished in time – the weather, the cement, the wrong size of bricks, the window frames. They obstructed me at every turn. 'Christmas, lady," one of them said. "You'll be lucky if it's ready by Christmas." Eventually, I had to bribe them. Pay them a bonus.'

'You ought to have saved your money.' I spoke carefully.

'We thought it was worth it. The bonus was only £200.'

'Cash in hand,' said Alan. 'That was how they wanted it.'

'I was not referring to the bonus,' I explained, 'but to the amount of money you paid to have the extension

197

built. You spent a great deal and, in my experience, it is never wise to spend money on an assumption.'

'An assumption?' asked Alan.

'You don't like the flat?' said Jean.

'The flat is pleasant,' I said. 'It is bright and well-equipped and sufficiently spacious to accommodate an elderly person. It is the sort of home which I imagine an elderly person would be happy to live in. I know,' I added, 'of four or five women at my bridge club who would give their eye-teeth to exchange their draughty, inconvenient homes for a flat like that.'

Jean looked pleased. 'The architect said it was ideal. He assured me you would like it.'

'I like it,' I said, and the word had never before seemed to me so inadequate, or so ironic.

'I'm glad. I'm so very glad, Mother, that you like the flat. It's a great relief to me, you know. I was afraid you would find fault with it. Quibble about the wallpaper, say the kitchen was too small, find the carpet too dull. I was afraid you'd think I was rushing you or behaving in an underhand way by getting it built without telling you. I spent sleepless nights worrying about what you would say, whether you would be furious with me for not telling you, whether – '

I interrupted Jean then. I spoke quietly and with my customary firmness. I told Jean that I would never live in the flat. I told her what I had told her, oh so many times before, that I wished to remain in my own home, that her interference bordered on harassment, that my privacy was priceless and could not be bought. I told her that her duties as a daughter lay not in forcing me to live with her but in leaving me alone. And I told her she was foolish and selfish and presumptuous.

'You're upset, Mother, that's all,' she said. 'It's been a shock for you. You'll change your mind in a day or two.'

198

I told her I would not change my mind.

'But it's your birthday present. And it cost thousands to build. We had to take out the most enormous bank loan to pay for it. The interest rates are crippling. Of course, I expect we'll recoup some of the money when you sell your house.'

I explained that I would not sell my house.

'Don't be absurd, Mother. We agreed. All this was arranged months ago. We made an agreement. I said it would be the most sensible thing all round if you were to live with us. We made an agreement.'

'I agreed to nothing.'

'You agreed that house of yours was old and damp and quite unsuitable.'

'If you remember, Jean,' I parried, '*you* told me it was old and draughty and unsuitable, and I could not deny it. It is nevertheless – despite its age and its draughts and its unsuitability – *my* home and I do not intend ever to leave it.'

The silence that followed may have lasted a second or a minute or even five, I cannot tell. I remember sipping the last of my brandy and I remember blowing my nose as if to remove from my nostrils the smell of fresh plaster. I remember Jean silently weeping and Alan pouring himself another drink. I remember the look of reproach and the sense of betrayal; I suppose the only thing we shared that afternoon was the sense of betrayal, that it skulked in the corner of that comfortable room and ambushed us all.

I left shortly afterwards, and Alan was kind enough to offer to drive me to my door. In the car we were silent, as though we both knew further words would only compound the damage already done. Alan spoke only as I got out of the car and even then all he said was that Jean would not give up. 'She means to have you in that flat by Christmas,' he said, and though the wind was sharp, and tried to tear the words away, I heard them clearly.

Inside the house, I locked and bolted all the doors. I pulled the curtains tightly across in my sitting-room and I made myself a cup of lemon tea. And then I sat down at the table with pen and paper and wrote a list of all the materials I would need to barricade myself in by Christmas.

16

Roff got used to the detention centre. Used to rising at
six-thirty in the morning, used to making his bed Army-
style, used to eating his breakfast in five short minutes.
He became accustomed to peeling potatoes every morning
from eight-thirty until ten, to chopping vegetables from
then until lunchtime, to spending his afternoons in a cold
classroom where he learned about the population of
Washington DC and the location of the world's highest
mountain and the habits of jungle animals. He became
acquainted with the centre's rules and regulations and
with the small humiliations that accompanied these rules
and the greater punishments that followed their infringe-
ment. He learned the quickest way to remove shit-stains
from the lavatories and the easiest method of avoiding
the screws and the best chair to sit in the television room.

The warders watched him and made notes and were
generally agreed that the lad had settled down.

At the beginning of Roff's third week in the centre, the
resident counsellor beckoned him into his small and
untidy office, invited him to sit down, offered him a
cigarette, put the kettle on to boil, stroked his beard, and
began to ask questions. The counsellor's name was Bob
Paine. He was a tall man, thin, in his mid-thirties, much
given to wearing corduroy and to chewing the tops of his
pencils. An ex-social worker, he debated hourly with
himself which of his two careers – his present or his
former – was the more frustrating, the more likely to lead
to failure, the more akin to banging his head repeatedly
and frequently against the stone wall of the chicken house

at the back of the kitchens. Despite this chronic pessimism about his chosen career, Bob was a man who prided himself on his perspicacity. He claimed that he could tell, by astute and incisive questioning, whether a boy would commit another crime after being released from the centre or not. In this – as in many other things – he was often, though not invariably, proved wrong. The adolescent, released early on Bob's recommendation, who had caused grievous bodily harm to his sister three days after his release and who was returned to the centre a week later, reminded Bob of his own fallibility.

Bob sighed, passed Roff a mug of instant coffee, and began to speak. 'We're all outcasts here,' he said, speaking slowly and intimately and crouching to retrieve a chewed pencil from the floor. 'All of us. You, me, the warders, even the Governor. We live up here on the moors, miles from the nearest town, we seldom receive visitors. We can't any of us do the things we would like – visit the cinema, the theatre, chat to our mates over a pint, buy a new pair of jeans. We all live up here deprived of normal social intercourse. We're all in the same boat.' Bob liked to encourage a feeling of intimacy between himself and the boys, to speak longingly of pints of beer and visits to the cinema, to foster the view that he knew how it felt to be stuck behind concrete and barbed wire. He wanted the boys to know he was on their side, that he was gunning for them, that he shared their sense of deprivation and alienation and dislocation. He told Roff to look upon him as a friend and a confidant, an older brother or a sympathetic uncle. He told him that he was always available for a chat, and that Roff should feel free to come to him with any problems he might have. He spoke earnestly and when he had finished he leaned back in his chair and waited for Roff to speak.

Roff was, however, silent. He thought the coffee tasted

202

like shit and that the low-tar cigarette Bob had given him was like smoking cottonwool. He didn't understand many of the words Bob used but was disinclined to ask him what they meant. He watched Bob perch himself companionably on the side of his desk, his legs dangling over the edge to reveal striped socks. *Paine fucks boys,* he had read on the toilet door only the other day, and he wondered whether it was true.

'You queer?' he asked.

'Queer?'

'Yeah. It said you was. On the toilet door. In big letters.'

Bob paused, removing the pencil from his mouth. 'Homosexual, do you mean?'

'That's right, yeah,' said Roff. 'Are you? I've never met no queers.'

'No,' Bob answered.

'Just wondered.'

'I'm not queer,' said Bob, raising his voice.

'Only asked,' Roff told him, flicking his dimp on to the floor, grinding it into the carpet with his foot. 'What's the time?'

'Ten past three.'

'That all?'

'Time hangs heavy in this place, doesn't it?' Bob remarked, and asked Roff whether he played snooker. 'One of our boys learned while he was in here. He's now North-East amateur snooker champion.'

'Yeah?' said Roff, without interest.

'He was a car thief,' said Bob, 'and now he's a snooker champion.' But Roff did not seem impressed. '*Apathetic,*' wrote Bob in his case-notes, '*and slightly hostile.*' He lit another cigarette and told Roff about the centre's library.

'Videos, is it?' asked Roff. 'A video library?'

203

'Books. A library full of books. Dickens, Trollope, Orwell, Greene, Thackeray. Even Spillane.'

'Who?'

'Mickey Spillane,' said Bob and sighed again. 'Thriller writer. Lots of sex and violence.'

'Oh,' said Roff, thinking of the arcade at home, hearing the noise of the Invaders in his ears, the flash of lights jolting his eyes, the speed with which his hands pressed the buttons. 'I'm not into books,' he volunteered. 'Me Mam reads them,' he added.

Bob asked him whether his home life was happy. 'You and your mother, do you have a good relationship? It says here your father left home when you were a baby.'

'He'll be back,' said Roff, though he no longer believed it. 'He's on an oil-rig, Saudi Arabia. Sends me money regular. And postcards of the desert.'

'Ah.'

'Wants me to go out there, see. When I'm eighteen.'

'And you get on well with your mother, do you?'

'She's a waitress,' Roff said.

'That's interesting.'

'I don't see much of her.'

There was a letter from Annie in the pocket of his jeans; it had arrived at breakfast, but he hadn't yet opened it. He knew what it would say. She would hope he was settled in. She would tell him the hotel was getting busy coming up to Christmas. She would complain that the boiler had packed up again.

'You communicate,' Bob wanted to know, 'you and your mother, do you?'

'She's wrote me a letter.'

'When you're at home, I mean. You discuss your problems, do you? Talk about the important things in life?'

'You what?'

'Tell her what matters to you. Do you do that?'

'Naw,' said Roff. Annie wasn't interested in his score on the Invaders. She claimed they was all a waste of money.

'You see,' said Bob, patient, 'what I'm trying to find out during the course of this tête-à-tête, is what you want from life. What your aspirations are, your fears, your hopes. What, in essence, makes you tick.'

Roff noticed it was getting dark already. The evening was a small square behind the window, a shadowed tree and a slice of darkening blue sky. Once the sky turned completely dark, he would mark off another day. He always marked off the day as soon as darkness came for it made the time seem shorter.

'For instance,' pursued Bob, 'have you any hobbies? Woodwork? Or football? Or running? Or drawing? Or bird-watching? Or – '

'Seagulls,' Roff told him. 'There's seagulls where I live. They come in our back yard, sometimes, for the dustbins.'

'Really? Fascinating, that's fascinating. Good. Such a gentle pastime, bird-watching. And plenty of opportunity for it here.'

'No gulls here,' Roff pointed out.

'Well, no,' Bob had to admit. 'But we do get the occasional kestrel. And plenty of partridge, of course, on the moors.'

'Oh yeah,' said Roff, asking again what the time was.

'Half-past,' Bob told him, suggesting it was time they got down to essentials. 'Like telling me why you hit the old man.'

The question surprised Roff. That afternoon on the beach seemed years ago, long gone, done with, past. 'What made you do it?'

Roff shrugged. 'He was there, the old man, wasn't he? He was there, so I threw a stone at him.'

'He was there. Like Everest.'

'Everest? That some mountain or other, is it?'

'Yes,' sighed Bob. 'Some mountain or other. Hillary climbed it because it was there.'

'Who?'

'Forget it. So you hit the old man, you threw a stone at him because he was there.'

'Well,' said Roff, 'yeah.'

'And the dog?'

'The dog was barking. Following me, see.'

'So you don't make a habit of killing dogs, would you say? It was an isolated incident, was it?'

'Yeah,' said Roff. 'An isolated incident.' He liked the sound of the phrase. 'A mistake,' he added, because he thought that was what Bob wanted to hear. He watched Bob light another cigarette; he smoked more than anyone else he'd ever met, more even than Annie did. 'You wanna watch it,' he said, 'all them cigs.' But Bob had started talking again, waving his cigarette in the air, going on about the need to curb aggression, saying that killing dogs was anti-social, telling Roff he'd have to conform, using words like expectation and progression and remission, words Roff had never heard before, not even in school. He could hear shouts from the activities room, a thud, more shouting, the raised voice of one of the screws. Roff thought all the screws were wankers.

Bob was asking him whether he missed his friends.

'Sorta,' Roff replied.

'Tell me about them, about your friends.'

'Okay.' Roff told Bob about a mate of his, his best mate, a boy called Arthur, with whom he spent all his free time. Arthur lived in the same street, he was on a Youth Opportunities Course, training to be a brickie. 'We go fishing,' Roff said, never having been fishing in his life, never wanting to neither. 'Once,' he embellished, 'we caught a pike.' He said the afternoon he'd threw the stone at the old bloke he'd been waiting on the beach for Arthur, that they was going fishing together off the end of the pier. He'd waited for Arthur for an hour, it was raining, Arthur never showed. 'I got angry, see,' he explained, "cos he never turned up. Let me down, Arthur did. I was soaked and angry.' He said he'd never of dreamed of hitting anyone except that his mate hadn't come. 'I'd rather of went fishing,' he said, thinking of the old buggers who sat at the end of the pier staring into the water, catching fuck all.

'Still around is he, this friend?' Bob asked, not believing a word.

'Oh yeah. Comes for Christmas dinner every year. His mum and dad was killed in a fire. Like a brother to me, Arthur is.'

'Really?'

'Well,' said Roff, wondering if he'd gone too far, 'a sort of brother.'

'You've a sister,' Bob reminded him. 'How do you get along with her?'

Roff smiled, thinking how easy it was, telling lies to Bob. They got on smashing, he said, him and Sheila, great. He missed her, being in this place, missed watching telly with her and meeting her boyfriends and going ten-pin bowling down the town Sunday afernoons. 'She's got hundreds of boyfriends,' he said, meaning she was a slag.

'She hasn't been to visit yet,' Bob pointed out. 'Nor has your mother.'

'Well,' Roff replied, 'that's on account of her bad leg, Sheila's, see. She can't get about much.'

'Only ten-pin bowling.'

'And me Mam's busy,' said Roff, hastily. 'Works all day.'

'A waitress, you said?'

'Yeah. Posh hotel. Tips are good,' he added, not knowing whether they were or not, caring even less. He looked towards the window, at the outside darkness, imagining the colour the sea would be now. A dog barked, one of the alsatians. They was kept in a hut, someone had told him, four alsatians, trained to go for the balls. With dogs like that, Roff reckoned you didn't need barbed-wire fences or searchlights, the dogs was lethal.

'I expect', said Bob, 'your mother misses you. She's probably lonely by herself. She'll be glad to have you out of here, back home.'

'Oh yeah,' said Roff, 'she's wrote me a letter, saying how she wants me home.'

'She loves you.'

Roff frowned, not knowing whether this was a question or not, whether Bob expected him to answer it. He didn't think much about love; love was like CSEs, it didn't matter whether you had any or not. He heard, from the direction of the dining-room, the sound of feet and voices and water jugs being plonked on the tables. Tea soon. He realized he was hungry.

'Well?'

'Suppose so,' said Roff, answering the forgotten question.

'You think your mother will want you back? After what you've done?'

'Sure she will.'

'Good,' said Bob, 'because you're getting out of here the day before Christmas.'

Bob was tired; adolescent sullenness exhausted him, questions without answers enervated him, the boy's very presence made him yawn. 'You can go now,' he told him, waiting until the door was closed before lighting another cigarette, chewing another pencil. He finished writing up his case-notes and picked up a book on Gestalt therapy he was in the middle of reading. He read two chapters, not because the book particularly held his interest but because it stopped him thinking about the boy he had just seen, and the boy he would have to see after tea, and the essential pointlessness of doing a job like this, and the fact that his wife had begun an affair with a local comprehensive teacher.

After tea, Roff wrote to his mother. Suspecting all mail was opened before posting, he said in his letter that he missed her and Sheila and that the food in the centre wasn't half bad. At the end of the letter, he added a ps: 'I shouldn't of done what I done to the old man and I'm sorry now.' But on rereading the postscript, he decided the Governor might see through the lie, so he rubbed it out. He slept well that night, thinking of the fairy lights they always put up in the promenade for Christmas and how stupid they looked.

Roff's letter took four days to arrive, landing on the hall linoleum of a stranger's house amidst a scatter of Christmas cards. The woman who opened the letter over her breakfast realized at once it was not intended for her, and propped it against her teacup, meaning to return it to the postman when he called the following morning. While she was preparing breakfast for her three young children, her youngest reached across the cup for the milk-jug, spilling not only the milk and the tea, but also knocking over the pot of honey. By the time the mess was cleared up and the child comforted, the address on the envelope was illegible and the letter itself soggy, smudged and sticky. Not wishing to pry, she had only read the first line of the letter, and as she put it into the waste-bin she hoped it had not been of any importance.

Three streets away, Annie was crying. She was crying because Des had just told her that he loved her. 'I'm a very lucky man,' she heard him say through her sobs, 'and you're a fine woman. We'll stay here,' he said, accepting more toast, 'until the stretch cover business really takes off. Who knows, we might be in a nice modern house on an estate by next spring.' She poured him more tea while he said again that he loved her, and while he wondered aloud if she would want more children, and while he promised her the best Christmas she'd ever had. He said they could go shopping at the weekend together, where he would choose her a nice piece of jewellery and where they could buy a turkey and some fancy decorations and a tasty plum pudding. Annie wiped away her tears and blew her nose vigorously, thinking it was a blessing Sheila had a flat now and Mikey was away, that she and Des would be alone. Thinking how pretty fairy lights would be, strung across the window.

17

The assistant at the home-improvement store looked at me with some amusement when I told him what I required. He was a young man with a curt moustache and an excess of eagerness.

'I need a hammer,' I repeated, 'some nails, a dozen, perhaps more, and several pieces of wood.'

He smiled. I could see he was about to ask me what kind of hammer I required, the size of the nails I would need, the type of wood I would prefer, but he surprised me. 'What,' he asked, 'are the materials for? Only it would help if you told me.'

I had not anticipated his question, and I could not reveal the fact that I needed the wood and the hammer and the nails in order to barricade myself in, in order to stop my daughter from gaining entry into my home. The day was stark and cold, but in the store the heat made me irritable and the excessive curiosity of the young man did little for my temper. I was anxious to make my purchases, for I had a taxi waiting and a great deal to do before I could begin my siege. I explained that I wished to build a potting shed.

The young man smiled. 'You want to build a potting shed,' he repeated, as though I had just announced my intention of flying to the moon.

'I have the measurements here,' I said, but when I presented him with the list he shook his head and explained that the lengths of wood I had specified would scarcely build a rabbit-hutch, let alone a garden shed.

'It is to be a small shed,' I said, peremptory.'An extremely small shed.'

'We sell sheds here. Ready-built.' He pointed in the direction of the exit. 'They're all outside. Big ones, little ones, whatever you need.'

I said again that I wished to build my own.

'A do-it-yourself expert, are you?' he asked.

'I am,' I replied, not knowing quite what he meant. 'The building of potting sheds is a hobby of mine.' I smiled, wondering quite how long I should have to partake in this preposterous conversation before I could leave with my purchases. 'It does not matter what kind of wood I buy, as long as it does not give way easily. Perhaps you would be kind enough to have the wood delivered to my home this afternoon? I am anxious to get to work, to have the shed completed and erected by Christmas.'

The assistant paused to stroke his moustache. 'Sheds we deliver,' he informed me, 'wood we don't. Wood you'll have to carry home yourself. Now if you want yourself a nice ready-made shed, we'll have that round your house by two o'clock this afternoon. You don't want to go messing about with bits of wood and hammers, not at your age. You want to get yourself something that's properly built.'

'I am perfectly capable,' I replied severely, 'of building a potting shed. I am not a fool.'

'No,' he said, meaning yes, and asking me to wait while he measured the wood.

I waited for several minutes. People passed me, carrying rolls of wallpaper, large pots of paint, lampshades; carrying all the paraphernalia that is deemed necessary for the improvement of one's home. Am I to be classed as a fool, I asked myself, simply because I wish to defend *my* home?

When the assistant returned, I almost confessed my true intention. 'I am not building a potting shed at all,' I almost admitted, 'but defending my home, guarding my privacy, making a stand for independence.' Of course I said none of this, for I knew the young man would not understand. The behaviour of the old is amusing to some, pathetic to many, misunderstood by all. I paid for my purchases and permitted the young man to carry the wood to my waiting taxi.

In the back of the taxi I smelled the wood and ran my hands down the spine of each plank and felt the beginnings of a small, but irrevocable triumph.

And now I am at home and it is the day before Christmas Eve. On the radio, the shipping forecast warns of gales in inshore waters and the weatherman apologizes for the absence of snow. I am dressed in a very old pair of slacks and some flat slippers, and the two candlesticks on the mantelpiece appear green with age even in the dim, erratic light of the candles. I have turned off the electricity and lit the candles because one cannot barricade oneself into one's own home and leave the lights blazing. Lights are such an invitation; they signify warmth and comfort, the prospect of refreshments offered, the promise of an easy chair, the exchange of trivial pleasantries. Darkness is essential; I cannot risk callers at the door seeing a light from inside, becoming suspicious when the door-bell remains unanswered.

I wonder if the siege will be a long one? I have prepared myself for that eventuality. Yesterday I bought not only my wood, but several other items – denture powder, soap, three bottles of excellent dry sherry – the sort of things without which life can be, if not altogether disagreeable, then certainly uncomfortable. I also bought goods of a more essential nature – food in tins and in packets and in cartons, food that will keep for as long as is necessary. I bought tins of smoked oysters and anchovies in oil and tins of spaghetti and ravioli and tins of orange juice and packets of breakfast cereal and cartons of something called long-life milk. I bought dried fruit in packets and soup and tinned vegetables and a tin of cod's roe. I bought some books and a magazine and some lavatory paper. But I did not buy a Christmas card, nor a present, and I avoided the man who was selling holly in the street. (Jean, I am certain, will buy some. She has a habit every Christmas of spraying berry-less holly with silver paint, sticking the stems into a glass bowl, turning the natural into the artificial.)

Outside, the wind is screaming, mauling at my barricades. I waited until dark last night before beginning my task. I stood on a chair and I placed the pieces of wood across the inside of each downstairs window. When I was quite certain they fitted, I nailed them into position, hammering gently but steadily until they were firm. I closed the curtains, pulling them behind the wood, between the window and the planks so that from the outside the house retained its appearance of normality. I repeated this with each downstairs window, with the exception of the scullery window, which I deemed too inaccessible and too small for anybody to enter through. The task took several hours, the hammer made my wrist ache quite intolerably, but the glass of sherry I drank to celebrate each barricaded window numbed the pain.

The windows secure, I then attempted to fortify the doors, both front and back. I locked and bolted the back door and placed the kitchen table beside it, as close to the door as I could manage. I rather suspect the kitchen table will turn out to be a superfluous fortification, for the back door is made of thick and solid wood and, when bolted, will not give easily. But it is as well to take every precaution.

The front door posed rather more of a problem. I did not deem its locks and bolts sufficient deterrent against the battering-ram of Jean's duty; I suspected the lock might give, the bolts possibly even break if enough force were exerted from the outside. I moved the small oak table in the hall towards the door, but its ineffectiveness as a bulwark was obvious. If the door were to give way, the table would topple under the door and my siege be at an end. I therefore concluded that stronger defences were necessary, and it was only through the determination that can overcome the exasperating frailty of age that I succeeded in dragging the large mahogany dining-table across the dining-room floor and along the hall. I pushed it as close to the door as possible, wedged against it. It stands there now, and I confess it looks somewhat absurd, its wood unpolished, its surface bare.

So. I have completed my task. I have erected my barricades. My house is a stronghold and quite, quite impregnable.

It is now early morning, the morning of Christmas Eve. Jean will come tomorrow, of that I am quite certain.

Christmas Eve.

In the shops of the town, assistants looked forward to receiving their Christmas bonuses and shoppers bought unnecessary gifts for those whom they disliked. Children giggled with pleasure at the sight of Santa Claus, and cried with disappointment at the plastic presents he gave them, presents that would soon break, presents they had not wanted in the first place. Office staff held their celebratory lunches in hotels and pubs and restaurants, reading out the jokes from the intestines of crackers and laughing too loudly. In the Ladies of one of these

215

restaurants, an office clerk wept because she had drunk too much, and an audio-typist sobbed over her husband's infidelity.

In the suburbs, frozen turkeys were placed in garages to defrost, and Christmas cards fell from mantelpieces and windowsills each time a door was opened, and pine needles dropped from Christmas trees on to patterned carpets which had not yet been paid for.

At the hotel, Annie served traditional Christmas luncheon to forty-two members of the Rotary Club and hoped the ensuing tip would enable her to buy Des a digital watch.

In the extension to her home intended for her mother, Jean arranged dried flowers in a vase and sprayed air-freshener in all the rooms. She thought of her mother and of the row that would inevitably erupt when she and Alan arrived on Christmas Day to remove her from her home.

'And a quarter of brussel sprouts,' said Henry Jones at the corner greengrocer's, searching for the correct change. His daughter had sent him a large, extravagant Christmas card, inviting him down to London to spend Christmas with her, but the thought of the train journey had frightened him and he had declined her offer. 'I'm too old to travel long distances,' he had said in his letter to her. Bunches of mistletoe caught his eye and the greengrocer looked inquiringly in Henry's direction. Henry said, 'I think not,' and looked away, not wishing to admit he had nobody to kiss under the mistletoe, ashamed of his loneliness.

At the railway station the probation officer who had escorted Roff from the detention centre and accompanied him on the train journey, warned him about getting into trouble again, passed him a five-pound note and wished him the best of the season's greetings. He did not expect his greeting to be returned and was unsurprised when Roff walked abruptly away.

Having nowhere else to go, Roff began to walk towards home, noticing without much interest the gaggle of carol-singers outside the bank, the man selling holly on the corner of the High Street, the huge tree by the town hall. Christmas, like God and love and hard work, was something other people believed in, something he did not much care for. In the centre, multi-coloured paper decorations had been hung across the dining-room and on Christmas Day a film was due to be shown after tea. 'Christmas,' the Governor had told him that very morning, 'is a reminder to us all of hope. The birth of our Christ is a message to each and every one of us that redemption is possible.' He had asked Roff whether he felt redeemed, appearing satisfied by Roff's negligent nod of the head. If redeemed meant glad to be out of the fucking place, then, yes, he felt redeemed. Firmly, the Governor had indicated the distress he would experience at ever seeing Roff back in the centre, and with equal firmness Roff had replied he would never be back. The weeks he had spent in there had been the worst years of his life, an ocean of horror in which Roff had almost drowned. One thing, and one thing only, had made him smile during all this time in the place and that had been the arrival, four days before his own release, of Mick.

Mick's unexpected appearance at tea on Sunday night had cheered him up no end. Not because of any pleasure in seeing a friend, a familiar face, but because Mick was no longer a friend, because Mick had just arrived and Roff was soon to be released. Having ignored him throughout the meal, he only discovered later the reason for Mick's detention. Mick had raped a girl, a fifteen-year-old. He had raped this girl and he had beaten her about a bit and the girl was now in a mental hospital, where she was likely to remain for some time. Mick had been given not weeks in detention, as had Roff, but months. When he was older he was to be transferred to prison, where he would stay until his six-year sentence had been completed. Hearing this, Roff thought it served Mick right, not for having raped the girl, but for walking away that afternoon on the beach. Somebody said Mick was a psycho, a statement with which Roff had quickly agreed. 'I used to know him once,' Roff had said, 'but we was never close mates.' It was generally agreed that having to rape a girl proved you hadn't the nous to get into her cunt any other way. All he hoped was that Mick had a fucking awful time in the centre, it being only what he deserved.

Approaching home, Roff couldn't decide if he'd be glad to see Annie or not. He'd get fed proper and sleep in his own bed and the telly would be colour instead of black and white, but Annie would ask him a lot of daft questions and pester him about why he hadn't written every week. One thing, though, he was sure of: better to be at home with her than in the centre. Better to listen to her nagging than the screws shout at him.

Being out was good, like the feeling he got when swimming in an empty sea. Like things was possible. On impulse he entered a shop selling novelties, buying for himself a penknife he had always wanted and for Annie an ashtray with the words, '*A present from the seaside*' embedded round its rim. Buying presents for people was not something he had often done and that, too, made him feel good, good enough to tell himself that when Annie smothered him with a welcoming, damp kiss he would not turn immediately away.

The house looked like Disneyland. Fairy lights framed the net curtains of the living-room, blinking on and off every few seconds, red, blue, green, yellow. On the front door a large plastic Santa Claus beamed above a circle of holly, and a lantern hung beside the door, swaying ever so slightly in the wind. The Santa Claus hid the door-knocker and the door-bell didn't seem to be working, so Roff went round the back, coming in through the yard, going up to the kitchen window.

The man was sitting at the kitchen table, his back to the window, intent on some task. Sheets of Christmas wrapping-paper were spread on the table, a large roll of sellotape, a pair of scissors. Roff watched him take a small object from his pocket, place it on the table, begin to wrap it in one of the sheets of paper. Large red hearts decorated the paper – these Roff could see quite clearly. What he could not see was the object the man was wrapping up, or the man's face. He noticed, however, balding on top of his head, which Roff took to prove the man was not young, and a cigarette in the ashtray, which proved he, like Annie, was a smoker. In the centre Roff had given up fags; not because he'd wanted to, but because the no smoking rule was strictly – and viciously – enforced. He ought to have bought himself a packet instead of the ashtray or the penknife, but he'd forgot. Maybe he'd go off them anyway. Smoking wasn't allowed in the abattoir neither; the smell, said the foreman, made the animals jumpy. He didn't know if he'd get his job back when he turned up for work after Christmas. One thing he'd found out in the centre was that he missed working – getting his own pay-packet every Thursday teatime, chatting with the men there, *doing* something. Not that he'd admitted it to Bob or anyone. It wasn't normal, was it, actually saying you liked work?

The man finished wrapping the present just as his Mum came into the kitchen. She was wearing a dress he'd never seen before – black, with silver bits at the neck and sleeves, and she had that stuff on, over her eyes, stuff

219

that made her look like someone had duffed her up. When she came in, the man pushed the present quickly into his pocket, like he didn't want Annie to see it. Roff saw her say something and laugh and walk towards the table and lean over. And kiss the man on the mouth. He was reminded of all the plays on telly Annie was so keen on; people laughing and kissing, people he didn't know in a room he'd never been in. Strangers, he supposed. After kissing, the man said something and Annie walked over to the sink and filled the kettle. While she was doing this the man got up, folded the wrapping-paper, put the sellotape in a drawer, hung the scissors up on a hook beneath the kitchen shelves. He was wearing a cardigan over a shirt and his tie was loose. He looked comfortable; he looked like he felt at home. Annie plugged in the kettle and then they both went out of the kitchen into the other room.

A drunk accosted Roff as he walked around the town in the dark. 'Got enough for a drink?' the drunk pleaded. 'Cup of tea?' When Roff gave him the ashtray he frowned, before placing it carefully in his oversized coat.

It seemed like he walked for hours. Along the promenade where the fairy lights jiggled about in the breeze from the sea and where some old drunk pissed against the railings. By the harbour where the boats looked sort of sad. Past the public park which was closed and empty. Along the streets, across the roads, through alleys, down avenues. Somewhere in the distance people sang carols and somewhere else, further away, a dog barked like it was demented. The further he walked, the tireder he became and the angrier he got. 'Some fucking Christmas,' he snarled at a stray cat, but the cat just hissed back at him, before jumping on to a wall.

The street he found himself in was at the posh side of

town, away from the railway station and the chip shops, a street of large, standoffish houses and long, long, front gardens, of trees and bay windows and ivy. In one of the houses someone was holding a party. Roff heard people's voices, someone singing, another shout, a third cheer. It hardly seemed right, people getting pissed on Christmas Eve in their big houses and singing, while he was outside with just a flimsy jerkin on and the zip on it broke. 'Fuck you,' he shouted. 'Fuck you all.'

He walked further, coming to the end of the street, ending up by the front gate of a house that was dark and looked empty and sounded silent. The number of the house was on the gate: No. 19, it said. Tracing his fingers round the numbers, his hand came away thinly spread with green moss. The gate was wooden, but the wood was rotten right through, split in places, smelling of damp. When he leaned against it, bits of the wood flaked off. For some reason the number of the house coupled with the name of the street reminded him of something, but he couldn't think what.

Empty, the house looked. More than that, almost like a person had died in it. Mick – who had done a few burglaries when he was younger – had told him once that the empty houses were the ones you never touched. The empty ones was the houses where the owners was inside, watching telly or screwing together in the bedroom. The houses that was safe was the ones with lights on all over the place. But this house looked really empty; shut up and empty and silent. He pushed open the gate and walked up towards the house.

And then he remembered who it was lived in the house. It came back to him sudden and he couldn't think why he'd ever forgot.

The penknife was still in his pocket and he took it out, looked carefully at it, and walked quickly, quietly up the drive.

18

I was playing patience by the light of two candles and the dull glow of the gas fire when I heard the noise. The breaking of glass, a harsh sound, loud and ugly, and so sharp that it made my ears ache and my eyes water and caused me to drop the six of hearts on to the floor. 'Jean,' I said, addressing the room, the card-table, the empty chair opposite me. 'Not yet Christmas Day and already she has begun to force an entry.'

But I continued to play. The noise had come from the back of the house and I found it amusing to think of Jean attempting to squeeze her ample form through the small scullery window, damaging both her clothes and her dignity. Wax dropped from one of the candles on the card table and I leaned over to touch it, allowing the wax to dry on my finger, peeling it off to see a perfect waxed fingerprint. Waiting for further sounds, I heard a thump, tins falling in chaotic clatter on to the scullery floor, the soprano of small pieces of glass landing on concrete. And I recalled that as a child Jean had always been prone to clumsiness, that at her touch cups would crack and electric irons cease to function.

At the back of the house a door opened, was closed again, and I began to be aware of footsteps approaching. My heart beat, anarchic, and I felt a little fear, some dismay, and an immense and overwhelming determination. Slowly, I turned the cards over – the five of clubs, the king of diamonds, several small hearts. Behind me the door opened, and I was ready to do battle.

'Good evening. As usual you are early,' I said, without

looking round. 'Do, please, close the door. The candles are nervous of the draught.'

Gathering together the cards, I shuffled them as I waited for Jean to speak. Outside, the wind menaced and I imagined I could hear the sea, tendentious and irascible.

'I have never known you to be bereft of words before.' And that was when I turned around and saw that it was not Jean who stood by the door, but a youth of perhaps sixteen or seventeen.

'The door,' I said.

'You what?'

'Do close the door.' I indicated the candles, indecisive in the draught. 'I was expecting my daughter. I have been expecting her for some time. Whoever you are, you have timed your entry into my house at a most inopportune moment.'

The boy stared at me; even in the dimness I could make out his frown. He appeared bewildered and, closing the door, looked about the room as though he had never before set eyes upon chairs, a card-table, a snug gas fire. Finally he spoke.

'You crazy?'

His question made me laugh. 'Possibly,' I told him. 'My daughter certainly thinks so and my doctor seems to agree with her. How did you get in? Through the scullery window, I presume.'

He looked at me, as though unfamiliar with the word. 'Broke a window,' he said, proud. 'Cut meself, 'n all.' He stepped closer, holding out his arm towards me. In the candlelight the blood across his wrist looked black. I sighed, thinking how immensely irritating it was of this odd youth to have broken into my home, to have destroyed hours of work.

'This is not a first-aid centre. I am not accustomed to

receiving wounded boys into my house. And I have no bandages. I presume the window is broken?'

'Yeah.'

'In that case, I suggest we mend it. If you managed to get inside, then I can only assume that despite my elaborate precautions my daughter will also be able to break in. Though, of course, she is less slender than you and the scullery window will present her with more problems. Perhaps you wish me to explain the reason I have barricaded myself in?'

But his answer was a negligent shrug. 'No,' I continued. 'Of course you do not want to know. The young are often less curious than people like to think. You see me simply as a dotty old woman, nothing more.'

I waited for the boy to answer, watching him pull from the pocket of his jacket an unsavoury handkerchief and wrap it inexpertly around his wounded wrist. For the first time I noticed the small penknife in his unbandaged hand.

'You wanna know who I am?' he challenged. The menace in his voice was laughable, and I tried not to smile. From the kitchen familiar sounds reached me – mice scuffling for their supper, the smug thrum of the refrigerator.

'I know perfectly well who you are. I am nobody's fool. Even in this light I recognize you. You are the young person whom I saw attack Mr Jones, the young man sentenced that day in court to a spell in one of those places – detention centres I believe is the correct term. Well, I presume you have served your time, finished your sentence, though I can hardly say it has improved your manners. And you have put on weight. All those institutional carbohydrates, I suppose. I do not know why you have come here, but I suspect it may be to do me harm.'

The boy nodded and looked at the penknife in his

hand as if for reassurance. I thought of him purchasing it in one of those ghastly little holiday shops on the seafront, touching it, sleeping with it under his pillow. I told him to sit down and he looked at me with what might have been gratitude. 'Your hair is different.'

'They cut it off. It was you what sent me there, to the centre. You got me put away.'

'No,' I told him, and in the kitchen the mice fought over the pieces of dark chocolate I had left earlier for them.

'It was your fault.'

'No,' I repeated. 'You are wrong.'

For a moment I closed my eyes. The room smelled of candlewax and of the sardines I had eaten a few hours previously for tea. At the windows the wind yelped, disappointed. Perhaps I dozed for a minute and when I opened my eyes again the boy was staring at the penknife, swopping it slowly from one hand to the other. Without his outrageous hairstyle, without that bright proclamation of rebellion, he looked ordinary – his features plain, mimicking those of thousands of others. I wondered whether he was a tiresome adolescent at home, if his father and mother were glad to have him returned to them, whether he dared to think of the future. He shivered and I turned up the gas fire, though the room was already warm. The clock on the sideboard had stopped days, weeks before, and I had no idea of the time, though I guessed it to be late in the evening, past the time Jean normally retired. 'She will not come now,' I thought, 'she will wait until Christmas Day to claim me.'

Too loudly, the boy spoke. 'I've got this knife, see. And I might just kill you with it.'

My laughter startled him, and the candles flickered. I

leaned closer towards him, peering at the knife in his hand.

'And that is to be the instrument of my death, is it? That cheap imported penknife? How strange life is, how very strange. I had always expected a less melodramatic end, a trivial, unadventurous death. To be run over by a bus while doing my weekly shopping. Or suffer a series of mild strokes. Or abrupt heart-failure while preparing one night for bed. But it seems now I am to be murdered. Is that your intention?' I asked. 'To kill me?'

'I dunno. I oughter. Kill you, I mean.' But his voice had bewilderment in it, and when he held the penknife towards me I think he understood that as a weapon it was manifestly ineffective, an instrument more suited to the opening of letters than to murder.

'You are not the first person to express a desire to kill me,' I said, and it was a relief to know that I was about to speak of George to this strange boy. 'My husband threatened my person on several occasions. Oh, it was a long, long time ago, when he returned from the war.'

'The war?'

'The Second Wold War. George was a captain, he was away for four years. The Far East. The war damaged him permanently, you see. When he came home he had changed. His mind had defected, you understand, turned towards a dark recess which nobody, not even I, could reach. Oh, on the surface he was quite normal, he gave every appearance of being the returning officer, the modest hero. At dinner parties and bridge evenings friends and acquaintances would ask to see his medals, they would pester him to relate how he had won them. They took his reluctance to do so as modesty. They did not realize how much he had changed. I saw the change as irretrievable, but nevertheless I did my utmost to help him. During the sleepless nights I made him hot drinks

226

and after the nightmares I would hold him in my arms and speak to him of the garden, the sea, of things I thought might help to soothe him. We had not been close for many years, but I thought we might be close again.'

'Was he took prisoner? I bet it was the Japs. I've read about them in comics. Seen about them prisoner-of-war camps on the telly.' The boy moved closer to me, his face alerted. 'Torture,' he said. 'I know about that. Brainwashing, 'n all.'

I shook my head. 'Not the Japanese, no. George was never a prisoner. George led his men over a distant hill in a hot and unfamiliar country, and he killed. The men he killed lay on the ground and George said there was surprise in their eyes. The story is an ordinary one, it has happened to other men in other wars.'

I paused. The boy waited, expecting more, waiting perhaps for me to tell him why George had been so changed, but I asked him instead if he had a cigarette. 'I smoke seldom,' I said, 'but a cigarette sometimes aids the memory.' But I remembered, oh so well. Distantly, I could make out the sound of car doors slamming, of voices. The wind had abandoned the house to tease the trees in the avenue outside.

'George was not a cruel man,' I said. 'He had been unkind to me in the past, there had been other women, but he had never been intentionally cruel. And then, one evening, two months after his return home, he asked me to accompany him into the hall. "I have something I wish you to see," he told me. I remember thinking the request bizarre, and then the thought came to me that my birthday was the following week. Perhaps George had bought me an early present – jewellery, some perfume, a new frock. I smiled at him, I may even have laughed a little in anticipation of my gift, and I got up from my chair and followed him into the hall. The evening was chilly, George led me towards the small glory-hole beneath the stairs, and I saw the door was open. "Really, George . . ." I began, before I felt his hand upon my arm and he pushed me into the glory-hole, bolting the door from the outside.'

'He locked you in?'

'He left me there for an hour. When he let me out, he smiled at me, but said nothing. Later that night George had another nightmare. In his sleep he wept. I asked him if he wished to see a doctor but he refused. Two days later, shortly after we had finished supper, he led me once again into that small prison, bolted the door, left me for an hour, perhaps two. Each time he released me, he said nothing. *I* said nothing. To protest might have been unwise. And after all, I was not locked in for long. I knew George would always come to unbolt the door, that after an hour or two he would release me. Until the last time, that is. Until the night he did not come to release me.'

'Left you there, did he?' and the enthusiasm of my listener's voice amused me.

'For nine days. He locked me in for nine days. Without food, with only soda water to drink. After those first hours, I slept. I pulled the coats from their pegs and made a bed. The place smelled of must and disuse. On the floor were wellington boots, forgotten newspapers, a framed picture I had never liked. It was dark and comfortless. I slept and I woke and I slept again. The silence made me afraid, but as the hours passed I thought I could hear the sea. "The tide is in," I told myself when the sound of water became louder. I think it was the sound of the sea that kept me sane during those days. When I could not sleep, I listened to it and occupied myself by undoing the stitching of the coats. I picked at the stitches with my fingers in the dark and pulled them out with my teeth. A pointless task, I see now, but rewarding at the time. When George came on the tenth morning, I had unstitched every coat.'

I stopped talking. My throat ached, I was tired.

'That it? That all?' the boy asked, as though expecting further horrors. I told him how George fed me that day of my release, on consommé and warm milk; how he carried me upstairs to bed, how he nursed me back to health. 'But even after my strength had returned to me,' I explained, 'I said nothing to George. He said he was sorry and I said nothing. I made no protest. And I told nobody. My daughter was away at the time, she was grown-up, she knew nothing of what had happened. Shortly afterwards George found a new mistress, a much younger woman. He came home only rarely. And when he did come home he was scrupulously polite. He lived for seventeen more years, and when he died I gave his clothes to Oxfam.'

I got up from my chair. The room had become stuffy. My companion looked tired. 'I have talked too much,' I said. 'It is late.' I thought that if I had told Jean of this she would not have built the extension to her house, there would have been no need of barricades, she would have understood. 'I will tell her tomorrow,' and the boy looked puzzled. 'When I explain, she will leave me alone.'

And I thought, 'I have exorcized George. After all these years I have finally told somebody of what he did to me.' I knew my mind would no longer be stained with the memory of his tyrannies, and I felt incalculably grateful towards my uninvited guest, towards this odd, bewildered boy who had listened to my tale and who had passed no judgement.

I stood up, fancying for a minute that I could hear the sea sliding down the pebbles of the beach, tugging the seaweed from the sand.

'Supper.'

'Yeah, ta.'

'Are you partial', I inquired, 'to baked beans?'

We ate the beans straight from the tin, accompanied by toast and peanut butter, both eating quickly, greedily, as do young children when not under the scrutiny of adults. When I reached for the peanut butter to spread it on my toast, the boy solemnly handed me the penknife and I took it – a trading of trust, a communion.

'I wasn't going to kill you, you know,' he said. 'Just wanted to see what you'd do.'

'I know.'

'Bought it earlier, see. In the shop where I got this present for me Mam. Bought her an ashtray, for Christmas. Went round to the house, only there was a man there. Some man, sitting in the kitchen, wrapping up a present. Never seen him in my life before. Me Dad run off, before I was even born he run off.' He sighed, unwrapping the handkerchief from his wrist, and I saw the blood had dried. 'She won't want me home now. She was always on the look-out for a man, and now she's found one.'

'In that case,' I suggested, 'you might like to stay here. I have spare rooms, extra blankets, clean linen.'

He blinked. 'Stay? In this house, you mean? With you?'

'Why not? I have sufficient provisions for a week. Bread and milk and freshly ground coffee and tinned fruit. Most of my life I spend my time alone, but solitude can often be a tiresome companion; a guest over Christmas would be welcome. We will strike a bargain, you and I. You shall be my guest for as long as you wish, but in return you must promise to help me man my barricades. You can be my bodyguard.'

'Bodyguard? You serious?'

'Naturally. Tomorrow, on Christmas Day, I expect my

daughter to try to break in and to do her utmost to remove me from this house. She wishes me to live in a granny flat, she has had it built on to her house for that specific purpose. In the living-room is a green fireside chair and the view from the window looks on to a duck pond. The kitchen is small and functional and the bedroom is pink. Pink,' I asserted, 'is my least favourite colour.'

'Green's mine,' said the boy. 'All the walls in the centre was painted green.'

I smiled. 'You understand,' I said. 'You know. And you'll be my bodyguard?'

'Okay. It's a deal.'

I showed my guest into the largest of the spare rooms upstairs. Its shadows shrank at our approach, as though dismayed by the candlelight, and on every surface – the mantelpiece, the chest of drawers, the windowsills – the dust was thick and grey. A motorcycle passed outside and somewhere in the town a clock struck too many times for me to count.

'Twelve o'clock,' said the boy, taking off his shoes. 'Christmas Day.'

He was humming to himself when I wished him a merry Christmas and made my way across the landing to my bedroom.

And now it is five-and-twenty past two on the afternoon of Christmas Day. I know the exact time because I have dressed as if for a special occasion: my gold watch is upon my wrist, I am wearing my favourite pair of black stilettos, this morning I put on my red velvet frock. My guest – I have discovered his name to be Roff – said he had never seen a dress like it, and this I took as a compliment. He looks less pale than he did last night, though the colour on his cheeks is due more to this

231

morning's exertions, I fear, than to general good health. Roff has been of inestimable help with the barricades – moving the sideboard from the dining-room to wedge against the back door, boarding up the scullery window, advising me of the risk of leaving even the small windows upstairs ajar. During our coffee-break this morning he told me a little of his background, of his mother who was a waitress, of a sister he despised. He is a sad youth, inarticulate, and life seems to bemuse him. But he does possess a rather endearing sense of humour, and the tales he tells of his spell at the detention centre are fascinating to hear. 'The knives is all plastic,' he explained, 'and the stew's so tough some nights they break when you try and cut the meat up. And the Governor, he goes on about sin a lot. One of my mates there, he said sin was a long way off. He knew that, he told me, 'cos his Mam said that was where his aunt was living and that was why they never visited her no more.'

When I inquired after his plans for the future, he shook his head. 'I had this job, see, in the abattoir. But I dunno if they'll want me back. It was great there,' he explained. The money was good, the men were friendly, he felt that he belonged. 'I'll go over next week, see if they want me.' But to see his face, so plundered of hope, saddened me and I knew he would not get his job back, that at the age of sixteen he was already shipwrecked upon the sands of unemployment. He told me about working in the abattoir, boasting of its cleanliness, telling me how sometimes the lambs panicked at the approach of the humane killer, how they could sense death in the air.

As he talked, I scrutinized his face. Even after his long sleep, his eyes betrayed a restlessness of spirit and I guessed that this, together with a feeling that he lacked worth, would always attend him, would wait to ambush him on lonely nights and solitary days. In ten years' time,

I thought, I shall be dead, but this boy will still be without work, will lack close friends, will have as his only solace the sea. He will be married by then and his wife will be unsympathetic, the kind of woman who uses the word 'love' only in order to cause pain, and who will laugh when he takes longer and longer walks by the sea. They will have a child who will be colicky and who will cry deep into the night.

I shall ask Roff if he would like to stay with me for a few months, I thought; I shall give him the memory of a batty old woman to carry with him in the years to come. We will take walks together along the promenade and when we have become bored with each other's company we shall part. 'You shall stay with me,' I announced, 'for a while. A month, two, three; until you find work, at least. I will give you an allowance which you can fritter away. We can eat anarchic meals together without the encumbrance of knives and forks, and watch too much television.'

My offer startled him and I smiled, pouring him more coffee. 'We are alike, you and I,' I said. 'The sea is a bond between us, we both recognize it has a soul.'

'I missed it,' he admitted. 'Stuck up in that place on the moors, miles and miles away from the sea.' His mother thought the sea was merely a nuisance, bringing too many people to the town, people who stayed at the hotel where she worked and who complained about the food and the service. 'She can't even swim,' he said, dismissive. 'We will swim together,' I suggested, 'when the siege is over.'

And we shall not have long to wait. The curtains are tightly pulled across and I have draped a shawl over the small table-lamp in the room. We have laid the table and set out a feast in this dim-lit sanctuary of ours. Bread is on the table (I have scraped off the mould), and smoked oysters and anchovies, tinned peaches, a bottle of French brandy, a pot of excellent jam, frankfurters in a tin, a packet of water biscuits. I expect Jean to arrive shortly. Even now she may be clearing away the dishes from the Christmas lunch, placing them neatly in the dishwasher, putting on her coat. Even now she and Alan may be getting into their car, driving through the emptied streets. I laugh, thinking of my daughter's sigh, the resignation with which she may say, 'Oh, I do so hope Mother is not going to be difficult.'

'What'll happen?' Roff asks. 'When she comes?'

'She will ring the doorbell, wait a few seconds, ring again. She will wonder why the curtains are drawn, the house in apparent darkness, why I do not answer. She will ask Alan to go round to the back of the house and peer through the windows. He may see the faint light behind these curtains, he may not. She will ring the doorbell again, keeping her hand pressed firmly against it, she will rap at the windows.'

'And then?'

I open the tin of anchovies and smile. For I think I know what will happen next, when Jean realizes that I have barricaded myself in. Underneath her winter coat she will shiver a little, as though aware of a sudden drop in temperature. 'She has barricaded herself in,' she will tell Alan, leaning against him for support. She will be dismayed, appalled, disturbed. 'Barricades,' she will whisper, waiting for Alan to tell her she has made a mistake, that it is not true. 'My own mother!'

'We'll go home now,' Alan will gently say, leading her back to the car, allowing Christmas music from the car radio to soothe her. At home, he will pour her some whisky, ensure the central heating is on, suggest they discuss things. 'You see now,' he will explain, 'how much she wants to stay in her own home, how determined she is not to move out.'

'I see,' my daughter will answer, 'just how much she hates me.'

But she will know this to be both unjust and untrue, and during the course of the afternoon she may gradually be brought to reason, may begin to understand. 'It would never have worked out,' she may say with commendable pragmatism, 'Mother and I living under the same roof. We neither of us would have felt at ease.'

I sigh, for I may be wrong. Jean may persist in her tyranny, continue to thump upon the front door, even enlist the help of the police. But I have Roff to help me, Roff and George. George is my trump card. If I must, I will tell her about her father, how he wished me to die, and I shall remind her how like him she has become. And she will not dare to take me away from here, she will not dare.

The prospect of victory makes me smile, and far below the house the sea applauds me.

'More anchovies?' I say, and pour out the brandy.

The world's greatest novelists now available in Panther Books

Doris Lessing
Novels

The Grass is Singing	£1.95	☐
The Golden Notebook	£2.95	☐
Briefing for a Descent into Hell	£2.50	☐

'Children of Violence' Series

Martha Quest	£2.50	☐
A Proper Marriage	£1.95	☐
A Ripple from the Storm	£1.95	☐
Landlocked	£2.50	☐
The Four-Gated City	£2.50	☐

'Canopus in Argos: Archives'

Shikasta	£2.50	☐
The Marriages Between Zones Three, Four, and Five	£2.50	☐
The Sirian Experiments	£1.95	☐
The Making of the Representative for Planet 8	£1.95	☐

Non-Fiction

In Pursuit of the English (autobiography)	£1.50	☐
Particularly Cats	£1.95	☐
Going Home	£2.50	☐

Short Stories

Five	£2.50	☐
The Habit of Loving	£1.95	☐
A Man and Two Women	£1.95	☐
Winter in July	£1.95	☐
The Black Madonna	£1.95	☐
This Was the Old Chief's Country (Collected African Stories, Volume 1)	£2.50	☐
The Sun Between Their Feet (Collected African Stories, Volume 2)	£1.95	☐
To Room Nineteen (Collected Stories, Volume 1)	£1.95	☐
The Temptation of Jack Orkney (Collected Stories, Volume 2)	£2.50	☐

To order direct from the publisher just tick the titles you want and fill in the order form.

The world's greatest novelists now available in Panther Books

Simon Raven
'Alms for Oblivion' series

Fielding Gray	£1.95 ☐
Sound the Retreat	£1.95 ☐
The Sabre Squadron	£1.95 ☐
The Rich Pay Late	£1.95 ☐
Friends in Low Places	£1.95 ☐
The Judas Boy	£1.95 ☐
Places Where They Sing	£1.95 ☐
Come Like Shadows	£2.50 ☐
Bring Forth the Body	£1.95 ☐
The Survivors	£1.95 ☐

Other Titles

The Roses of Picardie	£1.50 ☐
The Feathers of Death	35p ☐
Doctors Wear Scarlet	30p ☐

Paul Scott
The Raj Quartet

The Jewel in the Crown	£2.95 ☐
The Day of the Scorpion	£2.95 ☐
The Towers of Silence	£2.95 ☐
A Division of the Spoils	£2.95 ☐

Other Titles

The Bender	£1.95 ☐
The Corrida at San Feliu	£2.50 ☐
A Male Child	£1.50 ☐
The Alien Sky	£2.50 ☐
The Chinese Love Pavilion	£2.50 ☐
The Mark of the Warrior	£1.95 ☐
Johnnie Sahib	£2.50 ☐
The Birds of Paradise	£1.50 ☐
Staying On	£1.95 ☐

To order direct from the publisher just tick the titles you want
and fill in the order form.

Outstanding women's fiction in Panther Books

Muriel Spark
Territorial Rights	£1.25	☐
Not To Disturb	£1.25	☐
Loitering with Intent	£1.25	☐
Bang-Bang You're Dead	£1.25	☐
The Hothouse by the East River	£1.25	☐
Going up to Sotheby's	£1.25	☐
The Takeover	£1.95	☐

Toni Morrison
Song of Solomon	£2.50	☐
The Bluest Eye	£1.95	☐
Sula	£1.95	☐
Tar Baby	£1.95	☐

Erica Jong
Fear of Flying	£2.50	☐
How to Save Your Own Life	£1.95	☐
Fanny	£2.50	☐
Selected Poems II	£1.25	☐
At the Edge of the Body	£1.25	☐

Ann Bridge
Peking Picnic	£1.95	☐

Anita Brookner
A Start in Life	£1.95	☐
Providence	£1.95	☐
Look at Me	£1.95	☐

To order direct from the publisher just tick the titles you want
and fill in the order form.

All these books are available at your local bookshop or newsagent, or can be ordered direct from the publisher.

To order direct from the publisher just tick the titles you want and fill in the form below.

Name _____

Address _____

_____

Send to:
Panther Cash Sales
PO Box 11, Falmouth, Cornwall TR10 9EN.

Please enclose remittance to the value of the cover price plus:

UK 45p for the first book, 20p for the second book plus 14p per copy for each additional book ordered to a maximum charge of £1.63.

BFPO and Eire 45p for the first book, 20p for the second book plus 14p per copy for the next 7 books, thereafter 8p per book.

Overseas 75p for the first book and 21p for each additional book.